THIS AWFUL
SMALL MERCY
OF
MISS MIRIAM MALONE

Stuart Ayris

Beaten Track
www.beatentrackpublishing.com

The Awful Small Mercy of Miss Miriam Malone

First published 2022 by Beaten Track Publishing
Copyright © 2022 Stuart Ayris

Paperback ISBN: 978 1 78645 455 3

Cover Design: Debbie McGowan

Beaten Track Publishing,
Burscough, Lancashire.
www.beatentrackpublishing.com

Contents

Layer Marney Ward – Colchester General Hospital, Essex

Small Mercy (1)

1. One of Those Nights

THERE WAS A dull yellow glow to the outer edges of the bleak night. It was there, but briefly, if ever it was there at all. The solid air clung to the very last remnants of the day. A squalid fog kept doleful watch upon nothing at all. The single moon had been banished; the stars consumed. It was the sort of bleak night that would cause all good people to cower hapless in their skin and in their bones.

The village of Small Mercy was silent and still until the cracked Judgement House bell clanged thrice. The fog gulped down the very tremors of the clang and then that clang was gone – banished like the moon, consumed, as were the stars. There was silence once more.

John Dawlish heard it all. He heard the clangs, the tremors, the banishing and the consumption, but most of all, he heard the silence. John Dawlish had never been one to cower in his skin and in his bones. Furthermore, he held the pallid pink dawn in violent contempt. By no definition could he be considered one of the *good* people, not of Small Mercy or of any other place.

The colourless autumn had been preceded by a tepid summer. Some said that winter had been creeping sullen into the scene from as early as late August. It had been the way of things these past few years. Even the sumptuous revelations that spring can bring had become ever more joyless. Where in former times the crops had been plentiful, the fields surrounding Small Mercy bore now but paltry fare, largely sprouting little but sorrow.

John Dawlish uncrossed his legs and stood. He leaned back against the riven trunk of the oak tree beneath whose crooked dry branches he'd latterly been sitting. He drew a raw comfort from the feel of the rough bark upon his back. The thin over-shirt that hung inelegant from his wide shoulders to just below his waist was snagged in places by ancient barbs as he took to swaying slow from side to side. The more immediate and harsh the pain, the more soothed was he. Finally, satiated as only he could be, he rolled himself a crude cigarette. A light flickered into being as if sparked from the filth beneath the nail of his gnarly left thumb. The rancid phosphorous blazed. Dawlish sucked the flame into whatever was within the limp paper tube that protruded ragged from the gawp of his mouth.

For a while, the only indication of life in or around Small Mercy that bleak night was the putrid smoke that rose and fell from the hole in the face of the stranger by the oak tree. There was no wind, not even a breeze – just that smoke and that stranger.

John Dawlish smoked his cigarette right down to the rusty blotches on his thumb and forefinger. What remained of the paper clung damp to his thick lower lip. Twice, he tried to spit it away. He then slapped at his mouth with the ruinous palm of his right hand and successfully rid himself of the stubborn remnant. Dawlish became aware of the taste of blood in his mouth, upon the thick of his tongue. It meant nothing to him. He coughed and grunted loudly into the bleak night. The night and its bleak meant nothing to him either. He was that sort of fellow, was John Dawlish.

The banishing of the moon had deprived the stranger of the company even of his own shadow, and that suited him just fine. He stared dull-eyed into the corpulent gloom. He tipped back the brim of his cloth cap and scratched at his head where the loose strands of his dank hair met the broad morass of his brow. He had a lot on his mind on this particular night. There was much to consider. The coldness of the air lapped against him as gentle waves would insist upon caressing a misshapen rock.

He was never one for temperature of any kind, John Dawlish. Never would he shiver in the freeze nor be found panting like a dog in the rare summer heat. He was not like any other, nor had he ever desired to be. The fact that there was only one John Dawlish was as much a comfort to him as it had been to the inhabitants of the town way over yonder across the northern hills of which he'd in recent days taken his leave. It had been a sour and charmless parting.

The squalid fog paid no heed to the quaint follies of the bleak night.

By the time the pallid pink dawn spread with more fortitude to the north across the shallow river that ran parallel to the Small Mercy dirt track, John Dawlish had settled himself upon a plan of sorts. If the craggy grimace upon his awful face was any indication, it was a worthy plan indeed. He smoked another cigarette – smoked it right down to the bone. He retched up a good quantity of phlegm. Closing his eyes, he took a moment to indulge himself in the taste and aroma of it. With a sudden blurt, he expelled the glob of his innards onto the glistening grass. Tiny drops of dew dispersed aghast at such a demonstration of unholy and voracious disdain.

"How d'you like that then?" growled Dawlish. "Not so clever now, eh, you useless little bastards?"

The pallid pink dawn was fortified by first orange then yellow as the haze of the day beat back the ooze of the squalid fog and the bleak of the night. The sky resolved reluctantly to don a blank white visage. Just as the moon had missed its cue, the sun declined to perform. Even the very stalwarts of the firmament it seemed were not immune to a little ennui when John Dawlish was on the prowl.

A songbird chirruped heroically from a twisted grove of stunted birch trees midway up one of the hills to the east. It was a song of no beauty, just notes was all. No sooner had it begun than it came to an end and was gone.

The stranger stepped away from the base of the ancient oak tree and extended his arms out wide. His elbows clicked. He rotated his wrists and bunched the fingers of one hand into the palm of the other whereupon he proceeded to push down hard before stretching each inelegant finger out to its fullest. His nails were scratched, jagged and blackened with the dirt of his existence. Small clumps of grey hair protruded from the knuckles of the fingers on his right hand though none garnished the fingers on his left. It was one of the rare anomalies with which he had been afflicted – the fact that the back of his left hand was smooth and without blemish, almost *normal* you might say. He was a monstrous brute of a man.

It wasn't that John Dawlish limped when he walked, more that his bowed left leg could not keep time with the right. It was a rhythm thing, something wholly unmusical. There was no fluency to what most would consider an autonomic motion. His lumbering gait was not helped by the fact that almost any useful bone of his wretched frame had at one time or another been broken, crushed, stamped upon or by some other means rendered less than holy.

The stranger measured somewhat less than six feet in height. He was disproportionately broad across the shoulders and across the expanse of his chest. He was heavy limbed and brutal, more simian than human in the application of the overwhelming majority of his basic functions. He was animalistic, inordinately untamed. Yet he was no dolt. His mind ever churned with a restlessness that inspired him to delve deep and long into the merciless well of his darkest drippings.

"Little useless bastards," he muttered vile. "Fucking useless little, useless little bastards."

Dawlish narrowed his pale blue eyes before opening them terrifying and wide. He adjusted his cloth cap and rolled his huge shoulders a little. His functional mouth was almost fully open, revealing the full extent of the blackness of his deep. The three teeth he possessed were all bunched together crooked in what was ostensibly just a hole in the front of his face. He looked skyward to where the black of the universe had latterly held sway.

He saw no black.

The black was all gone.

There was barely even a hint of bleak to quicken his heart, just a horrific pink straddling the dawn. John Dawlish had never been one for pink. He was not what you would call a *pink* fellow.

"Always good to have a plan," Dawlish mused as he clomped oafishly eastwards across the rutted brown field that stood between him and the somnolent village of Small Mercy.

A light flickered from the window of the last house at the southernmost tear of the village. Dawlish grinned.

By thine light may I be led, the stranger chuckled hollow. *By thine light may I be led.*

It had been one of those nights.

And it was about to be

one of those

days.

2. Inelegant Shapes

THE BAKING OF bread is a serious business, and so it was for the man whose sweat splashed in ever-increasing swathes upon his red face. The baker toiled away in that last house on the southern edge of Small Mercy, from whose window a faint light had caught John Dawlish's gaze. The night had already given way to morn by the time the baker had shaped sixteen loaves. He had been entirely oblivious of the turning of the earth, so deep in himself was he. Picking up a huge wad of pale wet dough from the wooden keg to his right, he raised it above his shimmering, bald scalp and brought it down with a gormless thud upon the heavy bench behind which he stooped.

"Where is that damned woman?" he barked sullen.

The baker began work on the next batch. The dough consumed his fists and his fingers almost to his wrists. He pulled and pummelled it, that magical mixture that had started off in some place as a dry seed in the earth and now battled with him on equal terms. There was nothing magic about the pounding to which that lump of wonder was then subjected. It was being thuggishly beaten for its own good, ravaged and stretched to breaking in order that others may partake of it once brought to high heat.

"Woman! Where are you? This bread is set for its baking!"

"Now, now, Sullivan. Such rage so early in the day will do nobody no good, now will it? Particularly yourself. Of course, it is only for you and your health that I worry so."

Sullivan manfully suppressed his fury. Sarcasm, particularly in a woman, he had long deemed a trait of the devil. There would be time for her to come to heel. There was always time for that. The woman whom he had so gruffly summoned sauntered to the opposite side of the wooden bench and deftly picked up the two trays of ready-formed loaves. She turned like a ballerina and almost in one sublime motion slid the trays deep into the black aperture that had been cut into the wall above the red and yellow fire.

"About bloody time."

The surly baker had earlier resolved not to speak to the woman until at least the afternoon and was somewhat irritated that he had succumbed so soon. He simmered as he ruminated upon the long list of aberrations for which he held her accountable. Of late, there had been a facile coquettishness about her demeanour. Experience had taught the both of them that such tawdry spite was never destined to sustain.

The woman came to stand behind the baker. "Were you not taught as was I that to be miserable whilst performing your chores is to be inefficient, and that inefficiency is akin to blasphemy in our trade as it is in most all others?"

The woman tilted her head to one side and looked up at the baker's pulsating face with her wide, brown eyes.

"And were *you* not taught, Mary, that there is nothing as *ine*fficien*t* as being akin to a stinking corpse 'neath its shroud when the fourth chime sounds and your working day commences but a spit and a breath after?"

Sullivan slammed down ferocious the dough he'd latterly been assaulting.

Mary pushed back a strand of dark morning hair from her damp brow. It was a small room in which the bread was baked, and during working hours it was ever incredibly hot. Mary had not the flaccid, rotund face of Sullivan, though she did possess fingers as slender and nimble as he. They suited her well; him less so.

They had lived together, these two, since she was barely fifteen and he twenty-six. She had noted, with sadness at first, how he had so swiftly grown old. The sadness turned irreversibly into pity and the pity into a remorseless contempt. The loss of his hair by the age of thirty, the expansion of his waist, the sloping of his shoulders and the ache in his back had of course not gone unnoticed by the man himself. More irritating to him, though, than the physical consequences of his work was the fact that Mary appeared to have been entirely untouched by the very processes that had rendered him wretched. It was one of the many things for which he had grown to despise her.

In the darker moments of his most drunken stupors, the baker would oftentimes envisage himself standing over a hole in the ground at the bottom of which would be Mary's lifeless form. It was as close as he ever got to a tender dream.

Sullivan and Mary had never married. According to The Constitution of Small Mercy, to cohabit was commitment enough. Just as the concept of marriage did not exist, separation once together was permitted only in death. No weddings. No divorces. There were funerals aplenty, of course, each of which was conducted with emotionless brevity.

An odd place, this Small Mercy. An odd old place indeed.

The baker and his woman were a couple only inasmuch as they lived beneath the same straw and mud roof, ate their meals together and bickered almost constantly. There were four rooms in their small home – Sullivan's room, Mary's room, the baking room and the room where they ate. Perhaps in many ways, they were not unusual in the relentless dull misery of their days.

It had been no more than a few months into their courting that Sullivan and Mary were informed they had not been chosen to conceive future inhabitants of the village. He would sire no child and she would suckle no young. No reasoning was given for the decision handed down to them by the village elders, and no questions did they ask. They sought no recrimination, nor did they wallow in the cruelty of their fate. It was how it was. The consequence was that never were they to engage in love-making. Fornication was for the purpose of procreation alone. Small Mercy was not a place in which chance was permitted to linger bold.

The smell of fresh bread hung in the air of that small room like the fragrance of a fine red rose on a heap of dung. When the smell was *just so*, Mary withdrew the hot trays from the black hole and used the hem of her thick apron to prevent her pale and perfect hands from burning. She took the baked loaves over to the window to cool. Had she taken the time to look out into the morn, she may have seen the approaching outline speck of a figure far off in yonder rutted field.

"Don't dawdle, woman! Put these others in to bake. Be quick about it. The fire be burning low on account of your tardy rising."

Mary curtseyed as Sullivan rubbed grime and sweat from his small, red eyes.

"I'm to my room for ale."

The baker departed to his room for ale.

The woman put the final tray of loaves in to bake. Her coquettish defiance was only ever brief.

Despite their difference, Mary and Sullivan had always agreed on one thing – there were worse roles in Small Mercy than those which they'd been assigned. You were always warm; the smells were more than tolerable. There was, of course, the early starts to the day and, in their particular case, the close proximity within which each had by necessity to toil. But it was not all bad despite how so often it felt immeasurably intolerable.

Mary took out the final trays of bread at the appointed time and set them atop the others by the window. Forty-eight loaves had been baked and would soon be ready for collection. Those villagers for whom that day was Bread Day would take a loaf each from the piled wagon outside the Judgement House and consider not at all how that bread came into being.

Mary watched as the fire burned down. She opened the heavy iron door to its fullest extent and fanned her face with the bottom half of her apron. The flames had to be observed until they were fully out. This was Small Mercy, after all. Not even something as momentous and ancient as fire itself was free to boogie.

Mary had long considered the sole intention of the baker's animalistic snores as being to cause her misery. Just half an hour ago, Sullivan had left her presence to indulge in his allocation of ale, and now, by way of his awful somnolent gasping, it was as if he were right there beside her in his entire ugly wrath. Choosing to suffer in the heat rather than be assailed by the tuneless rumblings of that man, Mary shut herself in the baking room.

The sun was by now fully formed and glowing between the way-off northern hills. The wind had set aside its mischief for the moment. Fresh colours eased into being. As each minute passed, the shadows of buildings and trees struck ever more inelegant shapes. The huge round stones in the mill by the river far to the northwest of Small Mercy had begun to grind into turgid motion, powered by the four wooden sails.

JOHN DAWLISH'S DAYS had rarely been simple and untroubled. This, however, felt to him as if it could be one of those singular times when things would be *just fine*. The smell of fresh bread had lured him from out of the hard mud furrows of what was once a field teeming with greens and yellows and reds and golds.

It was as Mary was poking the embers of the fire into final submission and the loaves had cooled sufficiently to be touched and Sullivan lay flat on his back on his bed like a lump of beaten dough, that John Dawlish came to stand within the black shade of the baker's doorway. He breathed in deeply, tottering a little on his misshapen legs. He gulped down the scent of the baked bread though even that gorgeous wild failed to penetrate the fetid wad of slime that perpetually inhabited the irregular black holes in his nose that passed for his nostrils.

Give him his due, John Dawlish could have pushed open the wooden door and gained entry without invitation. Though he didn't know it just then, no doors in Small Mercy were permitted to be locked. His lack of knowledge of such a regulation does therefore render his actions somewhat laudable. Had the door been secured, it would have taken him very little effort to break it open with one or other of his huge fists. So the fact that, on that morning, he knocked with something approaching civility – well, fair play to him.

Knock.

Knock.

There.

Mary assumed it was the boy come early to collect the loaves. She rose to her feet from having been kneeling at the hearth. She breathed deep and straightened her apron. She approached the door to the home she had shared with Sullivan for what seemed like an eternity and prepared the cheerful smile which she had taken to adopting in recent times with ever-increasing chagrin.

Just as the stranger was about to knock once more upon the door, the woman pulled it open. Thus was the first sight she had of him being that of his fist replete with hair on the knuckles, dirt in the nails and the wretched skin of the back of his hand hovering but six inches from her flour-dusted face.

3. Whooooaaa

John Dawlish's voice was even more staggeringly unpalatable when he bent it to making a rare stab at civility.

"Fine morning, ain't it? This one, I'm meaning. This morning 'ere, ma'am, that we have upon us. Not last one or one afore that. Not them mornings. Them was both shit as shit can be."

Mary was no longer aware of Sullivan's snoring. Perhaps he had died. Or maybe it was because every single one of her senses was now fully attuned to the man before her. She was neither repelled nor appalled by what she saw. The extremes of emotions, both positive and painful, had been constricted over the years by the sheer glib inevitability of her life to date.

"A fine morning it is, sir." Each syllable Mary offered into the air was dry with a delicacy so at odds with the latter's wet rasping.

"Fine morning, ma'am. We are agreed on that, it seems."

"Yes sir. It do seem we be."

Silence.

For a moment or two.

Silence.

For a little moment more.

"Never seen you round here before, sir. You come from far?"

"From far enough," Dawlish muttered. He coughed harsh and open-mouthed directly into the woman's fragile aura. The stench of him was almost as grotesque as the sight of him. Sad to say, even at this, young Mary was undeterred. Some life to have led which makes that possible. Some life indeed.

"You been travelling all the night? Not much for miles around, they say, though I don't rightly know. Lived all my days in this village. Been in this house here for most of them days, truth be told, or near enough for it to be true, anyways." She was rambling now. She knew it. The stranger knew it too. Of course he did. He knew her type and all types there ever was.

"I come from where I come from," Dawlish, atonal. "I come from where I come from and I go to where I go to. Just so happens I done got to going to here on this fine morning."

"It is a fine morning, sir, as you say," breathed Mary.

"Fine morning."

"Yes, sir."

Silence.

For another moment or two.

Silence.

For a little moment more.

"I was a wondering," Dawlish began.

Then nothing more did he add.

"A wondering what, sir?" asked Mary too quickly.

"A wondering, as I crossed that there field, how it be that my nose be filled with the smell of fresh bread when for as long as I can recall my old nose here has been filled only with the smell of the devil's shit."

"Your nose ain't deceived you none, sir. I do declare there must be something of the hound about you, if you forgive me saying so. Freshly baked bread been made here this very morning."

The stranger stepped forward until the ragged toes of his old boots were across the threshold, Mary's ghostly frame no more than a few inches from him. "My old nose may not be much for looking at, but it don't often do me wrong and that's a fact." He grinned awful.

It was the grin and the subsequent attempt at a conspiratorial wink that finally saw the withering of Mary's fortitude and in its absence an emerging stark foreboding. She knew it. The stranger knew it too. Of course he did.

Not a sound was there from up above, down below or anywhere between. Just the smell of Dawlish and that emerging stark foreboding.

And then.

"Woman! Is that fire full out? Well, is it? I will have answer! And I will have more ale!"

There was a dreadful thud as Sullivan wriggled his way off the bed and lurched himself into standing.

Mary had rarely been more pleased to hear his voice.

"At the front, my dear! We have a visitor – a stranger it seems!"

"A stranger? I have no time for your nonsense! If it be that idiot Chuck boy come early for the bread, then you tell him I be giving him a belting if he ain't gone by time I get to 'im!"

John Dawlish scratched his forehead

John Dawlish straightened his grubby cap.

There was a sheen to the stranger's eyes that Mary had not noticed before. It wasn't that he was about to cry, nothing of *that* sort. It was as if his eyes had in some way *emptied*.

"I'm very sorry, sir," Mary murmured soft to Dawlish. "I think it best you leave just now. I wish you safe travels and bid you a fond farewell on this fine morn and hope you don't take no offence in the manner of this here parting."

Dawlish howled a silent yawn, giving Mary a full view of his rotted teeth and gums. On closing the cavern of his mouth, the stranger proceeded to slowly lick the cracks of his lips with the lolling of his lolling tongue. Satisfied with his preening, he slowly nodded his heavy head.

"We are agreed that the morning is fine. On that, if I be not mistaken, we have agreed more than once."

John Dawlish noticed the appearance of Sullivan in the scene before Mary did. The baker had with eerie stealth taken a position behind the woman.

"Now I really do have to ask that you leave," Sullivan stated with all the firmness he could muster. Shouting at Mary had always come so much easier to him than even the most innocuous of conflicts with any other than her. "We have more bread to bake and other things to do besides. I bid you good day, sir. Now in with you, woman so I can close this door to the chill."

Dawlish said not a word. He just stood there, his eyes all vacant, his lips freshly wetted. Mary was about to venture that she could feel no chill at all, but the words stuck jumbled in her jaw.

"Stand aside now, woman. Get out of the way so I can close the door and we can get back to our business."

"I'm sorry, sir," said Mary, head bowed as she closed the door. Once inside, Sullivan gave it to her good until even the bread lost its fragrance and the last of the embers lost the last of their warmth. That such a happenstance was inevitable was of no solace to the woman, who within moments of bidding the stranger farewell was curled in a quivering ball beneath the table as ferocious kicks were aimed at her between the foul curses and spattered spit of the baker.

One hour or so later, the Chuck boy arrived to collect the bread for the day. To his bleary-eyed surprise, he discovered there was somebody already there standing at the miserable baker's door.

"Hello, sir," chirped the boy. "Now if you wouldn't mind stepping aside a bit, I just need to get by you and get the bread for them as is up the hill there waiting. It's me job and that, and it be their Bread Day, after all."

There was no response from the stranger, who, the entire time since the door had closed upon him, had neither blinked nor even let go a single malodorous breath.

"Come on, Mister," the boy laughed, "too early for games, ain't it? Need the old bread or people will be getting on my case, and that ain't good, I can tell you. Ain't hardly got a case left these days, it done been gotten on so much."

Still no nothing from the stranger.

"You alright, mate?" The boy tentatively poked at Dawlish's arm with his forefinger.

And that dishevelled, ancient lump of a man, who had that fine morning arrived from who knows where to the village of Small Mercy, simply toppled sideways and crashed into the dirt like some grotesque gargoyle that had been blown off some cathedral roof.

"Whooooaaa!" yawped the boy, stepping back.

SULLIVAN'S CHIDING OF her having stumbled into a fraught hiatus, Mary just caught the end of the *whooooaaa*. With her only thought being that an excuse had been presented to her to avail herself of some relief from that baker's wrath, Mary rushed to the front door and flung it open. Her eyes fell first upon the boy and then upon the focus of his dismay.

"Stafford?" She spoke plain in addressing the trembling young lad.

"I did nothing, Miss! Honest! I just popped my finger at him, and he went over like I don't even know how to say! And there he be! It was all mad, it was! I didn't mean to do nothing but get him to move aside of the door so I could get the bread like I always do. Is he dead, Miss? Please tell me he ain't dead! I ain't got no case left. You know that better than any of 'em!"

During his imploring of Mary, Stafford did not for a moment take his startled eyes off the lifeless form before him. The tone of his voice could not help but betray the fear he bore as each syllable passed his lips. With every word he spoke, the timbre sank little by little until his final utterance was no more than an inarticulate gasp.

"He hasn't moved at all?" the woman asked sweet as she could, given the peculiarity of the circumstances.

"Not bone or breath, Miss."

"No sound?"

"I've done killed him, Miss, ain't I? I just done killed that man when all I wanted was to do what I do in collecting the bread you and Mr Sullivan make. I done poked him and he ain't done nothing since but not move and not do nothing. I can't even recall which finger it was I killed him with, Miss!"

Stafford began to weep and to sob and to sob and to weep. Mary pulled that poor boy to her.

"You done nothing of the sort," she said steady to him. "You ain't killed him, you hear? He a stranger, and a strange stranger at that. First thing that came to me when I saw him earlier was that there was something not right about him, something not right at all."

Stafford shuddered away from Mary's grasp and sniffled himself dry upon the sleeves of his filthy shirt.

"You know him, Miss?"

"We exchanged words in this very place not an hour ago is all," she replied. "I bid him farewell, yet it seems he ain't fared too well at all."

Stafford Chuck sniffled once more into the ragged fabric of his garb.

Before Mary could decide upon whether to check the rigid body of John Dawlish or to try to reassure the boy further, Sullivan barged past her with as much rough as he had left in him after the divine beating he'd delivered.

"Are you here to pass the morn with pointless babble, boy, or are you here for bread? Now what is it?"

In response to the baker's terse interjection, Stafford straightened his right arm and pointed to where John Dawlish lay.

About to object forcefully to such insolence, Sullivan instead turned his head, having first glowered at Mary, and in that moment experienced a swift alteration in his demeanour. His sullen disdain for the imposition of ineptitude upon his daily routine ebbed as a soulless curiosity took hold of him.

"Well, well," he mused. "Now what do we have here?"

Stafford inched forward a little until he stood beside the baker. Mary stepped out from the doorway and positioned herself on Sullivan's other side. The three of them were as still as the ragged form before them.

John Dawlish's body had fallen in such a fashion that he faced away from those who looked down upon him. His dirty cap had slipped from his head and rested upon the side of his thick, grimy neck, giving no easy means by which his features could be appraised. Thus was he able to take a moment to lick the grains of dirt that had gathered upon his wet lips as he'd hit the ground. It didn't taste of no bread, he acknowledged as he lay there, but at least it was something. It had been a long time indeed since he'd been touched by another and longer still since the fat flesh of his lips had come into contact with anything other than the phlegm and spittle that ever gurgled in his throat.

"Is he dead, Mr Sullivan sir?" Stafford breathed. "I killed him, ain't I? I know I did, even if you say I ain't."

As the boy, the baker and the woman peered over his huge and wretched body, it was all the stranger could do to suppress the wave of giggle that consumed him, for he absolutely could not wait for what was going to happen next.

4. Murderous Lad

It will ever be extraordinary how individuals of whatever standing will respond when confronted by the weird this curious world has, on occasion, to curious offer.

Sullivan knew how to solve the issue of transforming flour and water into edible form, adding more of each as and when required to produce dough ready for baking. For as long as he could recall, that was about the extent of the challenge with which his mind had been enticed to engage.

Mary had learned to manipulate fire and flame and to distinguish the scent of her fired loaves from the fetid air of her existence. She could judge when more logs should be added and precisely when the trays from the black hole in the wall should be rescued from their ultimate crematings.

The boy Stafford had been taught to use the sun as a timepiece and as such had come to rely upon it in terms of when he should rise and when he should fall, giving due regard to the cruel vagaries of the weather and the extent of weariness in his young bones.

The mind will only shimmer when enlightened. If neglected, it will respond with a shrug and a sigh and serve you with no more relish than would an unfed dog.

Stafford, Mary and Sullivan possessed no particular qualities that identified them as more adept than any other of their brethren. It was for them alone to solve the puzzle with which the indubitably fine morning had presented them. The shit mornings were long gone, long gone.

"Go get them loaves and load up the cart, boy," Sullivan ordered Stafford. "Say nothing to no-one about, about…all *this*.

Then you be sure to come back when done with your chore. You got that in your dullard skull?"

"Yes, sir," the boy replied, all high tones and wavering.

Stafford Chuck leapt by Mary and Sullivan in an instant and returned swiftly, piling the bread into the wooden cart like he was hurling soil into a grave. He set about pushing his wonky, laden cart with more tenacity and more urgency than ever he'd set about pushing it before.

Mary watched the poor lad's slender legs turn almost as fast as the wooden wheels of his cart as he did as the baker instructed.

"That boy will be out of breath by time he gets to where he needs go," she said sad. "He'll have no spare air in him to tell this tale even should he wish to."

"For a rare once, you be right, you foul woman," Sullivan did commend her. "You and your idle talking with this stricken stranger have done nobody no good," he added fierce.

"What would you have had me do?"

"You should have done how all are instructed to do in this place from the time we can talk and hear."

Mary made no reply but hung down her head fraught and in chagrin.

"Constitution item four," boomed the baker. "*There will be no Strangers in Small Mercy. Any Stranger that do find himself within the bounds of Small Mercy shall without delay be delivered, dead if need be, to the shadows of Judgement House.*"

"And you are so innocent?" Mary sparked. "You addressed him too, if I recall, and you made no mention of no Judgement House or Item four, five or any, far as I know."

Though he had the opportunity to concede the truth of Mary's statement, Sullivan chose to do no such thing. He was in no mood to give ground to her given the events of the day, given his sway of her, given his intolerable enmity.

"Now, woman, if it is heard that there was a stranger about here then you, and doubtless me, will be summoned up the hill to explain all. I ain't been before Judgement in my life, and I don't intend to be doing so now."

John Dawlish had long ago mastered the task of inhaling and exhaling air without recourse to the use of muscles that would ordinarily attend such a function. His urge to break into a horrific fit of laughter quelled, he had been listening attentively to the ruminations of this baker and this woman. More than once was he tempted to stretch his limbs, gain his full height and accost his hosts with the most ridiculous gabble of words he could mischievously muster. He chose instead to pursue the glory of a denouement far more satisfying and rank.

It has to be said that it came as some surprise to John Dawlish that Sullivan's chosen course of action plucked from the paltry set of options with which his dull mind presented him was to bring down with full force a rough-hewn length of wood upon the stranger's static head. Not once did Sullivan complete this crude act but twice. It would have been three times or more had Mary not interceded at the point when the side of Dawlish's head resembled more the remnants of a slaughtered beast than anything remotely identifiable as human.

Sullivan trembled momentarily with the barbarity of his action. Mary stood behind him. She was at first appalled, then transfixed. In truth, each was to varying degrees appallingly aroused.

Perhaps it was just as well that Stafford returned just then, for had the baker looked in that moment upon the woman that would never bear his child and she gazed full into the wrath of he whose life she had tainted with her once-innocent beauty, it is likely they would have engorged on one another in an act as ruthless as that in which one had just lustily partaken and the other dutifully observed.

"I did not do *that!*" the boy did most inelegantly exclaim.

Sullivan grabbed Stafford hard by each shoulder. "Now, you listen good," he said stern. "We here make the bread that feeds the people of this place. You do no more than would a horse or a cow! Only difference is you clear up your own shit and everybody else's shit! You will ever be no more than a horse or a cow, and you will clear up my shit and Mary's shit until we are dead in the ground and not able to shit no more."

Mary had the good sense to stay silent, Stafford the requisite amount of fear to respond with a quickening of his breathing and a drying of his mouth.

"So given that," Sullivan continued, "if I were to attest that it was you who beat that there stranger with that there wood, then there is no doubt at all that what may not have *been* a fact will *become* a fact, and it would be you, you little bastard, who would face Judgement and not I. You understand what I say, boy? It will go ill for you if you don't."

Stafford nodded with awful resignation. The emptying of his spirit had as much to do with the words to which he had been subjected as to the dreadful silence that oozed from the woman beside him, the woman who had but that very morn held him close, making him, for an angel moment, feel all safe and gorgeous.

"What are we to do now?" the meek woman enquired of her man.

"We get the creature inside. Mary, you help me move him. Boy, you hold the door open. Shut it firm behind us when we are in, mind."

Transferring John Dawlish's crooked frame from the ground outside to the table inside, beneath which Mary had earlier cowered, was less arduous than any of them had thought. Fuelled by adrenaline allied with the dread of being observed brought agility to Sullivan and strength to Mary. Stafford performed his task without error, and the three conspirators came to be assembled once again about the body of the stranger. The location had changed, but that was all. The puzzle was still the puzzle, the stranger still the stranger.

Mary and Stafford sought refuge in heartless subservience whilst Sullivan, red-faced and grumbling, paced the small room with increasing rancour.

"Have to see if there is still life in that thing," he barked at the others once he'd had his fill of tramping from corner to corner. "We should be sure as sure can be of that, at least. You, woman. See if he lives and quick about it. This ain't no time for your tardy dawdlings!"

As an automaton did the baker's woman approach the table and bend across Dawlish's body. She leaned her bloodless, pale face in close to where John Dawlish's mouth hung open. She turned her ear to the stagnant hole that would have been unrecognisable in terms of form and function had it not been for the few jagged teeth that clung to its depths. She closed her soulless eyes. The room was submerged in a stultifying silence. It was neither warm nor was it cold. Even the very air in that place had skulked away to an arena less odious.

"I hear nothing," Mary said low, her eyes tight shut, her ear almost touching Dawlish's misshapen bottom lip.

"Keep on," Sullivan instructed. "Do as I ask until I ask it no more. Just you keep right where you are until we know for certain he is dead."

Mary did as she was asked, steadily easing back away from the table only when Sullivan finally grunted his order for her to cease in her awful task. "I heard no breath," she reported dutifully. "No breath at all in sound or feel. If he ain't dead and gone then I don't know what he be, honest, I don't."

"Boy, you see if she speaks the truth. I have tarried with this woman long enough to know she is weak of constitution when a strong one is demanded and has a lying tongue in that mouth of hers that she is apt to flap with spite whenever she so please."

Stafford did not move at first but did so with much haste at the sign of Sullivan approaching him. He was too small to lean across the body as Mary had done so instead went around to the other side of the table and bent his head down to see if this stranger was dead.

"Not sure, sir," he murmured after what seemed the longest time. "Could be I hear something. Could be it's just meself that I'm hearing."

"Get closer, then, boy. Is this dolt breathing or is he not? Is he living or is he dead? That is all I ask!"

When at last he could endure his task no more, Stafford, head bowed and wretched, took his place beside Mary and informed Sullivan that the man was more than likely dead.

"*More than likely?*" Sarcasm and contempt mingled freely with the white spittle on the baker's unkissed lips. "*More than likely* is of no use to me, and *more than likely* is definitely of no use to you. Now get out of the way, you indolent pair!"

Sullivan pushed through them, giving one a jab with his elbow as he did so, the other the full force of his slumped shoulder. He stood over the body on the table and glared at it as if the hatred that flowed in torrents from his small, red-veined eyes would be sufficient in its ravenous intensity to stamp out the ragged embers of life that may still be lurking within. A loud crack resounded as he slapped the unbeaten side of John Dawlish's face. The lack of any response from the motionless stranger only heightened the irritation that consumed the baker. With a fist that still contained dough that had since dried hard in the crevices of his knuckles, the baker pounded three times Dawlish's stomach and once the chest. Nothing. He stepped back and wiped the sweat off his wretched brow.

Sullivan leaned sullenly against the far wall, slid down in stages and brooded. Mary and Stafford exchanged fearful glances.

From being as motionless as the body on the table, Sullivan suddenly came abruptly to life. He slid back up the wall, his knees crunching with pain, and clapped his hands together. There was a rancid grin upon his face, a shimmer in his squinting, red eyes.

"We bury him!" he did joyously declare. "We bury him deep and we bury him good. Alive or dead, the ground will see to his fate, and then we will have an end to all this *inconvenience*."

Perhaps Mary hadn't been totally deserted by all that rendered her more human than animal, for her response to what had been postulated was evident first by the startled expression that formed on her face and culminated in the manner in which her words cut through the putrid air between herself and Sullivan.

"We will do no such thing, I tell you," she said calm. "Enough evil has already been done on what was a fine morn. I'd rather throw myself at the feet of Judgement than be any more a part of your devilish designs."

Stafford felt he should say something but instead cowered back against the damp wall.

"Is that your position, woman?" Sullivan crooned sweet.

"It is," Mary replied. "Do to me what you will. Bury *me* in the earth, I pray, and bury me deep. It would be the kindest act you ever did do to me, I do declare.

"Is that so?"

"It is so. This madness of yours has an unholy reek to it. For many a year now have I caught the faint scent of it, but now I am filled to the brim of my being with it."

"This madness of *mine*?" the baker said soft and slow. He moved close as can be to Mary now, and with each step, his voice lowered until it was almost a whisper. "I do believe it was not *I* who entertained our stranger when I should have been at work. Not *I* who no doubt teased him with my sweet words. And I am certain it was not *I* but that boy there who caused the poor fellow to fall to the ground with one of those clumsy fingers of his. Is that not so? My dear?"

Stafford came out from the shadows to stand beside Mary. He was doing his best not to tremble too much, though he had no idea at all how he had not already collapsed and died.

"Sir," he said plain. "I do confess that the fault is all mine. Most likely if he is dead then it was me that did the worst of it by prodding him like I did. If you say he must go in the ground then I won't go against it, sir. If doing such a thing would put a finish to what I done then I'd do it myself, dig the hole and all and carry him and throw him in and cover him up. I am but a weak boy, though, sir, as you see. May I beg of you and ask sir if you would help me do what must be done?"

Sullivan breathed in deeply and exhaled full and long. His shoulders rose a little. His knees lost their ache.

"Now, Mary," he said, coming forward to ruffle the boy's ragged, black hair with his sweaty hand, "will you join us or will you not?"

"I will not."

"Then best you get to doing something else for you are more hindrance than help in our time of need. I declare that has likely ever been so and ever will be."

Mary strode out of the room and made the short walk to her sleeping area, closing the door gently behind her.

The baker ignored her egress and instead bent his damp head but a blink from the wide of the terrified Stafford's eyes. "Come then, boy and show me just what a murderous lad such as you can do."

The two of them took up a position either side of the table upon which the body of John Dawlish lay. Unbeknown to Sullivan and Stafford, the majority of the bones beneath that fetid skin had been broken and smashed at some time or other over the years in circumstances banal and fantastical. What's a crack on the head with an old piece of wood and a bit of blood when your entire life has been a succession of beatings, thrashings, ragings and wailings?

Anyway, mused John Dawlish as the baker and the boy clumsily pawed at him in their comical attempts to complete their mournful task, *let them hury me. Let them cover me up with all that tasty dirt, and I'll gulp it all down and I'll swallow it all into me until I've had my good old fill of it.*

Having managed to hoist John Dawlish's body off the table and onto the floor, the boy and the baker proceeded to take an arm each and took to dragging their bounty outside. Such was the effort and dedication each applied to their task, neither noticed how the stranger beat back the yellow Small Mercy sunbeams with the wild and rank of his lamentable lashes beneath which his ancient eyes howled as horrific and unholy as hell itself.

5. Proved and Risen

THE FACT THAT Sullivan and Mary resided in the very last abode at the southern extent of the track that ran through Small Mercy was undeniably advantageous given the events of the morning. None of the other citizens ever had cause to pass by, for the outskirts of that end of the village had never been of any discernible use. They were not farmed or grazed upon. As far as anyone was concerned, Small Mercy extended only as far as the shadows of the baker's home. Even when their working day was done and the inhabitants were free to associate with one another – within the limits ascribed by The Constitution – it had never been the custom to casually look in upon a neighbour if in need of solace or company. Once you were done with your daily contribution to the continued functioning of Small Mercy, home was where you generally headed. And once that door was closed (though not locked), home was where you stayed.

Sullivan considered himself at last to have benefitted in some way from the rigid rules that had dictated the passage of his life. Where once they had deprived him of the opportunity to bring life into the world and to gorge unfettered upon the sumptuous offerings of carnal pleasures, it was an irony not lost upon him that he had been so ravishingly free to end the existence of another. He considered all this as he and Stafford heaved the stranger's body through the untrodden grass of a meaningless field in search of a spot to dispose of their burden.

The yellow sun shone high in the blue of the sky. There was not a cloud to be had across the entire expanse of the horizon. It was a Small Mercy sky in every respect – solid, unblemished, clearly defined. There were days when it rained and there were days when it did not. The rain would last all day or it would not come at all. As it was with the rain, so it was with the sun. The wind was a little more unruly, but that too had in time seen its capacity for caprice curtailed.

To all but Mary, Sullivan and Stafford, the entire day thus far had been a testament to how the imposition of order and the steady application of endeavour in the fulfilment of basic tasks must remain undefiled. One of the unwritten tenets of The Constitution of Small Mercy was an unwavering faith in the power of banality. To experience boredom was to know peace just as to indulge in such frivolity as desire, creativity and restlessness was to invite the unwelcome spectre of discord.

Ah, but it only takes a little wind to nudge a cloud into the scene, and suddenly all that has been so gorgeously stagnant is rendered at once fragile. Were that cloud to darken, a whole different set of outcomes is instantly possible. From the moment that little wind breathes that cloud into the incessant blue, control is wrested away. It may rain or it may not. The blue of the sky may fade into white or grey and the yellow sun seek solace in the rampant folds of it all. Then there may come a storm of thunder and lightning, roaring gales and hail maybe. Or maybe none of that will happen and it will be just blue sky and yellow sun from morning to night. The sum of it all is that no matter the fanaticism and ardour with which the rules, tenets and regulations that govern any community are applied, there will always be that which cannot be legislated for. It is a wonderful sultry that those whose existence oozes on within the tepid confines of overwhelming monotony will be the very ones who miss the coming of the cloud, the forming of the storm. The first they will know if it is when they are drowned in the rains or set afire by the flashes. And then, of course, it will be far too late.

The satisfaction felt by Sullivan when he came upon the ideal place to bury John Dawlish's body was short-lived.

"Spade! Bloody spade!" he cursed. "Boy, run back now. Go to the back of my house and bring me back my wretched spade. Go!"

Stafford, as ever, did as he was told. Much to his relief, he somehow managed to return with the desired article within what the baker considered to be a reasonable amount of time.

"Now dig away until you are spent, and then I'll take on the task if need be. Dig deep, mind. Dig deep then dig deeper still, right on down to the other side of this world if you have to."

The hole in which they intended to bury John Dawlish was within a clearing of dark soil surrounded by sturdy trees whose trunks were thick and cracked, whose branches were tangled and bare of leaves. There was no birdsong to lessen the gloom nor was there the frantic scurry of tiny creatures to bring innocent motion to the stagnant and stark.

Stafford dug deep as instructed. He dug until he was spent.

"Is this right, sir?" the boy panted. "Deep enough, I mean? Just how you would want it? Ain't the other side of the world, far as I can tell, but I be all done, I'm sorry to be saying."

"Hand me the spade," the baker barked.

Sullivan chopped at the earth with his spade and hurled dirt and soil up and onto the clearing floor. He felt that same rush of excitement he'd experienced when he'd crashed that piece of wood against the side of John Dawlish's face.

Satisfied at last, Sullivan hauled himself out of the dark hole. He stood behind the upper half of Dawlish's body and called Stafford to come stand beside him.

"Roll him in is all we do now."

"Roll him in?"

"Roll him in."

And roll him in they did.

"Fill up that hole now and we be done."

Sullivan withdrew to the edge of the clearing and sat down with his back against one of the old trees. He had not felt as good about life in many a long year. He smiled. He closed his small eyes. And he listened to the scraping of the spade and the spatter of the dirt as it was deposited into the hole.

The filling up of the horrible grave had been less arduous for Stafford than the digging of it, and soon his task was complete. He informed the baker that the work was done. Sullivan, somewhat irritated at being wrenched from his reverie, sullenly grunted his approval. Without a look back at the scene of their labours, the baker and the boy returned to their village. Not a single word was there that passed between them the entire duration of their solemn return.

As the day wore on, the sky very slowly began to lose the bold and brash of its blue. Furthermore, unnoticed by man, woman or child, a little cloud was blown gently into being. Inherently nebulous by nature, it was inevitable that what had begun as an innocuous puff of pale air would take a form far more menacing.

Afternoon had turned fully into evening when there was heard from within that last house in the village a knocking upon the door. This time, still revelling in the success of his day, it was Sullivan, fair full with more than his quota of ale, who took it upon himself to rise and see to the matter at hand. The woman, Mary, had stiffened the very moment the dull thud entered her being. As if pulled by an unseen leash, she stood and followed the baker to the entrance to their loveless hovel of a home.

"What are you doing, woman?" Sullivan grizzled on becoming aware of her presence behind him.

Mary made no reply. The inevitability of it all overwhelmed her, rendered her vacant. She was shackled to the scene. Without word or effort, she slid her slender frame along the wall until it was she who stood before the door, that baker tyrant now in the gloom of her tender shadow.

Sullivan muttered something about ale and violence. His coarse utterances were nothing but hum and murmur to the spectre of a woman within whose penumbra he whined.

No more knocks came for none were needed. Sometimes all you can do is go through the simple motions such as when you reach out an arm, wrap your fingers upon a handle and silently pull open a door.

Dried blood was streaked and mottled across John Dawlish's huge, misshapen head. Almost the entirety of him was smothered in the dirt and ooze of the Small Mercy earth. The grin upon his festering face was devastating, the stench of him pure as the purest poison.

"Now then, Miss," said the risen stranger all singsong and dread in the bright, white dazzle of the bleak black night, "about that bread."

6. For the Birds

The sight of Mary sitting opposite the rancid stranger at the table upon which for years Sullivan had partaken of his tasteless fare enticed from him not one flicker of emotion. He had not the fair grace to faint or to suffer any other involuntary affliction that such a vision as the one to which he'd then been presented could rightly be expected. Such stoicism, of course, could not last. All that had been quelled suddenly gushed rampant to the surface of his consciousness.

The lower half of Sullivan's jaw divested itself of any pretence of form, revealing an oval hole of scant majesty. His small, red eyes blinked three times in quick succession before losing all discernible function. In sublime syncopation, his shoulders slumped, and his knees gave way. He was on the ground now, though it was unclear as to whether he was even aware of the fact. Without any conscious effort, his arms lurched forward, his rough palms steadying him with unwholesome pity as a means of preventing his face from crashing onto the rough-hewn flagstones. The artless fingers that had squeezed and tortured bread for almost their entire lives were splayed wide, the full weight of the baker's imbalance driving through them.

Mary observed the crumpling of her companion with a curious relish. She tilted her head to the side a little at the dropping of his jaw and leaned forward across the table at the culmination of his flaccid descent.

John Dawlish scratched the side of his head with the jagged nails of his misshapen fingers.

It was the woman who took it upon herself to move the madness on.

"I'll get that bread you been asking of," Mary said plain. She stood with care and shuffled past Sullivan, pressing her back against the wall so as not to be near even the stench of him.

By the time Mary returned to the room, the black of night had fallen hard. Though she was sure the light of the evening had only just begun to fade not a moment earlier, she questioned not the rapid collapsing of this odd Small Mercy day. She placed a loaf of bread upon the centre of the table along with a heavy knife whose wooden handle was chipped, scarred and woeful.

"I'll fetch some light," she said quietly, leaving and returning once more.

When at last the small room was lit, albeit with but a wan glow from a pitted, charmless candle, John Dawlish set himself to indulge in the freshly baked wares whose fragrance had so tantalised him when the pink did straddle the dawn.

Had he been conscious of the presence of the knife so close at hand to that ghoul of a stranger, Sullivan may well have feared his predicament to have become even worse than already it appeared. But he need not have concerned himself with such banalities as being murdered in his own home. For John Dawlish was, in some respects, a simple fellow. Thus did he pick up the loaf in both his hands and chomp upon the middle of the bread, his few rotten teeth performing admirably given their condition. He swallowed down the moist, chewed hunks with an audible gulp, the cavern of his mouth barely emptied of its mushy wad before the next came piling in.

Within just a few minutes that had been characterised by sounds of ravenous slobbering and the grunting and snorting of an increasingly satiated John Dawlish, the bread was gone. Crumbs lay strewn haphazard across the table. Mary reached across and swept them carefully with her small hands before gathering them up and putting what amounted to a good handful in the pocket of her dress.

"For the birds," she said to Dawlish, glancing briefly at him before turning away once more to gaze down at the head of the baker, who remained on his hands and knees on the floor at her feet.

"*Fine* bread," John Dawlish declared loud and certain. "I've had me some bread and such over the years, and that what you just served me up is *fine* bread."

"Thank you, sir. We never do have many who do complain of it. Not none, far as I recall."

Were it not for the continuing rigidity of Sullivan's form and aspect, the way in which Mary had never felt more at ease, or the presence of the stranger who had, within the course of the day, been buried in the ground only to rise again and fill himself with fine bread, it could have been just another late evening in any house in Small Mercy.

Ah, but nothing would ever be quite the same again around them there parts. Not now Dawlish was in town.

In time, the moon appeared. As the candle sputtered, so the moon grew. The room became sufficiently lit for Dawlish to proceed with whatever it was he had a mind to proceed with.

He began by giving due praise once more to Mary for the quality of her baking lest she not been fully aware of just how much he'd appreciated her hospitality. Having exhausted for the present his limited repertoire of what may be regarded as small talk, Dawlish took a deep breath, the very raggedness of which served immediately to smother the room in solemnity.

"Now, Miss."

Mary turned towards her filthy guest. There was a glint of white in her eyes, a thin smile upon her face for which she could not immediately account.

"Sir?"

"What we have here is what I would call *a situation*."

"A situation," Mary intoned.

"Yes indeed. We have here a *situation* and that's a fact."

Mary nodded, for how could she do otherwise? There was no doubt at all that this was indeed a situation.

"And in my many years, I have been in many situations. I have truly. Some have been situations that were in part like this situation, and others have been situations in part not like this situation. All of them have been situations, and I have been in them. There is no getting away from the fact that wherever I go, situations do somehow follow."

Dawlish looked at Mary as if seeking a response.

"Yes," she managed.

"I have learned not a thing from one situation to the other and that is the way it should be. Don't you agree, Miss?"

"You can call me Mary," the woman uttered sweetly, carefully positing no view either way as to his query.

Dawlish sniffed loudly and was about to expel a huge glob of whatever he'd formed within the wide recess of his crooked nose but chose instead to cough out the gloopy mess into one of his palms. He examined it close as if it had fallen from the black night and rubbed it onto the front of his filthy over-shirt. Mary watched the whole process in awe.

"I've never been one for names, truth be told, Miss. Never understood the need of 'em. I got given one or two of my own over the years, and they never did give me anything but bother."

Still Sullivan had not moved from his position on the ground.

"What I mean to say," Dawlish continued, "is that all my long life, I seen things and I done things. I done had things done to me and I been in situations of all kinds where it don't matter if I be called Mary or whatever you say you is or if I be called the name of the devil himself. No names never done me no good is all I be telling you."

"I'm sorry," Mary muttered.

"Ain't no need to be all apologising. How it is. How it always will be."

The woman nodded slowly.

"Anyhow," the stranger went on, "we only just been acquainted of late and, as you can see by that before you on the ground, we have one of them old situations that follow me around from place to place. Time, I reckon, that we get around to fixing our minds to it."

The moon was full and white in the window now, the mischief stars too. None of them wanted to miss a single thing. There's nothing intrigues the mighty firmament more than a little nighttime dread.

7. Just a *Thing*

B RING ME A pail of water," Dawlish instructed the woman. "Much as you can carry."

Without a sound, Mary left and returned some minutes later, dragging inelegant and panting half a wooden barrel. Errant waves shimmered silver and black, slopping from one side to the other, as devoid of rhythm as they were of purity. The contents could have been mistaken for oil such was their impermeable density. But it was only water. Water was all it was, just plain old water from the stream yonder, collected perhaps three or four days ago by Mary herself during one of those achingly beautiful moments when she would be far from the grasp of the baker and able to breathe an air less rancid than that to which her lungs had for so long been accustomed.

Dawlish jerked his head to the left and down, indicating a space between where he sat at the far end of the table and the static Sullivan on the floor a few feet to his right. "Just there. That's it. Close to his head as you can get it. Don't touch him, mind. He be just right where he needs be on them hands and them knees of his. Best if you get yourself over in them shadows, Miss. No telling what might get to being in a situation like the one we got going on this night. Like I tell'd thee, I don't make no habit of learning from one time to the next."

Mary swept silent behind the seated bulk of the stranger and squeezed into a chair that was midway along the length of the table. Once so ensconced, it felt to her as if she would never again be released. She was all but trapped in a vice consisting of the cold hard of the wall and the crooked of the wooden edge.

"Don't you move, and don't you say nothing now, Miss."

It was as redundant a comment as John Dawlish had ever made, and he'd made more than a few in his time, it has to be said.

Dawlish pushed himself back and launched himself slow and artless to his feet. He stretched out his arms and winced as he gained his full height. He grunted. He rumbled. Once fully formed, he seemed almost to fill the entire room. For a brief moment, the white moon was deprived of its morbid revelry. Dawlish took up a position whereby he was standing on one side of the half keg of water, the inert baker on the other.

Mary listened to the stranger's heavy breath. She leaned forward across the table and gazed upon Sullivan, who at a glance could have been mistaken for a sick dog. Just earlier, she had cowered unholy in the grime and the muck beneath the very table beside which her tormentor now knelt as if cast in stone. She felt no emotion when considering such a surreal reversal of fortunes, no emotion at all. It was all just a *thing*, as she was a thing, the table a thing, the baker a thing.

Dawlish proceeded to adjust the position of the barrel until the surface of the water contained a perfect image of the reflected white moon. So immaculate was the image, Mary had to glance quickly over her shoulder in order to assure herself that the moon had not been wrenched fully from the black night sky.

The stranger surveyed the scene before him from several angles before reminding the woman in a most ungracious manner that she should make no noise above a breath until what had to be done had been and got done.

With a terrifying display of inhuman agility, Dawlish reached across and lifted the unresponsive Sullivan full off the ground. For his part, the baker remained as he had been since struck down, his posture unchanged, devoid of all discernible life.

John Dawlish stepped back a pace until Sullivan's face hovered above the white moon water. At first, the white framed the face of the baker with a pale glow, but little by little, it began to merge into his sallow skin and into his open mouth. It oozed mournful into the wide of his eyes and crept into the hairy black holes of his nostrils. Dawlish held his prey thus, until the moon was indistinguishable from the man and the man indistinguishable from the moon. For more than an hour, this was how it was, this unholy melding of the ethereal and the malignant, a magical, tragical consummation if ever there was one.

Without hint of a warning, the stranger at last let go his hold on the baker. It was not that act itself that led to Mary failing in her adherence to maintain silent witness. It was what happened next.

For Sullivan's body did not come crashing down onto the half-barrel of water as surely should have been the case. It instead remained motionless and untethered in the air, some three feet from the ground held fast by no hand, supported by no plinth nor any structure of any kind.

Before Mary had even come close to quelling the terror with which her innards were then assailed, Dawlish lifted the barrel and poured half the contents over his own head and the remainder over Sullivan's. It was the splashing of the water as it hit the floor that finally broke Mary. The sound tore through her like a monstrous wave. She screamed guttural, her eyes clamped shut in sheer fear as the baker's body thwacked down heavy upon the flagstones.

As if roughly roused from the bleakest of slumbers, hewn no longer from the devilish medium of the stranger's devising, Sullivan lumbered to his sodden feet. He was pathetic of posture, gormless in demeanour, crude, hollowed out and terrified. He stared, as did Mary (who was still screaming), all wild-eyed and pitiful at the gruesome man before him. Where earlier, Dawlish had been all smothered in filth and black clotted blood, truly the image of a fellow who had been bashed about the head and buried in the ground, now he was as clean of skin and free of blemish or stain as anyone could aspire to be.

"Where I come from, Miss," he said low to Mary, who had seemingly screamed herself into silence, "a wailing like that which you did make is still what would be thought of to be a word when it comes to not saying a word. But it is done now, I do suppose."

Sullivan sank to the floor and shuffled back on his wet arse until he was all but under the table at Mary's feet.

"There," Dawlish said, plain and sombre, as he looked towards his hosts. "Now don't that look better?"

The baker shivered with cold and with fear. Mary trembled with foreboding. Somehow, she managed to find it within herself to speak.

"What just happened please, sir?" she whimpered.

"What just happened, Miss?" nodded Dawlish. "Well, what just happened is that the situation we was in has come to an end. There ain't no other way of explaining it than that. We have moved on is all. That's what happens, and that is what always will happen. You have yourself a situation. That situation comes to an end, and then we move on until the next situation comes and finds us. Now if that ain't giving you an explaining of what living life is then I don't know what is."

"But, I don't understand, sir." Mary began to sob. "I don't understand none of it," she continued, shaking her head slowly from side to side as each syllable left her young mouth. "I don't understand none of what went on since the minute I woke to this day. Not one bit of it."

John Dawlish sighed. He chewed on his thick lower lip with what remained of his teeth until he decided upon his response.

"It ain't about understanding nothing, as there be nothing to understand. I don't have an understanding of how my legs come to work, but it ain't never stopped me from walking, never in my whole existence. I don't know where my snot comes from or why I piss out from the front and shit out the back. All you need to know, Miss, all you need to *understand* if you be so intent on u*nderstanding*, is that it don't do nobody no good to rot and stink like an old corpse when there's wonder to be had. I can't put it no more plain than that."

Mary turned to the window. She saw only the black of the night.

"Where is the moon?" she enquired soft. "There still be light in here but no moon to gift it. How can that be? Oh, sir, how can that be?"

Dawlish scratched his face with one hand and adjusted his battered cap with the other.

"Some things just is," he said wearily. "And some things just aren't. Now best you two get to where you used to be going 'tween night and day, as I plan to sleep there under that old table of yours."

Without waiting for his devastated hosts to even get halfway out of the room, Dawlish curled himself up in his chosen spot and lay there untroubled throughout the night, his thick tongue drenched and dripping with the lascivious dregs of the startled galaxy's tears.

8. As a Babe

T HE BOY STAFFORD was eleven years old that day he thought he'd murdered the stranger with one of his fingers. His young life to that point had been one of basic chores and routine errands. Long and arduous days interspersed with dull and dreamless nights had comprised the tuneless rhythm of his existence. He had ever known only scant pleasure.

The nighttime hours that took shape following the treacherous events of that momentous day were filled with such visions and terrors that he was unable to immediately discern if the gasp with which he'd awoken was destined to be his first of the morn or the last of his life.

It was not just the pallor of her little brother's skin that alerted Grace Chuck to the condition his condition was in. An indescribable *ache* flowed from every pore of him that all but overwhelmed her to tears.

"Stafford?"

Grace leaned in close to Stafford's pale face.

"Stafford," the girl repeated, stepping back a little. "Stafford, are you sick? First tasks have already begun. You will be late to your work and you know how people get around here when those of the like of us are tardy."

The delicacy of her tone could not hide the worry in her soul.

Stafford turned to be on his side. His thin, naked body had at some time in the long night shed itself of the harsh and heavy encumbrance that passed as his blanket.

"Oh, Stafford," Grace sighed. "You are sick, I know you are. I see it. I *feel* it. Oh, my poor, poor sweet thing. I shall have to get Mother, though I hate to give her more woes than already she carries."

Grace was three years her brother's senior. It was her misfortune, as was common amongst the youth in Small Mercy, to bear all the trepidation of adolescence without any of the peculiar joys that should rightly attend those bemused and tender years.

Stafford's eyes were open yet he saw nothing but vague flitting shadows in the vague flitting light. In time, his mother, skeletal, hair grey before its time and limbs bent and wrecked by a lifetime of unerring subjugation, did her daughter's bidding.

It had been a long time indeed since she had been able to kneel, so instead, she did her best to bend low in order to gaze into her boy's face. Grace hovered fretfully beside her.

"Son?"

Momentarily torn from his torpor, Stafford glanced up into his mother's wide, brown eyes.

With all the woeful instinct possessed not just by one who has borne children but buried them also, Stafford's mother uttered not a word. Restraining her emotions in favour of a practical appraisal of the facts before her, she innately processed just what it was that was ailing her boy.

"Grace, dear," she said soft without turning. "Off to work now. Without cause or not, people will talk. Goodness knows this family needs not be the subject of idle talk in these times. So you go, girl, and be sure to give full attention to your chores."

Grace did as instructed, willing herself not to fear the worst as she stepped out timid into the burgeoning day.

"Now, my boy," sighed Stafford's mother as the front door clicked shut. "I see you ain't be dying and am thankful for that at least. Also, I see just as plain that it's not a sickness of the body that has you in its hold. I don't like to say you been up to no good because me and your father didn't bring you up that way. But you are a boy, and boys do have mischief in them and no amount of telling and loving will keep folly and fancy down when it has a mind to raise a lark. So, that being as it is, if it be a fact that *you* ain't been up to no good, then tell me, has it happened that someone has been up to no good with *you*?"

STAFFORD WAS AWARE of his mother's words only in as much as a calf may notice a breeze that crosses its face or as one of aged years may experience a sudden momentary chill felt by them alone and no other. Silence was left to fill the space between mother and son, persisting in benign solemnity until the woman creaked herself upright so as to let her son be.

The collecting of the bread from the baker had been a task assigned to Grace when she turned eight years of age, and it had remained her first duty of each day until she reached eleven. At this point, having been eight years old for little more than a week, Stafford took her place whilst she was reallocated.

Grace Chuck had ever been of slight constitution and was relieved and grateful when her bread-fetching days were done. Her demeanour improved further when it was deemed she be responsible for collecting the flowers from the meadow to the west of the village. Once gathered, she was to order the flowers into bunches and fasten them with a strip of willow. She would then deposit them on a barrow, from which they would be available to those for whom it was not Bread Day. On this particular morning, though, as her brother lay sick and her mother left forlorn, it was not to the meadow she headed but down the track to the baker's house. She fair flew on those dainty feet of hers, fair flew, fair flew, fair flew.

"My, you have grown." Mary smiled.

The cheeks of the gasping girl on the doorstep glowed tulip red.

"Thank you, Miss," Grace panted. "I come for the bread like I did when I was but young and silly."

Mary recognised so clear that look in Grace Chuck's eyes but said not a word. She turned and came back with a woven basket fully laden with freshly baked loaves.

Grace took the basket and settled it as best she could across her slender arms. It was as she was ready to begin her task of transporting her burden back up the hill that Mary addressed her in almost a whisper.

"Your brother. Where be he today then? Not unwell, I hope?"

Grace shook her head whilst all the while looking down. Had she not been so weary, the baker's woman would surely have picked up that skinny young thing and held her safe to her heart until the two of them were no more. But she had endured a very strange night indeed, despite having slept through undisturbed. Thus did she step back into the black of the doorway as Grace staggered as fast as she was able back up to where the village was beginning to rouse itself from its charmless slumber.

SMALL MERCY FUNCTIONED in almost every respect as an enterprise. Each villager operated within a rigid remit with the understanding that their efforts contributed to the smooth functioning of this particular patch of earth upon which they'd been destined to live out their life. It was with an unquestioning determination that generation after generation of Small Mercy inhabitants set about their endeavours.

Ah, but humans, no matter how mundane their lot, will always be susceptible to the whims and quirks that are as much a feature of their species as the structure of their bones and the wetness of their tears. That has ever been the case, and ever will it be. Where nature is perfect in form and function, man is no more than a work in progress, beset with incongruities, simmering with fatal flaws.

By necessity, therefore, it was recognised at the very outset of the village's conception that there would be a need for an individual whose sole role would be to ensure the maintenance of homogenous monotony in the face of innate human inadequacy. No cog could be allowed to fail, no wheel cease to turn. The one designated The Auditor would see to that.

The Auditor was second only to Judgement in the hierarchy of Small Mercy. Like all his ancestors before him, Franklin Singe, The Auditor at the time of this curious tale, took his work very seriously indeed.

It was said that Singe had been born not as a babe but as a lonely, grey-haired, fifty-year-old man. It was also said that he would die a lonely, grey-haired, fifty-year-old man. Such spurious conjecture, however, was never expressed too loudly for the reach of The Auditor was a thing of legend.

The Singe name had somehow managed to persist for as far back as when Small Mercy itself came into being. No Singe had ever been known to couple, yet each had unerringly produced offspring – one male child on every occasion. Franklin Singe was no different. He had but five years ago sired a sinewy, humourless boy who was cared for by the wan, joyless recipient of his seed in an unremarkable cottage far to the east of the village. The boy was seen only at funerals.

Franklin Singe was a master in his role. He would pace slowly up and down the main track, taking mental note of each and every person he saw. He could with but a scowl and a glare assimilate all he needed to know about the recipient of his unholy interest – their demeanour, the extent of their decay (physical and mental) and the level of their dedication to the greater cause. Some would say it was a talent of sorts, this ability to discern so much without recourse to words or simple enquiry. None would ever dare declare that of which all were so fearfully certain – that The Auditor, Franklin Singe, was without question a rank abomination who bestrode their drab environs with such sly rancour that even the devil himself would be revealed to be a crude imposter if the two were to be side by side considered.

9. A Most Human Kind

FROM THE MOMENT he became The Auditor, his father's body not two hours in the ground, Franklin Singe set about implementing the changes he'd through countless conniving nights considered necessary but had been in no position to pursue, owing to the infuriating ability of his predecessor's heart to sustain long after every other faculty had possessed the good grace to abandon him.

Although The Constitution did not explicitly express a view, the concept of ambition had never been encouraged in Small Mercy. Singe himself believed that if an outbreak of aspiration were ever to grip even a smattering of the imbecilic inhabitants of his village, only ill would come of it. Ambition required intellect and vision. Ambition was not for the fetid masses. Furthermore, he was unwavering in his belief that the greatest failing of his dead father and those who came before him was their reprehensible lack of ambition.

Franklin Singe began his reign as the second highest-ranking member of the Small Mercy elite with all the ravishing disdain that had fermented rotten within him whilst he'd sullenly awaited his father's demise.

Within a matter of days, he had sought out and appropriated half a dozen of the most anonymous and lonesome whose tragic and overwhelming absence of passion, conscience and imagination rendered them perfect for his Machiavellian designs.

He determined from the outset to become the stuff of myth and legend. If by the time he was done, the very whisper of his name did not inspire the kind of terror that engendered immediate and relentless subordination then he would have been an utter failure.

Blood congeals, dries and disappears. Bruises too must fade. Even bones will largely heal and muscles repair. As some are born blind or deprived of the power of speech, Franklin Singe came onto this earth equipped with a thorough understanding that true dread flourishes best when sown in the bleak shadows of the subconscious. Any fool can wield a club; it takes a certain type of genius to stalk unmolested within the nether reaches of the soul.

As soon as they were of an age to understand such concepts as fear and shame, each child in Small Mercy was made aware of The Auditor and his unseen companions who would number anything from ten to a hundred depending upon the severity of the reprimand being meted out by their parents. That suited Franklin Singe just fine. As far as he could discern, Judgement, his sole superior, held him in high esteem. Of all others, there was not one over whom he did not hold sway.

It was the callous spectre of The Auditor that loomed heavy on Martha Chuck as she went back and forth from the village to the stream collecting the water for the day.

A crushing pang of guilt assailed Martha as she emptied her pail into the deep well beside the Judgement House and peered across the track to the door behind which her little boy lay in pieces. Lest that brief glance of hers be observed and reported, she shook herself back into glib subservience and headed once more to the stream within whose cool waters she so longed to be submerged.

The sun had barely gained its full height when The Auditor was made aware that not only had young Grace Chuck been seen to have been more skittish than usual, but it had been she who had delivered the day's supply of bread from that idiot Sullivan. The Chuck girl was as foolish as she was pathetic as far as Singe was concerned, so the news that she had been particularly foolish and pathetic during the course of the morning was nothing but an irritation. Ah, but that business about the bread? Well, that got The Auditor's mind a-whirring.

It didn't take long for it to be confirmed that the boy Stafford had been absent from his morning tasks, hence his sister's facile efforts to minimise the impact of his insolence. Singe had suspected as much. He was invariably accurate in such matters. It was no mere instinct or gut feeling he had to thank for his remarkable intuition. Nothing as inelegant as that. There had been moments over the years when he had lamented just how unchallenged he was in the performing of his tasks. On this occasion, however, he felt himself becoming rather aroused at what the day may have in store.

It was in the subtlety of his actions that Singe's greatness lay. He was not of the devil as some would have him be. No demon was he, no unspeakable creature from the depths of the oceans or the bowels of the earth. His talents were of a most human kind. Had he been a painter, his works would have been displayed around the world. But he was not a painter. He was The Auditor of Small Mercy. His brush was his cunning, his palette daubed with every shade of malice any human could ever conceive.

After five consecutive hours of fetching and carrying water in order that her fellow villagers could drink their fill and relieve themselves of their accumulated grime, Martha Chuck returned home for her allotted break. It was then that she saw the inch-long nail protruding from the middle of her front door. She shuddered out a woeful sigh and in doing so reminded herself that not only was there no God, but no angels either. There was, as all in Small Mercy knew well, only action and consequence.

Within her home, Martha was all woman, all mother. She was no cog or wheel or pulley or lever. Once inside those sagging walls, she was more human than automaton, though as the years had worn on, the distinction between those two imposters had become increasingly blurred.

Stafford had remained naked upon his low bed throughout the morning. Other than turning awkwardly from one side to the other in moments of frantic panic, he had been motionless. Martha noticed when she looked at him that the colour in his face had returned somewhat.

"It be gone the middle of the day," she said soft to him. "There be a nail in our door already, though that don't surprise me none if truth be told. If you can bring yourself to something like even half alive then I beg that you do it, Stafford. You know as well as I the meaning of the one nail."

In the first indication since dawn broke that he was capable of anything but base action, Stafford rubbed his eyes and sat up with a mournful groan.

"I'm sorry, Mother," he muttered.

"Leave the sorry and such for later, dear. Just try and get yourself in your clothes and we can yet plead our case when called before Judgement."

Stafford heaved his little body to a standing position and pulled his filthy grey smock over his head. The bottom of it hung just below his bony knees. Already he could feel his skin begin to itch.

"Thank you, my darling," Martha said as she watched her little boy stretch out his arms and rub his eyes again with his fists.

It was only once Stafford had wandered to the door and out into the afternoon that Martha began to fully consider her predicament. One nail was never good, though the implications and consequences of one nail would in time pass. But should another from the shadows join it? Were there to be two nails banged into her door? The thought alone terrified her to the point of collapse.

It was well into the afternoon when that poor widow, that mother of two, mourner of three, began to wonder just what it was her innocent babe had got himself into.

10. Salacious Embrace

JOHN DAWLISH STIRRED beneath the baker's wooden table. He grunted, coughed and uncoiled himself. There was the semblance of a smile upon his desolate face. He manoeuvred himself into the centre of the room, stood, coughed once more and blurted out noisily a huge glob of phlegm into the two cracked palms he had fashioned into a receptacle of sorts. He examined his expulsion with some interest before wiping the product of his innards on the ragged material that had the joyful task of covering his arse. The deed done, he looked up to see that the baker's woman stood now before him.

"Morning to you, sir. I hope I didn't go waking you unnecessarily, like. It's just one of the young 'uns come for the daily bread."

"Only me wakes me, Miss so don't go fretting none," Dawlish rumbled. "A fine day it seems from where I be stood?"

"Indeed. You slept well, I hope?"

"Well enough. And you, Miss? You slept well?"

Mary paused a moment before making her reply.

"I cannot tell you how I slept or what passed during my night. I recall, of course, the events of the day, for how could I not? The last thing I remember was covering myself with my old blanket. After that, not a single recollection do I have. If I did dream then I can't tell you the nature of it, and if I awoke – as I am accustomed to do, four, five, six times during the course of a single night, I regret to say – then I know nothing of what passed during those times. Yet I do declare that I am *changed* in some way or another in a manner I can't get close to describing. It's a feeling is all, the like of which I never did feel before."

"That so?"

"Yes, sir. Forgive my wittering on. Something has come over me during this last night that, that…well. I will come right out and declare it, sir, if you don't mind, though I will sound like a foolish woman of the most foolish kind. It be like I went to my bed dead and woke to the morn *alive!*"

Dawlish clomped a thudding pace towards she who had been reborn. He stared directly into the essence of her.

"As to the events of yesterday," he intoned, "no mention will ever be made, no mention at all. You have woke all *alive*, as you say, and that is all there be to it."

"Yes, sir. Of course, sir."

"Now go tell that man of yours what I just be saying. No mention, no word. Ever it was a situation we had. And now it is a situation we have no more. Tell him plain and tell him over and again if need be."

Mary nodded.

"I wager it be that he recollects more than you. Could be his recallings will be enough on their own to hold that tongue of his."

Mary nodded again.

Dawlish farted.

Mary left.

Dawlish farted again.

Nobody farted like Dawlish.

"Now that's me all alive too," he did declare as the foul stench of his innards staggered out mischievous through the open window and into the unfurling of the day.

BY THE TIME the heat had subsided in the hearth and he had swept the floor clean, the baker was exhausted. He ached in every bone he possessed. Every sinew of his body appeared to have withered during the night into weak and useless fibres. To have observed him even then, you perhaps would have noticed little difference when appraising his physical form. You may have wondered why it was he who was attending to the chores ordinarily reserved for his callow companion but no more. He was of an age where bones will ache and sinews sag. He alone knew that something was very much amiss to a most disconcerting degree.

Where Mary had passed the night as if in a stupor, Sullivan had gained not one minute of rest. From the moment he'd entered his room, a terrifying rupture had taken of him.

With the moon ensconced in a salacious embrace in the stranger's gullet, no light was there to illuminate the baker's den. His eyes rendered redundant, he accepted with commendable fortitude that he had no option but to eschew any notion of resistance. And so it was that the very essence of that man for whom love had once but briefly dangled its delights was subjected to the full unravelling of all that as a consequence he'd become.

First, a surge of pure horror leapt from deep within the centre of his chest, and he watched as a pale dot of blue light flickered beneath his wretched skin and grew into a circle the size of penny right above where he knew his heart to be. He felt no pain as the circle of blue light popped out into the open and hovered in the blackness no more than a foot above where he lay.

As his sense of horror diminished, it was replaced with a feeling of absolute, unfettered rage. Sullivan was convinced he would explode into pieces. It was as the last remnants of his consciousness were about to shatter that he became aware of a crimson circle of light, perhaps three times the size of the small, pale-blue orb that still shimmered before him. The crimson circle glowed with such intensity it brought a pinkish sheen to the entire outline of that impotent man. Like the one before, its source was the old baker's heart. It too eased through from the in to the out and set itself beside its pale-blue brethren.

There was to be one final circle of light, this time yellow in colour and larger in diameter. So, in time, Sullivan could do nothing but submerse himself in those gentle, heavenly lights and turn himself fully over to their majesty.

The scintillating manifestations of malice, rage and shame that had for so long wrought havoc upon his once-decent soul had taken now their true form. Out in the open, their beauty could not be denied, but like the Sirens of legend, theirs was a purpose most malign. The spectres three had crooned rampant in that man, and he had in time willingly conspired with them in the daily denigration of the woman whom once he'd loved.

Having been exorcised of the malice, rage and resentment that had sustained him all these last years, the baker had no choice during the remainder of that long night but to acknowledge that he was a man in form and function only. As there was no hateful aspect to him now, there was no love. His very essence, his soul, all that which renders a human magical, was no more. He was a collection of bones encased in a filthy, flaccid skin which was held together by dour muscles and kept alive only by the insipid blood that dribbled sullen through his veins.

Some night for that baker.

Some night indeed.

The embers in the fire had dulled, the floor was clean. His morning chores were complete. Trembling a little, he shuffled back off to his room, whereupon he made no effort at all even to look for ale. He just sat on his bed for a moment before curling up on his side. He thought about weeping but didn't. He forced his eyes closed for a few moments, hoping he would die. But he didn't die. So he stayed there all timid and hollow, bread baked, hearth cooled and floor clean, just wondering what was to become of him.

JOHN DAWLISH GAZED across the western expanse of torrid grassland that culminated far off in the stream from which Martha Chuck further up the hill passed her morning fetching and carrying water. He took sorrowful note of the pale, brown blotches that oozed unwholesome between the yellowing swathes of once-green pastures. Dawlish thought deep upon the elements and how each had it in their gargantuan power to both give life and to destroy life.

As the sun doth open the petals of the finest flower so it can drain dry the rivers and suck the life from the land. Where water may nourish and cleanse, it may also flood the crops and drown man, woman and child should it so desire. As the flames of a fire will warm the wet and sodden and transform base dough into bread, so it thinks nothing of destroying whole forests, towns and villages with the errant sputtering into being of an errant spark. And the land? Well though it staves off the oceans and brings forth beauty and sustenance from its very depths, it too has the propensity to crack open wide and feast upon all that tumble into its mighty chasm.

Dawlish considered all this, in his own peculiar way, as he stared across that western expanse. He had seen so much in his time – destruction, wonder, desolation, magic and tragedy. The stench of his two stupendous morning farts still clung to the air around him. In spite of the regularity with which he indulged in blasting out the fetid vapour of his innards, he could never conceive of a time when even the most timid of farts would not bring him great joy. And in that alone was he in any way akin to any other man who ever did tarry upon this wondabulous earth.

11. Not the Air

For Franklin Singe, the sight of a bent nail in a cracked door was something fine and solemn to behold. No hammer had he ever swung and never had he pinched a nail of any description between his slender fingers. All doors he had stood before had been opened to him without him ever having to signal his presence. He had but two hands yet an unseen number at his immediate disposal; two eyes but the vision of innumerable pairs. Within the bounds of Small Mercy, The Auditor was omnipotent. Though it was Judgement who, in his own fashion, presided over the village's various rituals and ceremonies, it was widely held that in the matter of punishment, it was The Auditor who reigned supreme.

It wasn't that Singe necessarily revelled in the distress of others, more that he had an insatiable lust for retribution in its purest form. Inaction, frailty, weakness – all demanded a disproportionate response in order that such malignancy not become endemic. He was one for symbolism, more than speeches, and if that symbol appeared to manifest itself from out of nowhere yet was visible for all to see, then so much the better. He doubted, even with his vast store of intellect, that he would ever again devise anything so perfect in terms of meeting all requirements as that nail-in-the-door abomination of his.

So, the boy had failed on the morn, and the mother, the woman, the widow, whatever she was in the whole scheme of things, had been complicit in that failure. Rather than come forth honest with the unwholesome ruination of the situation, she had sought to involve her foolish daughter in the ploy to deceive and to distract lest it be known she had nurtured into being yet another dotard.

In Small Mercy, more through repetition than design, it had always been that the parent would be held accountable for the action or inaction of their offspring. Martha Chuck's husband was dead, so it was upon her that the might of Judgement was destined to fall. The fact that Stafford had, with commendable courage, risen from his bed at midday to go about his afternoon duties – well, that was nothing but an act of impudent defiance as far as Franklin Singe was concerned. He knew not who had slyly observed the fetching of the bread by Grace and thereby provided proof of the boy's tardiness. Nor did he know which of his spectral charges had banged the nail into that Chuck woman's door. That was just the way the system was designed to function. Though never one for ostentatious displays of emotion, The Auditor permitted himself a wistful grimace and a slow shake of his head. Sometimes, he could not help but wonder just what a little ambition can achieve.

MARTHA CHUCK CEASED in the ravage of her heavy task at the sound of the Judgement Bell. The working day, regardless of whatever part you played in your contribution to the fabric of Small Mercy, came to a close at that much-wished-for sound.

The air was sullen.

The air oozed relentless.

The air was not the air.

By the time Martha Chuck returned to the village, more or less the entire population of Small Mercy had gathered in a ragged semicircle before the steps of the Judgement House. As a phantom, Martha nudged her way silently through the crowd until she stood between her two remaining children, who had no doubt been instructed to take their place in the expanse of dust and dirt around which the populace heaved. Grace quivered to the left of her; Stafford barely noticed the arrival of his mother such was the dread that gripped his very soul.

Then, from out of the bleak of the shade and into the tragedy of the bright, stepped The Auditor.

The clang of the bells shrugged off the last remnants of their shame.

The air was sullen.

The air oozed relentless.

The air was not the air.

The tragedy of the bright.

The Auditor.

This Small Mercy

(and all who sail in it…)

As he stood there ungracious before the woman and her sorrowful children, The Auditor marvelled at the wonder of autonomic function. Stripped bare, Man was perhaps after all something of merit. He was King and he was Queen. He wasn't so lost in the moment to notice the absence of the baker and that woman of his. Ordinarily, he would have been irritated by such an incursion of irregularity, but on this occasion, he found himself even further aroused than already he was.

There had been many Auditors over the years, but only ever one figure who went by the appellation Judgement.

The Singes had for generations produced Auditor after Auditor, male heir after male heir. They carried not bread from down the hill to up the hill nor fetched water from the stream all day long. Nor did they tend to the fields or impart knowledge to the ignorant, construct and erect, grind that which was to be ground or forge necessary implements in the red and orange fires of a black hole range. The standing of the Singe dynasty rested solely on their ability to identify, vilify and terrify their fellow brethren whose only misfortune was to have been cursed with being born a human in that Small Mercy.

WAY DOWN AT the southern foot of the village, John Dawlish was still looking out west through the bakery window. Were you to have followed his gormless gaze, you may have reckoned he was in a trance or a daydream, though day was almost at its end. You would no doubt, if asked, have assumed him to be in the process of counting the white butterflies that flittered here and there; maybe thought he was seeking out with those unblinking eyes of a creature for to snare and gorge upon when night truly fell. But no. Even by now, it must be somewhat obvious that this stranger of ours, whose inelegant stumblings began this curious tale, has more about him than at first was apparent.

As he stood at that window, the woman Mary emboldened in her room, the wretched Sullivan subdued and crouching by the doorway, more golem than man, Dawlish absorbed into his cavernous depths every flutter of every eyelash, every globule of sweat and each sly sigh of every human being who, in that moment, breathed from between the hills to the north and the woodland to the south.

"Always good to have a plan," he reminded himself low.

And in the profundity of the moment, he realised sweet that he was as close to tears as ever he'd been his entire life.

12. A Manner Incomprehensible

J UST THE ONE nail. Not two. One."

Those words whirled around in Martha Chuck's head as she stood motionless at the steps of Judgement House. Her children were either side of her, the ragged remains of the entire Chuck clan, arrayed before the assembled multitude, simply awaiting their fate.

Stafford had missed one morning of his chores. Grace had done the best she could. None of it seemed at all right to Martha. Expressions of varying degrees of bewilderment flittered in an and out of the shadows that struck out across the pale faces of those who had ever depended upon her for reassurance that their life would someday improve.

Dusk crept in upon the edges of this baleful Small Mercy scene.

Everything was as it should be.

Everything *is* as it should be.

Judgement had no name but Judgement.

Judgement *has* no name but Judgement.

There was no breeze yet, all the same, the breeze eased.

It was too early for the moon.

The sun skulked sullen someplace else, leaving in its wake only a smattering of light with which to beat back the dimming of the day.

Everything must

fade

in time

Franklin Singe, with all the silent rancour he could muster, stepped to one side in order that the only person who inspired more terror than he could take charge of proceedings.

Judgement stood well over six feet tall.

Judgement was swathed in a black hooded cloak that hung loose from top to toe.

Judgement wore no shoes of any kind.

Judgement breathed deep as the ocean and heavy as the mountains.

There never was anybody quite like Judgement.

At languorous last, Judgement did speak. The voice was as of a distant avalanche. Each consonant was a crack in the sudden of it all, every vowel the dread doom chomp of the final falling tree. There was a wail in the silence between each sound, yet that wail was the silence and that silence the wail.

Judgement spoke in thunder.

Judgement spoke in lightning.

Judgement spoke in drown.

Judgement spoke in quake.

Judgement's diction was something between the first desperate gasp of the newborn and the eternal exhalation of the damned and the doomed.

That being said, there was not a single sound that fell from the mouth of Judgement that was not utterly incoherent. If that stream of notes ancient and guttural were bound by the threads of some structured language, then it was one foreign to all then present. Even The Auditor with his unrivalled intellect had not then, or at any time before, the slightest notion of the specifics of the proclamation. He alone, however, could only marvel, albeit ruefully, at the inherent genius of his master. For he had long believed that holy truth that the subjugation of the many by the few is enhanced, not hindered, when justice and its composite parts is articulated in a manner incomprehensible to those whom it purports to serve.

Judgement spoke for but a short time.

Judgement spoke no more.

Judgement was done.

Judgement did leave.

Yet the image of Judgement lingered long into the evening and through into the dawn of the following day.

The cowed throng twitched back into some semblance of life only to be quelled into a graceless stupor once more. The Auditor was not Judgement for sure, but there was none dare doubt the awful acts of which he was capable.

"Judgement hath spoken," Singe did mournfully intone.

The Small Mercy villagers shuffled from one foot to another as if having awoken from an unsettling dream. Martha Chuck remained at the front, her head low. Grace tried hard to stem her little-girl tears. Stafford just stared into nothingness, wishing for it to engulf him without relent.

Eventually, Martha spoke. Her voice was a dull throb.

"Dear Auditor, I am no clearer as to the fate of my family than I was when I first saw that nail in my door yonder."

Franklin Singe cast forth a cruel and callous grimace despite having intended to avail himself of an expression of far finer subtlety. Internally, he upbraided himself for the crass application of this part of his duty before once again taking command of every faculty available to him.

"Judgement hath spoken," was all he would give that wretched woman in her pain and her ache.

"But I know not of what Judgement did say," Martha said, lost.

"Judgement hath spoken."

The Auditor cast down a torrid glare as the night took hold. He turned. And then he was gone.

The crowd dispersed slowly, walking in silence to their homes, daring not even to wonder if they would be greeted by a nail or two of their own. In time, Martha and her children were all that remained of the tragic proceedings of which they had played so pivotal a part.

"Come now," Martha murmured soft. She put an arm around first her daughter and then her son. "Let us get inside and be away from this day."

When they were once more stood before the door of their little home, Grace spoke in almost a whispered howl.

"Mother, I don't see no sense of what has just been done to us, if anything at all. What is the meaning of all this?"

Martha turned to look over her shoulder, then made her reply.

"Judgement hath spoken is all," she said.

And then she did usher them distraught into the weep of their night.

STARS SPUTTERED INTO life and the white moon did them the courtesy of a fleeting appearance. Clouds came and clouds went. The earth turned slow and remorseless. The Judgement Hall bells clanged the passing of each hour with faultless spite. Eventually, a pink straddled the dawn and the yellow sun did yawn up from between the northern hills.

It was Sullivan who first noticed just moments after rising to attend to his chores that the stranger had gone. He shuffled carefully through each room to assure himself of the fact, hoping not to wake Mary, whose sweet breaths he could hear drifting from under her door. Assured of Dawlish's disappearance, he began to feel a little less broken. When Mary finally rose, she knew within no more than a breath or two that the stranger was no more for the air was once more of freshly baked bread, not sodden with fragrant desolation.

MARTHA CHUCK PASSED a sleepless night. There was a hollowness within her when she shook off the detritus of her despair. A devastating inevitability oozed through her entire body with each step she took from the room in which she ever lay lonesome and into where her children ought to have been. No wail broke from her at the sight of the two empty beds, nor even a sob. She just lowered herself to the floor and sat there a while.

A mother knows.

A mother knows.

So AS ONE woman writhes within the ravages of her loss, another considers with some cherish the fresh nuances of her own particular situation.

The baker bakes without affection.

The Auditor is all snarl and all sneer.

Dawlish gone.

Stafford gone.

Grace gone.

Small Mercy, my lover, my friend, is all set for some kind of a reckoning.

13. Gleefully Gathered

S HE'S GONE MAD, I tell you."
   "Never did get over that man of hers though he wasn't much far as any who knew him say."

"More ale in him than sense at the end. Some reckon it was them babes that died when they were barely off weening that got him that way."

"Nagging woman will do that to a man just as much."

"You hold your tongue, now!"

"I'll hold what I please, woman."

"Will you now, my dearest?"

"Soon come a time when that door of theirs will be so full of nails it will be only nails holding it together."

"The bread be late and if the bread be not here then I fancy the flowers too will be wilting where they grow."

"What care I for flowers? A man cannot live by the frippery of blooms!"

"On that, you speak true."

"And on many other matters beside!"

"Really, my dearest?"

As the villagers went about their morning tasks, their conjecture weaving in and out of their air around them as they fetched, carried, pushed and pulled, not one of them deviated from their allotted tasks. A craven lack of empathy had ever been endemic amongst the Small Mercy population. Cogs and wheels and levers and pulleys. Up and down and around and around. Long live The Constitution!

MARTHA CHUCK TREMBLED beneath the rancorous silence that was right then her only companion on this earth. She stood slowly. She bit her thin lower lip. A pitiful drop of pink blood swooned to the ground. She examined the rough blanket that lay unruly on the floor by Stafford's bed, searching it with intensity and care as if she would somehow discover the boy within the dark folds. Five times and more did she pull back the stained covering that was Grace's blanket, each time smoothing it flat and neat upon the tawdry mattress.

She thought not of nails, be they one or two in number. She considered not the enmity of The Auditor or the indecipherable proclamations of Judgement. The bells clanged a thousand times as she floated within the walls of her home. Her children had gone. All else was of no consequence.

Eventually, two boys whose first chore of the morning consisted of sweeping the main track of Small Mercy free of the debris of the night were imposed upon to collect the bread from the baker whilst a gaggle of young girls gleefully gathered up the flowers in the absence of Grace Chuck.

"The Chuck boy came not again this morn," said Sullivan to Mary. His face was red from his efforts, his fingers raw and riven with dried dough.

"I say he must be ailing, is all," Mary asserted.

"Maybe he is and maybe he ain't."

"It is of no concern to me or to you. Ours is to bake the bread and that is what we will do."

Sullivan nodded, aching in his acquiescence.

Neither of them made mention of the stranger's parting. The stark memory of his presence and all that had occurred was as overwhelmingly tangible as if he were still beneath their roof.

Mary went to her room. Whatever else had changed following the devilish deeds of the stranger, there remained within her undaunted and intact a grim melancholy that would not abate.

Sullivan had begun ever so gradually to perceive that his transformation from lord to serf was perhaps not quite as indelible as first it appeared. He slept that afternoon with a grimace etched deep into the raw of his being.

BEFORE EVEN THE midday sojourn that signalled the halfway point of the Small Mercy working day, Franklin Singe had been appraised of the salient facts of the morning. The boy Stafford had failed once more in his duty to collect the bread. The pathetic girl Grace too had neglected to see to her task of fetching the flowers. The only sign that any life resided still within the Chuck household was the silhouette of a woman pacing back and forth, to be seen first in the window at the left of the door then in the one to the right. Back and forth it went, that silhouette. Back and forth. When some ill-advised of his invisible charges posited with crass excitement that the Chuck children were dead in their beds and that the pacing shadow within their home was not their mother at all, but some demon sent at the behest of Judgement, Singe dismissed them with a furious wave of his hand. When no more news came, he closed the door to his study and settled back in the large chair that had the look of an unadorned throne about it. And then he closed his loveless eyes so as to seek out the company of his most sinister self.

It was a credit to the impregnable structure of Small Mercy that whatever new tragedy had befallen Martha Chuck and her children was essentially of no consequence with regards the fine functioning of that curious hamlet.

As morning rolled into afternoon, even the early mutterings had dissipated into nothing more than a faint recollection. In a place where the very concept of dreams and imagination were anathema, no event, no matter the magnitude, dwelled long in the minds of the villagers. The monotony of the chores allied with the rigidity of the routines that kept the whole thing going allowed for barely a flirtation with frivolous enquiry.

It was as true that day as any other that as powerful as Judgement was and as sly and callous as was The Auditor, The Constitution was the real force at play. Without that insidious and subtle diminution of spirit that began from birth onwards, Judgement would be viewed as a mere curiosity and Franklin Singe, that spiteful purveyor of all things malicious, would most certainly be cast far away to tremble breathless within the bounds of his own terror. Small Mercy had been long in the making. It had evolved into a formidable dominion, indomitable in every aspect.

People had disappeared before. No sooner had their absence been noted than they were forgotten even by those closest to them. An awful comfort was drawn from the fact that to be absent was a fate more desired than to be dead. Never was there one who gave voice to such a musing. The passive acceptance of those left behind, the admirable way in which they pursued their allocated role for the good of all, was sufficient. The act of mourning itself was perceived as an indulgence akin to dreaming. Both lacked the essential clarity of purpose to which a productive citizen should aspire.

One more Small Mercy day turned into one more Small Mercy night.

SOMEWHERE ON THE other side of the river from whose waters Martha Chuck would daily fill her pails, the white stars struck haphazard upon a sight that brought even the melancholy moon some semblance of interest. Thus was the scene afforded a focus more refined than otherwise it may have been. A slight breeze brushed the surface of the water, inducing slender ripples that flickered from black to silver and back again. The reeds along the bank swayed to a rhythm of their own devising.

Some ten feet or so from the western bank, two bodies lay motionless, one beside the other. They were identical in composition, knees bent up to chest, head largely obscured by a flaccid arm. They were foetal in every conceivable way.

The breeze that brought subtle motion to the black water and groove to the reeds had no impact upon that pair on the grass. And the breeze, the moon, the reeds and the stars could only look on in dismay as that stranger, that John Dawlish burst torrid and ravenous from the bleakest, blackest depths of that Small Mercy river.

Dawlish clambered crudely to the edge of the water and hauled himself out. He coughed and grumbled as he tried to rid himself of whatever detritus had sought to hold him back. The bodies but two clumping paces away remained unresponsive.

The ghoulish stranger who had entered Small Mercy just two mornings ago, turned his attention to the ground.

"Ah, now then," he nodded slowly, "I do believe that what we have here is another of them old *situations*." He bent down low until the shadow of his huge barbaric frame brought pure black to the yellow of the moon and the white of the stars. "You get your rest now, little boy, and you get yours too, little girl. There ain't no mistaking you be needing it or my name ain't whatever it be this time around.

The reeds along the riverbank still swayed.

Fair play to them for that.

Fair play indeed.

14. A Sparrow Jigging

The Small Mercy mill was situated far to the west of the village almost precisely on the same latitude as The Judgement Hall. Few had ever seen it, yet all reaped the benefit of its sublime efforts.

The wide circular base that spanned perhaps sixty feet in diameter tapered upwards ever so gradually, reaching into the skyway, its top being exactly half the width of its lowest point. Its simple construction consisted of huge timbers hewn from the trees that had once been so abundant in those parts, bolstered with woven willow, which was, in turn, covered with clay burned hard by the firmament fires of the remarkable universe.

The outer carcass of the mill was free of adornment. Function was all and all was function. At its very top, thick planks of oak swollen by the rain and the harsh of centuries long gone served to seal off its innards from the turning of the days. Thus was the mill as much mausoleum as womb. Despite its very remit being the grinding of coarse grain into the fine flour without which the loaves that played such a part in sustaining life would never exist, there persisted within a harrowing and dismal pall.

Four wide sails some thirty feet in length, made from the soul and ancient ruin of that which once oozed lush sap distinguished the mill from what may otherwise have been perceived as nothing more than a sullen testament to all that is artless and mundane. Entirely dependent upon the vagaries of Mother Nature's sighs and gasps for to turn and turn, the sails never did complain with so much as a squeak. Within the upper reaches of the wooden dome, an ingenious array of cogs was set in motion with each rotation and beneath them a pair of huge circular stones separated by the thinnest of slithers set to grinding against one another all a-moaning and a-groaning. The grain from the fields when crushed between those remorseless hulks wept dry flour-dust tears that floated down through into the main body of the mill, piling up mountainous and magical.

The Miller, Linton Gauge, lonesome and holy in his trade, approached his work with an unstinting solemnity.

So essential was the mill to the continued functioning of Small Mercy, it was not just its location that endowed it with unique prominence. The Miller was afforded a privacy denied all but a few. The shadow of The Auditor fell well short of the reach of the wooden sails. Linton was as free as it was possible to be this side of the northern hills. His mother and father long since in the ground, The Miller led a quiet and simple existence.

Linton Gauge was average in many an aspect. He was of no particular height, weight or muscularity. His hair was fair, his eyes light, his complexion unusually free of blemish. He was somewhere between thirty or forty years of age though had the appearance of one for whom life remained something of a mystery. His prevailing disposition was one of innocent melancholy. He was a sweet and delicate man, more flour than grain, troubled only by recurring bouts of insomnia that assailed him for no reason he could ever fathom.

The many hours he passed within the confines of his home – for the mill was where he both worked and resided – had imposed upon The Miller an unusually pale hue. In the full flood of a bright light, he was hardly visible at all. He slept, insomnia permitting, upon the dry ground to the right of the doorway, a single sheet for warmth and a small sack of cloth upon which to rest his head.

His interactions with fellow humans being limited almost entirely to a nod when accepting the sacks of grain from those who delivered them or when those same anonymous folk returned with their barrows for the flour, it would perhaps be of no surprise that Linton Gauge was given to genial discourse with birds and other creatures with a predilection for idle chatter. He had once attempted to extend his social milieu to include the fish in the river but even he, gentle and sincere as he was, had eventually conceded that his efforts would ever be in vain. He blamed not the fish for his failure, nor did he find himself in any way culpable in terms of the outcome. The fish were the fish and The Miller was The Miller. It was as simple as that.

On this particular morning where, unknown to Linton Gauge, John Dawlish had but moments ago emerged from the water to cast his black eyes upon the sleeping Chuck children, The Miller took some comfort in discovering a sparrow jigging about on the ground outside his door.

"Now then," Linton smiled sad. "What can I do for you, my fine fellow?"

The sparrow glanced up at The Miller, whose silhouette in the doorway afforded that man a form far firmer than that which in reality he'd been endowed.

"Don't be shy," continued Linton Gauge. "All is well on this morn, is it not?"

The sparrow paused. It is a known fact that of all the birds in the skyway, sparrows are given moreover to meditative rumination than most of their kind.

"For now, all appears well," the small bird replied.

Linton gazed into the eyes of the sparrow, who, in turn, met the soul of The Miller with the full deep of his glory.

"Have you a name?" asked Linton softly. "I do not believe we have met before, though I may be mistaken. Please forgive my failings, young sparrow. I mean no ill to you or any other."

"You may refer to me in any way you wish," replied the sparrow with all the dignity that small bird could muster. "I am here to inform you, however, that though we may be agreed that the morn just now may be well enough as far as these things go, it will not prevail for long."

The Miller was intrigued by the sparrow's dour prediction. Much later, he would come to berate himself for the facile nature of his response.

"You speak of dire things to come?" Linton smiled. "The sky is about to fall down upon us or some such? Please tell me it is not so?"

The sparrow began once more to skit from one little foot to the other. He turned a full circle, looked once down at the ground and then back up at The Miller.

"It is one thing to speak to the creatures of this earth," the sparrow intoned, "it is another to hear what they say. But to *understand?* Well, I forgive you your affliction, whoever you may be, in whatever place this is."

"I apologise if I have caused offence, sweet thing. It seems we must never have met before, in which case, my name is Linton. If you are a visitor to these parts, please know that you will always find a friend in me."

The little bird turned his back on The Miller. Following a short, inelegant run-up, he flew gorgeous into the expanse of the blue sky, descending in size from sparrow to dot to nothing. In that moment, Linton became aware that his feet had become as unwieldy as if they were of rock just when he would have given his very soul to have wings.

15. Bass Sharooom

THE CROP FARMER, Tobias Defoe, was a man in anatomical construct only. In truth, he was as much a product of the earth as anything he planted, nurtured and harvested.

In his sixty-something years, Tobias Defoe had ventured but twice to the outskirts of the village – once to bury his mother where the daffodils bloomed yellow, and once more to inform The Auditor that the disappearance of his father, though it be only a week or two following his mother's demise, was of no concern to him and therefore should be of even less concern to anybody else. He thereafter awoke each day with the fine understanding that one parent was out there somewhere in the world whilst the other remained at rest beneath nature's fearful symmetry.

Red of face, hard of skin, white of hair.

Tobias Defoe.

Unbreakable from the outset.

A creation as admirable as any who ever lived.

Tobias Defoe.

Not once did The Crop Farmer consider his lot to be anything less than holy. His possessions were but paltry, the extent of his wealth meagre. Yet he wanted for nothing. Rampant with desire, Tobias Defoe flowed through his days with the enduring shimmer of the river whose waters he'd never bathed in, propelled by the same waves of air that moved the sails that ground the grain that made the bread he never ate.

A man in construct only.

Tobias Defoe.

Just shy of sixty years, red of face, hard of skin and white of hair.

A marvel of a man if ever there was one.

As affirmed at the beginning of this tale, Small Mercy had for some years now experienced a paucity of produce due to the increasing reluctance of the surrounding lands to work their magic. Where once there were fields of wheat as expansive as the black of the night and the light of the day, Tobias Defoe's dominion was now no more than an acre in size. The earth would not be denied its show, however, nor The Crop Farmer his front-row seat.

The rickety shack in which Tobias resided had been built by his disappeared father. Much like its architect, there was nothing straight about any of it. All was crooked, ugly and cracked. It clung to its form by dint of a force unknown. Still, it kept him from freezing in the winter and from bursting into flame in the summer. But in these recent years where the weather, the seasons themselves, had become unruly, the walls of his home had struggled to adapt. With each day, a creak from the rotten wood or a crack of the hard clay that served to give form to the whole, would serve notice that nothing that is wrought by the sweat and blood of man is meant to last forever.

Tobias stepped out from his stinking hovel and thudded into the day. Beneath the ragged roof built by his father, his breath was foul, his soul subdued; but out in the ravishing wilds, he was mighty indeed.

Tobias Defoe viewed himself as blessed. There was not a moment of his waking day that passed when he was unaware of the beauty of his life. He indulged himself only in that which was wondrous. No ennui did he wallow in. In no pit of gloom was he ever tempted to shrivel. More beautiful still was the fact that Tobias accepted it all without question. This was life. It was his life. And he was living it. The turning of the earth was as vital to his existence as the beating of his heart. They were in tandem. The earth, in truth, rotated slow within his chest. That big old heart of his pumped sumptuous potions from the depths of the world as much as it urged red blood through his narrow unmagical veins.

There was a music to the existence of The Crop Farmer that was heard only by him, for it was meant for his aged ears alone. Songs were sung by the jagged stones that littered the surface of the ground, blues songs, mighty songs, thudding, whomping songs blurted out in the shadows of the wheat stems. Jazz clung to the air between each sheaf, easing sweetly this way and that as the breeze dictated the sway of it all. It was groove jazz, subtle jazz, luscious jazz, all so far apart from the dirty groove of those jagged stones below, yet all was music, all magnificent. The trees that stood solemn around the field boomed out their bass sharooom without hesitation. No jazz or blues for them, no notion other than that it was the deep of the beat that gave profundity to the mundane, rock to the roll. Tobias Defoe heard every single note, felt to his core each throb and each thrum, tingled with the shimmer and shone with the shine of it all.

Section 7.1 of The Constitution would not have sat well with The Crop Farmer.

> *Within the bounds of the village of Small Mercy there will be no recourse to the production, dissemination or expression of any combination of sounds, be they of human making or of a means more nefarious, whose sole purpose is to inspire behaviour unworthy of a citizen of this place. The Judgement Hall bells are excepted from the scope of this tenet.*

Tobias Defoe had never read The Constitution of Small Mercy. The chances are that he was entirely oblivious of its existence. Since the disappearance of his father and the death of his mother, he had remained beholden to no tenet, no regulation. He knew not that the jump and jive that accompanied him from morn to night was in its essence both unlawful and despised. Even the word 'music' would have been foreign to him. Had he been informed perhaps that what he experienced with such fundamental relish could even be contained in a mere word of two syllables and five letters, it is conceivable that he would have rejected the very notion with the full force of his incomparable spirit.

Of all the people within the environs of Small Mercy, Tobias Defoe was perhaps the most vital whilst being simultaneously the least considered. He was as invisible as the chains that bound the entire community together. And that suited him just fine. He was privileged in his life to observe the transformation of base seed into holy sustenance. Music was his alone to enjoy. Though his mother be dead and gone, his ancient father was out there somewhere, swaying with his old bones between the notes of the universe just as the wheat soft shoe shuffled in its raiment of burnished gold.

The only occasion when Tobias felt the need to speak was when he wondered whether or not he was still able. At such times, he would induce a cough in order to clear his throat and take a sip of water to wet his tongue and mouth. Initially, he would tentatively attempt to greet the day. His tone at first would be low, almost indiscernible, in fact, the sounds he emitted being no more than grunts and groans. When, finally, he was able to express himself audibly with simple words such as would befit an ordinary man, he would experience a surge of disappointment. It was as if being endowed with the ability to talk reminded him that he was not after all fully of the earth but more akin to a human being than was comfortable. These were but minor setbacks in the course of his days. The solitude of his station in the function of Small Mercy allied with the luscious outpouring of magic, song and nature that were the parameters within which he breathed and tarried brought him no end of sumptuous hours.

The morning sun gave gold to the fragile wheat that had these past few months emerged courageous from the fetid soil. With his home set upon a slight incline and the expanse of his canvas having been so inexplicably reduced of late, Tobias was able to apprise himself of each and every stalk and husk. He saw joy in each shimmer, lust in every shade. The slender determination of stalk after stalk that had defied all that is logical to burst through the tragic earth was to him a thing of inexplicable wonder.

So, way over to the west was the mill and its pallid custodian, conversant with the ways, and to this east, the river bisecting the two almost exactly, we have Tobias Defoe with his wheat and his music, his mother dead, his father disappeared. Between them, they were responsible for producing the very basic ingredients that sustained the folk whom they had never met and who had never met them.

Far to the north, however, there was one other whose efforts were of equal value to the maintenance of life in that curious village. His lot was to provide care and nutrition for the livestock for whom the pastures at the foot of the northern hills were his dominion. In essence, it was his duty to deceive his flock into believing they were loved like no other whilst in reality each day they swooned through was a day closer to their premature demise – all just so others could feast upon their lifeless carcass when the taste of bread and greens would no longer do. No prophetic sparrow did attend him in his duties. No symphony of booming oak or grooving crop accompanied him whilst he tarried. Yet, it could be argued that he was more remarkable than either Linton Gauge or Tobias Defoe could ever aspire to be.

Ladies and gentlemen,
I give you…
Nathaniel Wild.

16. Sumptuous Ravagings

WHEN OF SUFFICIENT cool, Man may be able to live by bread alone, but it appears he will oftentimes insist on replenishing his innards with a far bloodier fare.

Nathaniel Wild had lived and worked up by the northern hills for fifty years or more – almost two-thirds of his life. He had awoken one cold morning amongst the damp straw within a ramshackle barn. He guessed, maybe accurately, that he would have been about ten years old at the time, a boy, certainly, but no babe. He had shrugged himself free of his blanket and blinked himself alive. A heft of white light poured through the wide opening in the opposite wall, laying a path down upon the ragged ground, upon which he set his little feet. He had thus emerged into the midst of a green expanse that stretched as far as he could see. No memory or recollection did he have before that moment when he shook off the straw and stepped into the world. How he had come to be there, he only ever gave but brief consideration. Somehow, he knew that his name was Nathaniel Wild. All else that marked him out as unique, to the point of being remarkable, came to him in time. He questioned none of it. He accepted it all.

By any reckoning, Nathaniel was short in stature. In even his own estimation, he had to concede that his girth had taken full advantage where it came to testing the limits of bodily expansion. His face was almost perfectly round, though his huge, red beard detracted from what would otherwise have been a feature every bit as unique as his paucity of height and the immensity of his bulk. It was inevitable, given the aforementioned parameters of his constitution, allied to the rigours of his profession, that his bones gave out a perpetual groan even when in the deepest of sleeps. To refer to him as a short, fat fellow with unruly facial hair and indelicate features would be a little unkind but likely forgivable. He was as unprepossessing on the outside as were the pigs, cows, goats and sheep with which he shared his days. While the astonishing creatures whose status as the natural custodians of the earth has been usurped by those incapable of quelling urges most awful and primitive, Nathaniel Wild was never destined for such a fate.

Nathaniel did not walk. Well, he did, but he didn't. He clomped. That's what he did. Clomped. His steps were heavy and deliberate. Even when the land across which he roamed was at its most unyielding due to callous frost or intense heat, he never once failed to leave evidence of his passing. In all his days, he had never fallen nor even stumbled. His short, thick arms pushed through the air like pistons. His thunderous legs waded from dusk 'til dawn as if he were waist-deep in water. When changing direction, he did so as would a tanker on the everseas, such was the momentous nature of his indomitable frame. His beard, on closer inspection, was not just red but consisted of all manner of hues. There was white and yellow, even blue in places, or so he fancied. That outpouring of facial hair never ceased to bring him joy, whether foraging through it with his filthy fingers or twisting it into fine points that he never could quite keep from unravelling. He loved that beard of many colours. He really did.

"How be you, my darlings," Wild crooned to the nineteen sheep who bubbled in a huddle before him.

"Fare thee well, you sleepy lumps?" Wild oozed to the eleven cows, several of whom clung to the shade afforded by the leaning shelter whilst the others uniformly expressed a solemn indifference that, to their credit, could have been mistaken by one so enamoured with beards as nothing more than the product of a particularly fitful sleep.

"And you messes and mucks, with your farts and your harrumphs, I hope this day does find you all stinky and fine?" Wild enquired of the thirty-three whomping pigs, whose raggedy presence he stepped full into until surrounded on all sides, an ancient stump defiant in a snorting swamp of boisterous stink.

"I ain't be forgetting you, my timid beauties, so don't you go a-fearing or nothing," Wild called over to the four goats who stood a few yards up the gentle incline of one of the mammoth northern hills. "You all is as precious to old Nathaniel as this old beard of mine, and that ain't no lie I be telling, no sir, it ain't."

The sheep continued to munch low upon the dark grass, the cows to breathe deep and resonant, the pigs to persist in the frantic scrambling, majestic in their disregard for pretence, pride and platitudes. The goats looked on with an admirable stoicism.

Nathaniel Wild bathed not in the white light of the morning sun but in the stench of his flock. Never was he more aroused than when his black nostrils were engorged with the fragrance of his beasts. If ever the time came that his eyes could endure no more the sting of steam conjured by the melding of bovine urine, flatulence and excrement, well, he knew that he would already be dead.

Just as there was an archaic magic in the way John Dawlish bestrode the land, so the farmer Nathaniel also did possess a nature of indefinable majesty. An ogre is an unwashed angel, and that is the truth of the matter. Plain matter is the ultimate deception. Illusion is all. Love is all. To dream is to inhabit a realm that knows no parameters. The inhalation and exhalation of breath is the purest experience of joy to which any man, angel, ogre, gargoyle, sheep, cow, goat or pig can ever aspire. There is no evil. There never was no evil. Nathaniel Wild was born with that knowledge, and not once had he ever questioned the veracity of it. You wouldn't know when first you set eyes upon him, but breathe his air, imbibe of the sumptuous ravagings of shit, piss and sweat with which he lustfully availed himself from morn until night and, before not very long at all, you would have no choice but to accept the gorgeous wonder of that man.

For the villagers of Small Mercy, it was only by the practical application of skill and endeavour in pursuit of a variety of defined outcomes that balance was achieved. The very adherence to the concept of benign equilibrium was as inherent in the coarse fabric of that curious village this side of the northern hills as a slavish commitment to an omnipotent deity perhaps was to the denizens of some province far, far away. The governance required to ensure that each inhabitant had available to them the nutrients to sustain them from one day to the next was loaded with a complexity and forethought equivalent to those rules and regulations that bound the community together with regard to its moral and spiritual obligations. It was only in the tangible intractability of the one and the ethereal nature of the other that the two could be distinguished. They were accorded equal merit. The practice of feasting upon the carcass of a cow, a sheep, a goat or a pig went as unquestioned as a nail in a door or the indecipherable proclamations of the one known as Judgement.

As LINTON GAUGE rubbed flour dust through his slender fingers, Tobias Defoe breathed deep of a bouquet of yellow wheat and Nathaniel Wild stroked with a callused hand the rough back of one of his pigs, each felt a solemn tinge to their respective revelries.

It was in that moment that John Dawlish decided the time had come to do whatever it was he planned to do next.

The boy Stafford rubbed his eyes at the glare of the day. His sister, Grace, snapped free in an instant from the grip of the heavy torpor to which she had no memory at all of how or when she'd succumbed.

Linton Gauge watched in silence as the white flour danced slow to the floor.

Tobias Defoe glimpsed the gold of his wheat fade to a shade less startling in his hand.

Nathaniel Wild heaved into his lungs a scent for which no cow, pig, goat or sheep could rightly be held responsible.

"Awake, you young 'uns," that Dawlish did grumble.

"It's you," Stafford said low. His tone was more marvel than fear just then.

"It be me."

"You're supposed to be dead," the boy murmured.

"Lad," Dawlish barked as a black furrow cracked jagged across his face, "you have absolutely no idea just how many times I done been told that."

17. Chuntering Pig

To put it plain, Grace Chuck screamed. She screamed as if chased by the hounds of hell. You get the idea. That kind of scream.

With a terrifying ease of motion, John Dawlish reached up sharply with his right hand, grabbed the petrified young girl's yelping from the air and deposited it in ghastly fashion into the depths of his black and cavernous mouth. The silent moment that followed was curtailed by the crack of a belch and a gurgle of wet that had gathered in Dawlish's throat. He congratulated himself on the former whilst gulping down the sludge of the latter. Grace Chuck's thin lips remained parted, her eyes as wide as eyes can be, but try as she might, her scream was at an end.

The dark hole of the girl's open mouth was almost perfectly round. John Dawlish bent down as low as he was able and proceeded to peer into the aperture, as if he were attempting to ascertain the eternal essence of her – which of course was exactly what he was doing.

"My sister," Stafford stammered. "Grace is her name. She's called Grace."

"More Grace in what she be called than how she be behaving from what I seen of her just now," Dawlish mused. His attempt at a smile was as horrific to the young girl as were he to have licked her from head to toe with his malodorous tongue.

No flour, no crops, no livestock.

Just John Dawlish himself and the world swaying to the thud and the boom of his inimitable whimsy.

"I would take it upon myself to have a sit upon this wet ground as a way to make this black shadow of mine cast no more gloom upon you than it be doing right now, but these bones of mine just won't be obliging."

Stafford bravely stood up and then, as if finally becoming aware of his terror, immediately lowered his head and closed tight his eyes.

Grace experienced an awful agony in every tender part of her as she jerked herself upright to stand beside her brother. She too bowed her head, shut her eyes.

John Dawlish took a pace back. He turned his gaze to the blue of the sky and then to the slime of the ground. Eventually, after what seemed to Grace and Stafford like a day and more, Dawlish dragged the two children into the full gawp of his vision.

"There," he said. "There be you, young Stafford, and there be you, young Grace. And here be me if I ain't mistaken. And back down yonder, well, there be most everyone else."

Stafford and Grace followed Dawlish's stare as long as they were able then in unison dropped their heads as if they'd just been subjected to a hanging.

"Now, I ain't ever really been one for questions and the like," Dawlish went on. "This skull of mine ain't got what some would call an enquiring mind. It got other things, but questions never did sit well in my noggin. I knows what I know, and that always has been nothing I ever wanted to tamper with. So, what I be meaning to say, is that how you got where you be now and the why of it is of no interest to old Dawlish. What's been and gone is dead as dead, far as I be concerned. What happens next, well, ain't that a thing more interesting to discuss?"

John Dawlish spat on the ground, missing the black shadow of his left shoulder by no more than an inch.

Grace trembled without trembling.

Stafford breathed without breathing.

There were no birds in the skyway, yet there was birdsong.

Now how about that?

A scarlet mist oozed into Stafford's young cheeks.

"Sorry about the other day, Mister," he stated.

Dawlish made no reply. All finished, all done, gone, dead.

Grace stole a breath and looked across at her young brother, who in response turned his head towards her.

"This…man…is known to you?" she whispered coarse.

"We had a situation is all," said Dawlish, replying before Stafford was able. "And now, as is clear, and maybe I even said it as being so, we have another of them old situations."

Grace Chuck continued to look at her brother even as he faced front once more and the stranger's words drifted into the morning. She felt a subtle rejuvenation of her being, greeting each minuscule emergence of familiar sensations as she would the arms of her mother or the return of her father. In the first accomplished attempt at an interaction with the ghastly figure before her, Grace nodded.

John Dawlish inserted a filthy bent finger into one of the oval cavities of his nose until it was almost a finger no more. He withdrew it with a squelch, examined the conglomeration of blood, dirt and slime that had gathered upon the length of it and then did nothing more than allow his arm to fall by his side. He wiped nothing off, discarded no debris. Grace was appalled yet she somehow managed to present herself with the same absence of emotion so ably demonstrated by her barely recognisable brother.

"What will you do with us?" Grace asked.

The stranger was struck all quizzical.

"Well, ain't that a question on a day like this?" he replied. "There's me just a telling you how it be that whatever did occur to make me be where I am and you two be where you be a circumstance whose conjuring is of as much interest to me as where my shit goes when the sun comes up, and there's you, Grace my girl, all eager to get the future from me the first chance you get."

Grace looked swiftly to the ground. She sought out the black shadow of the stranger yet fell short.

"I'm sorry, sir," she murmured.

Still birdsong.

But no birds.

"You hear that?" Dawlish asked sweet of his two young companions.

Try as they might, neither Stafford nor Grace heard anything but the beating of their little hearts and the swish of the reeds along the riverbank behind them. Whether more emboldened by recent experiences or compelled by sheer innocence, Martha Chuck's lost little boy responded to the stranger's question.

"There is nothing in my ears I don't believe," he said with increasing certainty, "than them words you speak and maybe the sounds the river makes when it's being a river or whatever it choose to be."

It was no trick of the light that led to the diminishing almost to nothing of John Dawlish's black shadow as Stafford spoke. Just as it was a true fact and no illusion that by the time the boy's final intonation had by beautiful happenstance merged with the schlopp and tingle of the river ripples, the gargantuan frame of the man for whom but three days previous Small Mercy had never existed, grew at the very minimum a good six inches in height. The boy saw it just as the girl saw it. Despite there being no collaboration by way of the creaking of bones, the stretching of sinew of the re-emergence of black shadow, the truth was plain. The fact that neither Grace nor Stafford were in any doubt as to what had just occurred was a source of wry contentment to the ancient figure within whose ravaged and ugly palm their existence just then was crudely ensconced.

John Dawlish threw back his huge head and laughed from the deep of his chasm. He roared wild and tremendous, yet still all Stafford could hear was the sound of the river and the swish of the reeds on the bank.

In the far distance to the west, Linton Gauge was tethered to the tantalising dying tremors of the last dab of flour that touched the windmill floor. To the east, Tobias Defoe remained entranced by notes only he could hear; the wheat in his grasp finally had no more music to give. And up by the northern hills, Nathaniel Wild yearned for the return of the sensation that shuddered through him all rock and roll carooooom when his blunt fingernails made loving contact with the blushing hide of his chuntering pig.

Having gathered himself into a form less redolent of a chortling mess, John Dawlish availed himself of a demeanour more in keeping with the momentous nature of that which he was about to impart. With tangible ache and laudable testament to his unwholesome penchant for bathos, he assumed a kneeling position upon the ground such that his head was at the level of the boy and girl who stood before him.

The blue had fled the sky.

The shimmer was long gone from the water.

Even the reeds took a break from their grooving.

"All that has gone before was meant only to get me to you and you to me and us to where we be by this river here. Never again will you be what you been. There ain't no other way, far as I be knowing."

Dawlish then dropped his voice to a whisper that was astonishing in the soothing clarity of its tones.

"*Just let yourself go,*" was what he said.

"*Just let yourself go,*" was what the boy heard.

"*Just let yourself go,*" was what the girl heard too.

Birdsong but

no birds were there

to be found.

Just let yourself

go

Stafford experienced a burgeoning within his bony frame the like of which he had never known before. It was a lightness of being that began in the hard soles of his guileless feet and broke in a wave of joy across the full gasp of his heart before pouring out unabated through every inch of him.

As for Grace, it was a distinct discomfort in the extremities of her fingers that alerted her to something strange assailing her. What began as a jolt of pain eased into a tingling, which, within seconds, she experienced as a gentle bubbling in her veins – not just experienced it but actually *felt* it. Throughout that entire body of hers, Grace Chuck flowed to the very brim with such a surge of high passion that she all but exploded. True to the name that she had perhaps until then ill-served, young Grace bloomed from the stooping, cowering figure with which her years of ignoble servitude had imbued her. Shoulders back, eyes to the sky, red of lip and flush with ardour, that young girl became in that moment as angel as any angel that ever did giggle and sway.

John Dawlish surveyed briefly his young companions. A sudden bewilderment overcame him. It was as if he had never seen them or the like ever before in his life. And then, just as swiftly, that eerie feeling let him be. He then licked from his forefinger the scabby morass of gunk he'd earlier that morn pulled from the black deep of his nose and revelled in the ecstatic comfort of the moment.

18. The Gentle Kiss That Popped

S TAFFORD AND GRACE had lapsed into sleep not long after the stranger had so sumptuously acquired their complicity in whatever it was he had planned. They had awoken, like many others in the village far to the south and down the hill, to a sky conspicuous by the astonishing prevalence of its stars.

Dawlish sat at the bank of the river, his rancid trousers rolled up haphazard to just above his mountainous knees. His feet tapped out a grim rhythm upon the joyless surface of the water. Stafford sat to the right of him, Grace to the left. They too were bare of foot, and though their feet overhung the edge of the bank, they remained dry. The many months of only sparse periods of rain had significantly reduced the height of what was once a deep and free-flowing expanse.

All three, the misshapen man and the two lost children, took a moment to gaze up at the black sky. The white spangle stars danced without restraint, flashing and swirling all frenzy and incomparable.

"Fine bit of that old *letting go* I been telling you about, that is," Dawlish murmured as he turned his gaze once more to the river. "Be that as it may," he continued in the deep of their night, "I have to confess to getting ahead of my old self them hours back. Don't know what I be thinking, hitting you with the *just letting go* without you having the chance to know how it came into being. Them things don't just magic themselves up. What I be trying to say is that we can't go no further 'til you be knowing about the black of the black, the white of the white and the beat, the beat, the beat."

Neither Stafford nor his sister made any attempt to respond, both having discovered the reflection of the spangle stars in heave of the Small Mercy waters. Like those stars, the children were present, but they were not present, in the scene yet outside of the scene, motionless from a distance but close up churning with ancient wonder.

John Dawlish shuffled forward until his feet were fully submerged. In that moment, he resembled in stature and solemnity the form of an old tree. Even his voice, when next he spoke, had managed to avail itself of a key more sonorous. Moreover, the hitherto sparse array of words and expressions, which he had of late utilised and applied with a slovenly disdain for all that could be considered beautiful, well, that too had been ravishingly enhanced. There was no trick to it, no magic. As with so much about that fiend, it was just the way it was.

He spoke first of the black of the black and of how the black of the black had endured relentless and perfect at the incalculable outset until the moment of its holy relent, from which peculiar circumstance all else would inevitably be unveiled for good or for ill. It was no quantifiable phenomena that inspired the black of the black in its holy relent, just as nothing other than peculiar circumstance could be attributed to the emergence of all else that would inevitably be unveiled for good or for ill.

Relentless, perfect, incalculable – seven times did Dawlish repeat those words.

The children uttered not a single word, barely breathed in fact, hardly blinked. The stars too, both in real and reflection, were utterly enchanted.

In tones low and eternal, John Dawlish went on.

It was the coming of the white of the white, he asserted, that was the true and unassailable wonder of it all. For not only did the white of the white burn hot and sharp wherever it chose to burn hot and sharp, but in doing so, the black of the black, as a consequence of its holy relent, found itself bound in majestic union. Where the white of the white burned at its highest heat and in its sharpest form, the black of the black would attend with an intensity so relentless, perfect and incalculable that the white of the white could only be emboldened. Only with the presence of the black of the black could the white of the white exist, yet it was equally true that it was the consummation of the union between the black of the black and the white of the white that endowed the holy relent with its intangible power, which was incomparable in its sublime and ecstatic exultation.

The black of the black.

The holy relent.

The white of the white.

Sublime and ecstatic

exultation.

John Dawlish paused for a moment in his revelations. He slowly freed his feet from the starlit water and shuffled back awkward until his thick legs no longer hung over the cold, muddy bank. He then huddled all his limbs up close to his core and closed hard his wild eyes. As if being manipulated by a force unseen, his right heel thudded the hard of the ground, followed by his left and once more his right and on and on and on, a syncopation of a most hypnotic intensity which continued unabated for the entire remainder of his sermon.

"The beat, the beat, the beat," he crooned tender. "The beat, the beat, the beat, the beat." And all the while that syncopation of a most hypnotic intensity. "The beat, the beat, the beat."

Dawlish told in rhythm and in rhyme of the fundamental impervious necessity of the beat. He weaved words about and around one another, unravelled them and danced with them like a lunatic at dawn. He ranted and he raved in his frenzied depiction of the beat. His was a rapture from which it seemed he may never divest himself.

The beat, the beat, the beat.

Only the beat, the beat, the beat.

No union, no consummation, no relent, holy or otherwise.

Just the beat, the beat, the beat.

He damned the very notion of silence to an unspeakable fate, banished it to oblivion, consigned it to where the black of the black is not even the black of the black, the white of the white not the white of the white.

He roared, did that fetid ghoul, roared he did, as he told of the rumble of the mountains.

He howled, howled he did, all guttural when telling of the might swelling of the mighty seas.

The beat, the beat, the beat.

The beat was all, and all was the beat.

The beat, the beat, the beat.

His heels had been thudding into the earth with such ferocity that the skin cracked open. Trickles of crimson bled through the mud and into the river, yet still he went on with his raving, his ranting, his roar and his howl.

The beat, the beat, the beat.

The beat, the beat, the beat.

And then, at the very height of his tumult, as if the very concept of sound itself had been wrenched from the universe, he stopped.

The raving gone, the ranting gone, roaring no more, howling done.

No more spangle-star reflections.

A chill breeze drifted down from the cleavage of the northern hills, stayed a while and then retreated to its hollow.

John Dawlish dragged his wretched body forward and ploshed his lacerated feet in the cool of the Small Mercy waters.

The black of the black.

The white of the white.

The beat, the beat, the beat.

Mountains.

Mighty seas.

"So now, children," Dawlish said tender as both young Stafford and young Grace turned their sweet heads to his tones, "I done told you the sum of it best and only way I knows how."

Stafford leaned forward and put a small hand on one of the stranger's bulbous knees. Grace too did likewise.

Dawlish heard clear when the boy stated plain his gratitude. He missed entirely, though, the gentle kiss that popped from the perfect, round mouth of little Grace and came to nestle ravishing somewhere between the filth of his forehead and the rank majesty of his sorrow.

19. Irrevocably Ruined

THERE IS A certain tragic irony in the fact that had Martha Chuck attended to her daily chores in the manner ascribed by the strictures and tenets of the village, it is conceivable that she may have happened upon those whose cruel absence had rendered her so very broken. It is true that her daily foray to the river and back encompassed an area much further downstream to where that stranger had held her children in his thrall, but, even so, the instincts of a loving mother in desperate times can never be discounted.

Martha instead chose to confine herself beneath the crooked roof and pitted walls that comprised all she had ever known as home. Nails be damned. What more could be done to her than had already been done?

As each clang of The Judgement Hall bell seeped into her, so all recognisable emotions dissipated. Over the course of no more than six hours, she became a woman in form only, a mother and widow solely by dint of bleak fact. Her heart beat as a clock ticks, pumping blood through her veins and organs. That astonishing process designed to sustain life lost its lustre, for its function merely prolonged the agony of Martha's existence.

The sallow breath that stumbled from Martha's dry lips caused not the faintest puff of mist to form upon her kitchen window. Her lungs were flat and wheezy. In her spectral sauntering from room to room, the fall of her pitifully small feet was attended by a maudlin silence. Even her home, it seemed, was all cried out.

The closest anybody came to enquiring as to the well-being of that poor woman was when three aged men arrived at her front door. What began perhaps as a valiant effort to throw off the shackles of a lifetime of dour acquiescence in favour of an awkward indulgence in chivalry, soon became nothing more than a demonstration of shameful inadequacy. One of the men commented upon the poor condition of the nail that still protruded from Martha's door. One of the others shook his head in rueful lament at the insidious demise of artisan skills. The last of the three was content merely to wonder to himself how long it would be before the nail fell out of the dead wood of its own accord, such was the decrepit nature of both that which he had banged in and that on the receiving end of the banging.

Martha Chuck observed the three elderly villagers unseen as she peered out from her small bedroom window. Despite being of clearly advanced years, Martha did not recognise any of them. Had she been not so spent, she may have come to realise that other than her two children, she would perhaps be able to name only a handful of others within the community she had lived within her entire life.

The Small Mercy Constitution had, through a combination of technical brilliance and the charmless elevation of function over wonder, been successful to a remarkable degree. Even those born beneath the most spangle-star skyway would ever in time be denuded of the capacity to dream, to imagine, to indulge in spontaneous bursts of fancy. Thus it was somewhat inevitable that Martha Chuck experienced no contempt for the skin-and-bone men as she watched them scuttle back to the other side of the track. When denied access to the extremes of emotion of which a human being is so gorgeously endowed, be it rage, affection, despair or dismay, then that soul is in essence no more a man, woman or child than an ant is a dog or a tree an ocean.

That old Constitution was something else. It really was.

Whereas from the very founding of Small Mercy, Man's capacity to be irrevocably ruined through profligate dalliances with that most lurid of temptresses – imagination – was considered as being solely the preserve of the evil and the insane, the extent to which an individual was capable of eschewing adherence to any moral rubric in the holy pursuit of order inspired a nostalgic awe in those for whom the fear of public humiliation was far worse even than death.

Time turned in on itself.

Nobody noticed at first.

And then they did.

It was only when the stars were full in the sky that any remark was made of the absence of The Judgement Hall clangs for what must have been seven hours or more. A little more discomfort attended those who awoke sometime later to begin their early morning chores to discover not only that the pink had failed to fully straddle the dawn, but the moon itself, big and bright in the pale blue of the sky.

All agreed that something wasn't quite right. Not one of them, of course, was in possession of sufficient imagination to speculate just what it was that wasn't quite right about whatever it was that wasn't quite right.

Sullivan stood by the window and looked out across the muddy field that bordered the western edge of the Small Mercy shacks and hovels on that side of the track. It had been an odd few days for him, so perhaps out of all his brethren, he was a little less bemused than most. He barely recognised himself aside from the aching of his bones and hollow of his groans. His condition just then was somewhere between wretched and soulless. He felt some comfort in the paucity of his impulses. Then, of a sudden, a chill so stupefying as to be baptismal engulfed the entirety of him. It surged through his bones and his blood and his liver and his brain. It tore the sulk from his soul and ripped free the maudlin resignation in which he'd been wallowing. And as the chill shivered back out into the rabid bleak, Sullivan became aware of his reflection in the glass. A grimace was ripped across his face, and as he gazed upon it, he felt an arousal of such intensity even that treacherous woman of his would have never come close to matching it – even in her finer times.

Mary stood at the door of her sleeping quarters and remained there for a moment or so. Try as she might, she was no longer able to sense even the slightest waft of that stranger's stench. She brought her efforts to an end with a pitiful sigh. She trudged through to the kitchen and poked the embers for some sign of lingering flames, but there were none. She was aware of how Sullivan's shadow grew monstrous from the doorway behind her, though not once had she turned her eyes from the hearth.

Sometimes a woman just knows.

20. Desperate to Impart

MARTHA CHUCK'S SORROWFUL predicament drew not a drop of compassion from Franklin Singe. Whilst she was descending into spectral form, Franklin Singe, The Auditor, sat in his hard chair, reflecting with cruel relish upon his aptitude for devious designs whose elegant formulations were equalled only by the scintillating barbarity with which they were unleashed. That being said, he had long tired of the whole nail-in-the-door thing, though it clearly still had its place in his malevolent repertoire. It was the very inelegance of it that bored him, which in turn reminded him of all those imbeciles with whom he was cursed to live out his days. He determined that the disappearance of those awful children had presented him with the perfect opportunity to ensure his place in myth and in legend.

Singe chewed roughly upon the tip of his right index finger as he rocked slowly back and forth in his chair, ensconced within the bare walls of his soulless abode. Back and forth he rocked. Forth and back, chewing roughly on that bony finger of his, dead skin fluttering down to the floor like some rotten flurry of snow.

"The boy being absent from his chores? Did I err in my attribution of sloth and idiocy as the cause? Perhaps and perhaps not. The Chuck woman is no more vulgar or less insufferable than the rest of her kind and surely lacks the imagination to conceive of a scheme of nefarious and admiral cunning. Not even a dim harlot such as she would defy Judgement by wilfully keeping her brats from their chores. So it is clear on that alone those brats of her have fled their squalid nest. But what could that guileless mother of theirs possibly have to gain from their absence?

There is something else at play here. This is more than mere mischief, mere happenstance."

The discussions he had alone in the dark of his home were those The Auditor prized most, both in the intellectual stimulation he derived from them and the propensity for devilment they afforded him. He conversed with others only when crudely imposed upon, which, given his fearful reputation, was as rare an occasion as, well, the vanishing of a pair of loathsome imps.

"Now is not a time for nails or the garbled words of my cursed superior. A mind such as mine must ponder long and hard upon this matter. Let those dull creatures fetch and carry through their days and gawp and snore away the glib of their nights. And let that hapless Chuck widow scream herself into a wretched husband's grave for all I care."

Singe wallowed wild in the despair of all others as he chuntered on to none but himself.

And then he all but laughed aloud in acknowledgement of his genius. All that emerged from his depths, though, was an ugly crack that resounded but momentarily, an exultation that could in no way be mistaken for joy of any kind.

"No need for haste," he nodded as he set his feet firm to the ground in order to bring his rocking to a halt. "It is only right that a feast such as this be enjoyed morsel by morsel by morsel."

He closed his small eyes and slipped into a gorgeous slumber that lasted until the moon was full in the starless, black sky. The knocking on his door that had prompted his inelegant awakening fuelled him instantly with indignant spite, for never had he tolerated uninvited company. By the time he had steadied himself and flung open his front door, he was all but raging.

Sullivan the baker, however – for it was he who had displayed such insolence in the face of his better – was unperturbed by so surly a reception.

"It is not the hour at which you have chosen to impose yourself upon me, though that has raised my ire, Baker, but the very fact that you have chosen to do so at all."

Sullivan passively stood his ground.

The two men briefly regarded one another before Singe's rancour subsided with the same rapidity with which it had risen. He grudgingly took a step back as a sign that the baker may enter. Sullivan followed The Auditor in and shut the door to the outer world. The space between him and Singe was no more than a foot when the visitor was predictably upbraided.

"I can only presume your brains have turned to dough since last we met?" Singe sneered.

"Were you to have asked me such a thing but a day or so ago, sir, I would have had no choice but to confess it may have been so."

"And now?"

"I be as right in the head as I ever been, sir."

"Then your act of disturbing me in my thoughts is the act of a *sane* man fully cognisant of the punishment that would ordinarily result in such abhorrent behaviour?"

"Mr Auditor, sir, I have information that I be hoping will explain my intrusion. Just as my blundering into your night has, I fear, no precedence, so what have to tell you be of a nature without compare."

Franklin Singe considered the words of the baker. He studied his eyes, the blackness of his mouth from which his tongue flicked and the general comportment of that man. The Auditor had full faith in his instincts where such matters were concerned and thus did he step slowly towards his rocking chair before sitting carefully upon it. Sullivan remained standing just inside the doorway, his callused hands clasped behind his back.

"Without compare, you say?" Singe said, thin and low.

"Without compare."

"You understand that I will be the judge of that?"

"I do, sir."

"And you understand also that if I am not as enthused or intrigued as clearly you are with what you seem so desperate to impart to me then there will be consequences for you in line with The Constitution of Small Mercy?"

"Yes."

"You wish still to proceed?"

Sullivan nodded.

And proceed he did, until almost the black night was through.

His tale told in full and without embellishment – not that any was required – the baker returned down the hill, through the silent village and back to his home where that woman of his had not even bothered to light a single candle. His reaction to such insolence was not as rash as it may have been before the stranger had entered his life, for it burned with a more cunning kind of bitter now.

Alone again, Franklin Singe caused his chair to commence its rocking once more. His entire body tingled and throbbed with a tremendous arousal that was so overwhelming it was all he could do to prevent from gushing out from every pore and orifice at his disposal. In time, his blood began to pump with more decorum and his mind return to a state less frenzied. He was flaccid again, pale again, inhuman again. He was thoroughly engorged with the prospects of what lay ahead.

The baker would not go unscathed for his indiscretion, of course, but the details of such banal retribution were of little concern to The Auditor just then.

These surely were new times that would, Singe believed, find even Judgement himself wanting.

All hail The Auditor!

All Hail Franklin Singe!

21. A Big Old Baffle

Franklin Singe was not the only one to have received a visitation of import that particular Small Mercy night.

Linton Gauge, Tobias Defoe and Nathaniel Wild had experience simultaneously the momentous and rollicking the beat of the beat on the breeze though each man was spread far from one another across the huge swathe of land that lay between the toppermost point of the village and the foot of the northern hills.

The morning sky was blank in its blue. A slender sigh of mist sauntered slow from the east to the west, from the west to the east. The air had no charm about it. It was as if a certain strain of stagnant had infiltrated with malign malevolence that which ordinarily was at the very least indifferent.

"So, my fine swallow friend, though I have not the words to quite explain, I feel a change has attended the yellow sun this morn. Do you sense as much?" enquired The Miller of the bird, who had chosen to alight at his bare feet.

Without hesitation, the loquacious bird did with some relish reply.

"There is no moment when change is absent, my dear man. Change is the only constant in this universe. Of course, my experience in the upper skies lends any view I expound a greater credence than perhaps of those such as your kind who are destined ever to be tethered to the ground. Though I am just a small bird, as well you can see, I have ever been confounded by the curious manner in which your species insists on making complicated what was never meant to be complicated at all."

"Well said, sweet thing! I humbly offer up no defence for my brethren and their ways. I was just all of a wonder, more even than usual, is all."

The swallow ruffled straight its majesty of fine feathers and took to the air without further remark. Linton did not follow the bird's ascent but instead gazed downwards with a longish gawp. In time, despite the solemnity and unease with which he had awoken, upon his lovely face a lovely smile wowed into being that he was powerless in all good conscience to suppress.

Some ways to the east, Tobias Defoe lay heavy upon his back in the very epicentre of his wheat field. His thunderous legs were outstretched and his arms crossed above his shoulders. The back of his crude head rested upon the huge petal of his palms. He looked up at the sky and saw nothing, no colour, no haze even. The harsh wheat stalks were black at the base, easing from yellow into burnished gold at their peaks. The light of that burnished gold spread out in broad shafts across The Crop Farmer's heft.

Through the barely perceptible swishing of fabulous wheat companions, Tobias still throbbed with the beat of the beat that had thumped hypnotic and jive through his dreams. With no effort at all, he attuned his heart to the rhythm until all was syncopated. Once fully in the groove, he let his big old feet swing from side to side to the beat of the beat and the thud of the thud.

"Whatever this music be," he mumbled low, "at least there be a blues to it, even if the devil himself be its progenitor."

The Crop Farmer closed his eyes and fair bopped as well as any old bopper ever did bop whilst flat on his back in the rabid eye of somebody else's dream.

As for Nathaniel Wild, well, his assembly consisted of more than a single chatty sparrow and bossa nova wheat sweethearts. That fact alone did not elevate him in any way above the other fine fellows. It was just different is all, is all, is all. Just different.

"Now, my beauties, I known all of you too well over these many years, whether you be sheep, pig, cow, goat, for any of you to deny that old change in the air as is come upon us since the black of the black turned to the white of the white. And don't give me none of that *holy relent business*. I done had enough of that in times past, as well you all know."

With a wide grin upon his face and a fulsome wet in his eyes, he looked upon the assorted creatures who were formed in a ragged circle about him. Not one of them did anything but appraise him with deep, deep affection. The gravity of their conjoined ardour was sufficient a response for that indomitable Small Mercy legend.

"You're all a credit to yourselves and to me too, if that don't be too bold a bit of nonsense to say. Being all agreed in that there be this change in the air, I do declare I don't have the slightest notion of what it doth portend. This beat of the beat that came down through space and space and time and time from way down there on the other side over holy is a big old baffle, for sure. there. So what do you think on it then, lads and unlads? Anything to offer your everloving pal?"

The snorting of a particularly mucky pig was sufficient for Nathaniel Wild to bring his ruminations to a conclusion.

"Well, that settles it, I suppose. As always, I am indebted to the wisdom of you all, given how I am awful short where wisdom and the like be concerned. If the order of the day ain't filth and joy then you know better than all others just how short my comings be in all matters else."

The sheep, the pigs, the cows and the goats dispersed free and gorgeous to set about their day, burdened not by all that it means to be of humankind.

Dawlish was curled up asleep deep in the wet mud of the river bank when Stafford Chuck wrested his gaze from the flow of the mountain waters to reach across to touch his sister's shoulder. They had both been sitting in silence, adjacent to one another, cross-legged, for a time indeterminate.

"Grace," the boy whispered. "Grace?"

Grace turned her pale face towards her brother. Her expression was blank but not in a sad way; more blissful than anything if truth be told.

"Yes?" she said soft.

"Do you feel…I don't know…strange?"

"I feel different, for sure."

"Strange?"

"Not strange exactly. Just different, I suppose."

"Scared different or just normal different?"

Grace took her brother's hand in hers.

"Strange and different are as much alike as to be the same, sweet brother. I do confess, though, that whatever it is, I believe it fair suits me well, all things considered."

"That's good."

"Yes. I think it just might be so."

Grace pulled Stafford to her, and he rested his head on her bony shoulder. The both of them took again to gazing into the shimmering waters of the Small Mercy river. Such was the dreaminess of their reverie, the first they knew of their captor's rising was when his jagged shadow condemned of a sudden the diamond clear waters to rank and cataclysmic oblivion.

22. Wild Colour Being

IT TOOK BARELY more than a day or two for the inhabitants of Small Mercy to divest themselves of their interest in the interjection into their monotony provided by the sorry lot of Martha Chuck and her missing children. The bread got baked. The bread got collected. The water got fetched. The water got poured. The flowers, too, did come in bunches to the foot of The Judgement Hall steps.

How the baker's woman would have loved to have been one of that faceless majority for whom life just then reverted back to its fantabulous grind. The brief glimpse she'd been afforded of a life differently experienced had been so intoxicating that its sudden dissipation had hollowed her out in spirit and in joy. She deemed herself to be worse off than ever before that awful creature had tampered unbidden with the sweet comfort of her wallow. She cursed the blood that pumped from her heart and she cursed the flesh with which her bones were sheathed, though she no longer cursed Sullivan. Facile displays of petulant resistance were as burnt embers to her now.

Sullivan was determined not to overplay his hand. His gamble in divulging his knowledge with regard to the stranger and all that therein pertained had gone far better than he'd expected. Thus he did not, as well he may have done, go back to his old ways when Dawlish's devilry faded almost to a blush. He leapt not into the rapturous gruesome of brutish disdain. The emotionless manner in which he went about his business was, if anything, even more terrifying than the beatings and roars she'd been sure would flow. Sullivan was back, and Sullivan was wowed to the depths, revelling serene in the dismay of that woman whom he had once loved so very, very much but now held in spectacular contempt.

The bread got baked.

The bread got delivered.

The water ploshed to satiate its dry hordes.

The flowers wilted on arrival.

The indomitable wheels of that self-professed, civilised society churned on charmless.

How Martha Chuck would have loved to have been one of that faceless majority for whom life just then reverted back to its fantabulous grind. She found herself thinking back to what she'd been like as a young girl, a babe even, but anything she dragged up was ragged and blurry. It was as if her life had only begun the day she met her late husband.

The bread got baked.

The bread got delivered.

The water ploshed to satiate its dry hordes.

The flowers wilted on arrival.

The indomitable wheels of that self-professed, civilised society churned on charmless.

Such was the staggering speed at which Small Mercy regained its equilibrium, it is fair to say that the increasing infrequency of Franklin Singe's visitations upon the village from his house at the upper eastern edge went entirely unnoticed. The stark power of his propensity to do harm had grown to be so palpable over the years that his physical presence had become all but irrelevant. He had become a ghost, a spectre, a ghoul, a happenstance. Thus was he able to give full, uninterrupted attention to the tremendous challenge with which he had been so fortuitously presented.

Being a cynic by nature and a pragmatist by necessity, he began his ruminations from the standpoint that every element of the baker's tale had been the pitiful product of an irrevocably damaged mind. He did not, however, go as far as to dismiss it in its entirety. He slowly teased out that which was possible, feasible even, from the patently absurd.

For instance, it was possible, though improbable, for a stranger to arrive in Small Mercy. There was no physical barrier to prevent such an eventuality. So, yes, that may have occurred – for a stranger to stumble into Small Mercy. But for that same improbable stranger to be beaten to death by a baker and for that stranger to be then buried in the ground and then not only come back to life and return to the scene of his demise but to then rather than exact retribution instead enquire of his barbarous assailant if there was any freshly baked bread in the offing?

There are some things of which the very existence attests to the flourishing of a demonic and loveless paradigm whose unholy absence of tenderness speaks to the worst of humankind; the subjugation of a woman by a man is one example; the systematic admonishment of any who dare to dream by those for whom folly and fancy are symptomatic of some mental decay is a second.

There are some such things
'tis true to say
that should never be
but
are.

The fact that in spite of there being not an ounce of dreamy wonder within his odious composition, The Auditor was not one to exclude the possibility of forces unknown. Though the rigour with which he applied his implacable reasoning powers had no equal, his candid acceptance of the presence of some insidious mischief most malign was fundamental to his particular brand of genius. The arousal he experienced when the tragic fate that was wont to befall those of an indolent and feckless disposition was enhanced to a mighty degree when the dour results of his intellectual endeavours summoned into being an inexplicable swell of appalling majesty.

23. Down to the Bone

WHATEVER DAWLISH WAS about to say to his charges was temporarily delayed by the customary expulsion of his morning phlegm. This was followed by the usual spluttering and coughing as his putrid innards sought replenishment with an air far more fine.

Grace turned in a single lithe motion whilst still cross-legged. She looked up at the stranger and addressed him sweet as he somehow succeeded in steadying his asymmetrical collection of misshapen bones and slovenly sinews.

"Good morning to you, sir," she said plain. "Did you sleep well?"

"What?" Dawlish barked. "Did I what, child?"

"I was asking if you slept well, sir, for you been in your noisy repose for much of the morn by my reckoning."

Dawlish dropped inelegant to his blasted bulbous knees and leaned forward until his face was only inches away from the young girl. His black pupils flicked this a-way and they flicked that a-way, all the time imbibing of every atom and non-atom of her. He then sniffed up her scent through the black of his wide nostrils before contorting himself into a position whereby he was sitting on his arse on the wet of the sodden, muddy ground.

"And you, boy," he said, unable to hide the mischief in his tone. "Are you be wanting to know the whatnots of my night?"

Stafford's instinct was to pretend he hadn't heard the stranger's query. After a glance over his shoulder at his sister, though, he acceded that the whatnots were what he wouldn't mind knowing, if it be not too bold an asking.

"So," Dawlish continued, his tone dripping with a tone less crotchety. "If you must be knowing then I do declare I be rested in all them parts that needed resting. Do that satisfy the curious of you crafty whelps?"

"Meant no harm, sir," muttered Grace, lowering her eyes a little.

"She didn't, Mister. Me none neither. Hope you didn't take no fence and like."

Dawlish contorted his ghastly accumulation of features into absolutely no expression at all and was far more sinister as a consequence.

"Now you done had yours, old Dawlish here have something of himself he'd like to be knowing."

The pause between his statement and whatever he intended to ask of the two Chuck children was laden with menace, further enhanced by the blob of spittle that drooped slow from the thick of his lower lip and finally fell to the ground like an emotionless slow-motion tear. When his question at last did come, it came in the form of a bark, a blurt.

"Why ain't you gone running off when you had a chance to? Quick with your words now, and be knowing I ain't one to miss no falsehood, oh, no, I ain't and never have been."

Both the boy and the girl answered at once and in spectacular unison.

"The beat of the beat of the beat," said them both.

"The beat of the beat of the beat?" repeated Dawlish with simmering delight.

"The beat of the beat of the beat," the children once more intoned.

The stranger threw back his gruesome head and let out furious into the day what he must have considered to be the sweet, sweet chimes of sweet, sweet laughter. Once done with his howl, he stood sudden with alarming agility. He then began shaking his head wildly from side to side as he spoke.

"That old beat of the beat of the beat! Yeah, you got it, children! You done and got it deep in you now that old beat of the beat of the beat!"

Sputtering to a halt like a spent engine, John Dawlish turned away and smoked a cigarette right down to the bone. Grace uncrossed her little legs. Stafford did too. They both stood and watched the stranger as he walked up the ridge and away from the riverbank. When he was almost out of sight, Stafford grabbed his sister's hand and they ran up after him. He had stopped way before they at last reached him.

"What happens now, sir?" asked the boy, panting.

Dawlish bent forward slightly and put his filthy right hand on the top of Stafford's head and his filthy left hand on Grace's.

Dawlish chuckled a chuckle that resembled the awful blurts of a dying man.

"Damn it all, I say!" he declared raucous. "If whoever be responsible for what we be doing and what we have done and all what we say and all what we will be saying and doing from here to the end has not the wit or the sense to give full structure to this narrative then all may already be lost! I shook off my shackles many a moon ago with the help of the beat of the beat of the beat, and I reckon you two young 'uns have done some good old shakings of your own these last days."

Grace and Stafford both yelped in unison, though they were not entirely sure of the reason for their yelpings. They ran around that fiend in a perfect circle, not once but three times, until they were all yelped out. Once they had steadied themselves and regained their breath, they looked on in silence as the stranger proceeded to urinate with implausible force and range for a duration that was equally preposterous. Once done, he hauled back up his fetid strides.

The children were overcome with a shattering dismay, utterly yelped out.

Dawlish muttered a while with incoherent fury. Whatever words it was he expelled into the breeze were entirely subordinate to the venom of the tone with which they were delivered. He was of multitudes.

Time passed.

Time passed not.

Illogic was everywhere.

Time passed not.

Time passed.

Illogic

everywhere.

"Boy!" blurted Dawlish.

Grace Chuck watched silent as her little brother gulped in the bleak of his shimmer.

"Mister?"

"Take my hand."

Another unholy blurt.

"Girl!"

He asked of her the same, and she complied full.

He had them now, one in each hand, at the base of a gentle incline. He had them now. That Dawlish.

A bird invisible grey shrieked splinter. It had no name, that bird. It simply was.

A puff bulbous cloud dawdled east into dreary and hurried out of the scene.

Undeniable blue.

Decadent blue.

"What will you do with us now?" Stafford asked of John Dawlish.

No reply did that stranger make, for by then he was intent only on dragging them by their puny arms like two dead branches all set for the flame.

24. More Meritorious

JUDGEMENT.

Ah, Judgement.

Where Singe had grown to despise the artless way in which his superior went about his business, the inhabitants of Small Mercy were ever in terrible awe of that inscrutable entity.

Judgement was a necessary spectre, a necessary demon.

Judgement was the wow and he was the unwow.

Every eight days, it was The Auditor's duty to seek out Judgement and report upon those matters which were salient in the continued smooth functioning of Small Mercy. He found them increasingly tiresome and had reached the point where it was only his slavish adherence to The Constitution that compelled him to continue.

Judgement could always be found within the far reaches of The Judgement Hall – the wooden building on the western side of the track. It was the largest structure in the village and marked the northern-most dwelling. It was markedly unadorned given the unrivalled status of its lone occupant. The many thin windows that ran from floor to ceiling along each of the walls barring the front aspect shed sharp slithers of light upon the uneven stone floor. The flat roof was topped in its centre by a square wooden housing from whose central top beam was suspended The Judgement Bell.

Franklin Singe set for his meeting with Judgement. His demeanour was surly, his mind engorged with rancour. The sky was without stars, without magic. The full moon was nothing more than a tragic light whose only role was to give black and stark to the shadows that struck out from the ragged hovels of

Small Mercy. There was not a puff of breeze in the air. The earth turned stagnant if it even turned at all. Singe came to a halt at the narrow doorway of The Judgement Hall, pushed it open and walked straight on in. Once in the very deep of the black, he made his way to, even with so little light, he knew to be the middle of the room. And then in deep chagrin, he did wait for his master to deign to emerge.

Judgement entered at the far end of the black. Though Singe could not in any way make out his form, he knew without doubt that he was in the presence of Judgement.

Nothing was said.

And then something was said.

That was how it always went.

"Since last I came," The Auditor began, "there have been events most unusual."

No response.

Never a response.

"As ever, I will be brief."

No response.

Never a response.

"The two Chuck children are missing."

No response.

Never a response.

"It is said that a stranger has latterly visited upon these parts and that he too has taken his leave. It is also said that he has certain 'powers' of a most intriguing kind."

No response.

Never a response.

Judgement departed at the far end of the black. Though Singe could not in any way make out his form, he knew without doubt that he was in the presence of Judgement no more.

Franklin Singe turned and bled back out into the lesser black of the dismal night. The white of the moon appalled him. He went back home. His home appalled him. Life itself appalled him.

He wallowed in murderous malcontent until he simmered no more. He felt sharp pulsings within his brain as the last remnants of crass emotion trembled out into the gloom.

The moon went down.

The sun came up.

The sun went down.

The moon came up.

The reckless disdain of the night spurred Singe to ruminate no longer, his tolerance for tedium wholly spent. Thus did he ooze out silent into the dark to seek audience with that lamentable baker.

Sullivan pulled open his front door as if the visitation had been long planned.

"Come in," he said low.

The two men were standing in the bleak just inside the bakery when The Auditor stayed his host with a crude tug on the latter's sleeve. "That woman of yours. She sleeps?"

"She does. In her room back over there."

"She is deep in her slumber?"

"We have no need to concern ourselves with that harlot. She knows well enough not to rise unbidden. Follow me, if you will, sir, where a chair and table await you."

A single candle burned low and flicker by the single dining room window.

"You will have a drink, perhaps?"

Singe declined, intent only on matters of import.

"I'll get direct to the matter at hand," he stated. "This stranger of whom you spoke, you stand by your tale and all the details therein?"

"I do, sir."

"You tarried not with malign fancy or adornment?"

The baker shook his head slow and solemn.

"And none but that woman of yours and the Chuck boy know of this stranger and his deeds?"

"The woman, I can attest to her having held her tongue. For the lad, I can be not so sure."

"His absence then may prove to be more meritorious than even it first appeared to be."

"If you say so, sir."

"You are aware that you are still to face reckoning for your recent intrusion upon my quarters?"

Sullivan nodded.

"Then, Baker, I will have you assist me in bringing these events to a most satisfying conclusion."

"I be humbly yours to command. It's that ghoul that got 'em. I know it sure as I know anything."

"Idle speculation is of no use to me in this undertaking in which I have decided to employ you. Do not by your babble render that decision the action of a fool, for if you do, it will not go well for you."

"Yes, sir. Apologies, sir. I meant no harm, I hope you be knowing."

The Auditor breathed deep before replying.

"We must proceed in caution. You understand what that means?"

"I do. I be knowing what caution be and how to do it good as any man."

"That may be so, but what of your woman? Are you of equal certainty that she will keep her counsel?"

"I will see to it, sir. I'll cut out that tongue of hers if that be the only way!"

"You have a cruelty about you, it seems, of which I had hitherto been unaware, Baker."

"Cut it out in her slumbers and hurl it into the fields yonder! Then she'll yap and flap no more, not ever!"

"Into the fields yonder, you say?"

"Oh, yes, sir. Them be well matched, that jabbering tongue of hers and the mud and the filth."

Singe fell into a sinister silence.

Sullivan felt his heart beat slower, which, in turn, led to a brief and unpleasant churning of his innards.

"Then as we are agreed on the matter, I will take my leave of you. You will undertake your task, following which you will not on any pretext seek me out. When the time is right, you will be summoned. Is that clear?"

"Summoned, sir, yes. That be well understood. But that task you speak of? If you be so kind as to say it simple for me, I would be obliged. I ain't be wanting to be letting you down none, surely I ain't."

Singe let out a sharp sigh that dripped with irritation.

"How can it be that you have so easily forgotten that which you just so eagerly imparted?"

"Sir?"

"The woman, you dolt. Her tongue. The fields yonder."

"Ah, sir, I be only jesting in them things I said. Her keeping that silence of hers on that fiend and his devilry, well, you ain't got to be concerning yourself with that. I got my ways, and my ways is sure and sound."

"Jesting, you say?"

"Jesting."

"You recall perhaps that you are mine to command in these endeavours?"

"I do."

"Then you will do as we agreed. You will cut out her tongue and you will dispose of it in yonder fields."

Sullivan sank low into his chair and clasped his hands upon the table before him. He then looked up at The Auditor.

Singe brushed his clothes straight and showed himself out into the listless gloom.

Not a single person in the village heard Mary's scream when Sullivan first put one filthy hand over her eyes as she lay in bed then sliced off her tongue with a blade he held in the other.

Not even Mary heard it. She didn't even hear her own scream. There was bright-red blood everywhere, all over her face, over her neck, her shoulders, in all parts imaginable.

Sullivan considered his sloppy spoils carefully before hurling what was once his true love's tongue far into the fields yonder. He shook his head in mild disgust as he went back inside. He swept clean the hearth and set about measuring out the flour for the morning's bread, musing with some relish upon the recent series of events in which he had been so stunningly entwined.

25. The Devil is a Blurt

A S THE PLANETS do by some remarkable magic twirl with one another in their immortal galaxy waltz amidst the spangle stars, so on this sweet earth too there is ever occurring a happening somewhere, some place that has slipped the chains in defiance of the sinister application of reason. Enlightenment in its true form is not the thorough understanding of the possible but the unabashed acceptance of the thoroughly improbable.

How Linton Gauge, Tobias Defoe and Nathaniel Wild came to be in one another's presence way up there 'neath the gaze of the northern hills bears no examination. Each had for so long learned that to resist the keening call of Mother Nature's ancient sirens is to consign yourself to a most benign existence which has its equal only in death itself.

Though it be their first encounter, not one among the three doubted they had been companions from the moment they were born. They were more than mere men, barely of humankind at all. Where shadows should rightly have been, no shadows were there cast. The sky was an impossible crimson, the semicircle of grass before them, astonishing in its diamond gleam and its emerald tint. A breathless bold did fervently abound.

When your life has been led in holy solitude and any dialogue of which you have partaken has been with vegetation, the natural elements or creatures of all species but your own, the power of the spoken word will by necessity have become subordinate to the glorious panoply of the senses. So it was that not a word passed between The Miller, The Crop Farmer and Nathaniel Wild as they stood there together in the midst of the day. It And then, at last, that fiend, that vagabond, that John Dawlish appeared over the ridge to the west, the two Chuck children trailing behind him all rank and desolate.

Lumbering across the field and coming to a halt before the three men, Dawlish was of hideous aspect. Every ounce of him reeked of devastation. The little girl sighed herself into sitting upon the ground to his left. The boy ached so much but still managed to take his place without complaint on the stranger's other flank.

It began to rain.

And then it didn't begin to rain.

There was black and there was red and other shimmers inexplicable.

The devil is a blurt.

Even angels sometime must weep.

A fire blazed bright orange in and about them all. A blue crackle did spurt from the dull of the earth. There was magic full form just then, the veracity of which was questioned by not one of them there present.

Nothing was said, no instructions imparted. It just happened is all. The ravenous fire of orange and blue anchored them to the universe as they gazed eyes closed into the black of the black and the white of the white..

John Dawlish, John Dawlish, singsong and throb, it was he who, by way of his blam and his splintering, did bring an end to the eternal whomping silence.

"The time is now," he drooled low.

Nathaniel Wild said nothing.

Tobias Defoe said nothing.

Linton Gauge said nothing.

Grace Chuck was all in her drowsy.

Stafford, though, was electric.

"Time for what?" the boy asked.

John Dawlish swivelled awful and gruesome to engulf the little lad's pale and innocent face.

"The time is now," drooled Dawlish once more. "The time is now."

There were stars.

White and solid stars.

Oh, ogre.

Oh, beast.

White and solid stars.

Dawlish turned from the boy and addressed without discrimination the assembled company.

"Clear as any bright day, I do tell you all true that this here gathering ain't no chance encounter like you get in fables and lullabies and the like. Every tall tale so they say will harbour no sense on the way up and even less on the way down. So here we are. The lot of us from here and there and back again. I do confess, right here in this shade and this shriek, that what we got in days to come cannot be changed in detail or design. Don't be glum when I tell thee that not one of us from here on in is anything but a crude and simple dangle puppet of no brain, no soul, no heart and no blam. I been created back in the cloud of some tragedy to be in this moment. Best I can do to soothe you in your ragged is to tell you all true that not the one of us is real if, of course, you been a-wondering on the subject."

Nathaniel Wild looked at Tobias Defoe, who looked at Linton Gauge, who looked at Stafford Chuck, who looked at Grace Chuck. None of them had eyes for the stranger.

John Dawlish took his place in the centre of them all and then, without invitation, let loose from his rotten innards a single musical note that was so majestic that the round yellow moon shattered, the white stars shattered and the purple sky shattered.

It was beautiful.

So very beautiful.

Stafford Chuck was bemused.

"I am real," he murmured with all the dismay he had in him. "I Just know I am, so I don't know why you have to go saying I ain't when I am."

Grace Chuck awoke as if from a reverie.

Stafford frowned and turned to the young girl. "That's right sis, ain't it? You and me is as real as the trees and fields and the bones and the skin of us!"

Grace nodded.

Nathaniel Wild walked silently behind and between where Grace Chuck and her brother were seated on the ground. He put his heavy right arm across the boy's puny shoulders and his heavy left arm across the girl's.

"What you doing, Mister?" Stafford yelped.

Nathaniel did not reply. He just stayed like that with his arms spread wide across the shoulders of those children. And he stayed like that until the boy fell asleep and the girl fell asleep and the moon put itself back together after its shattering and the white stars put themselves together after their shattering and the purple sky turned to the palest of blues and...

and...

Linton Gauge was covered in the powder tumble of the beat of the beat of the beat.

Tobias Defoe was drenched in the wave swell sap of the beat of the beat of the beat.

And that Dawlish fellow?

Well, he was absolutely nowhere to be seen.

26. Everflow

JOHN DAWLISH SANG loud and wild to the upper skies.

He was a beast of song, a coyote, a howler, a shrieking mad demon, a long-lost lover, a mountain, a canyon, a torrent, a smoulder, a drowning, a fury, a tremble, a bombast, a wailing, a tragedy, a wilderness, a ravage, a cherish, an ecstasy, a wonder, a drunkard, a husband, a father, a shrivel, a dead, a dead, a dead, a dead, a dead.

John Dawlish sang loud and wild to the upper skies.

Still, through all that, he heard Mary the baker's woman scream when she was in the very hot of her scream and the very break of her pain. But it was nothing but a breeze to him when deep in his song.

It had been some while since he'd been alone. When you're one such as Dawlish, you can only stand company of any kind for so long. Those such as he had ever been destined to pass huge swathes of their time on this earth in solitude. Just as so many would find him barbaric and loathsome, he would consider them equally so. Yet, to his inevitable chagrin, he had oftentimes found himself drawn inexorably to those places where humans were wont to congregate.

In days long, long passed, John Dawlish, when he was of a mind, was able to exude a thoroughly delectable charm. When he was a younger man, his limbs were less misshapen, his facial features more adequately aligned. He would speak sweet at times and sing such notes as would blow clean away any remnant of whatever once ailed you. His lips would bloom pink and his entire being flow full and blissful into the sigh of you, the heart of you and the soul of you. There was a time when such occurrences were notable only by their absence. But these days, Dawlish was not just a stranger to those in Small Mercy but a stranger to all that ever knew him, ever fell deep into the deep of him; a stranger even to himself.

In agony did that ghoul remove every fetid rag in which he'd been garbed.

He stood as upright as he was able in the deep of the green grass.

He pissed, hands on hips, for what could have been forever.

Sometime later, he clothed himself awful once more.

He started to whistle the semblance of a tune but couldn't even get the semblance of it so coughed himself to a halt.

He studied deep the emptiness within him. It pleased him to do so. He studied deep that emptiness until there was no more empty left for him to be considering.

Eyes closed, he touched soft the crags of his face with the vast expanse of his palms. So gently did he move from his chin to his forehead and across to his cheeks then both sides of his nose before there came a time when one hand was on either side of his crooked skull. Without a warning even to himself, he made a devastating attempt to pull his ears clean off. His ears, it should be said, did not come clean off, nor even close. They stayed just where they were. Dawlish then took to trying to kiss sweetly his own lips, but no joy did he have. He had a mind to look into his own eyes, but this mad notion left with the same swiftness with which it had come and thus went untested.

He looked up at the upper skies blue and in doing so became a stretch of cloud.

He looked down at the earth and instantly sank deep on down into it, through the wet of the grass, the gawp of the soil and the rasp of whatever was beneath.

He looked up at the upper skies blue and in doing so became a stretch of cloud again.

He did all of this because he could.

That was the only reason.

He became the wow beat of his old wow heart.

He sploshed into the blood of his veins and floated with the pumping.

He became his fingers.

He became his toes.

He partied with the lice legions in his rancid hair.

He swayed sweet and steady in the hammock of his scrotum.

He pissed himself out of his penis just for the hell of it.

And then, as evening began to come around, John Dawlish, that ghoul, that ogre, that fiend, laid himself down to rest. He'd sought no shelter, no shade. Just slumped down right where he'd been standing and doing his stuff. He closed his eyes and then opened them and closed them again. He did that until the sun came up, that opening and closing of his eyes that was synchronised sublime with the raucous pulse of him. He got no sleep, but of course, it wasn't sleep he'd been after.

Dawlish shuffled himself into a seated position, coughed, spat on the ground, stretched his arms, stretched his legs and then scratched the black of the night from the bleak of his gaze.

Another day gone.

Another night gone too

in the relentless churn of that improbable man's life.

The everflow sweeps in mighty from the sumptuous startle of the outer sway.

The everflow doth persist.

The everflow doth groove.

The everflow doth saunter brutal.

The everflow always will be.

It sweeps in now,

The everflow

sweeps in mighty now,

the everflow,

sweeps in mighty now from the sumptuous startle of the outer sway.

The everflow

The everflow...

...

...

"What's that smell?" asked Stafford of his sister.

"I smell nothing strange, brother."

"Nothing strange or nothing at all?"

"I smell just the fields and the mud, though they barely have a smell at all."

"It be not that or them? You ain't be playing with me? Oh, sis, surely you must be getting up your little nose what I be getting up mine?"

"Could it be some remnant of a dream you just dreamed?"

"No, dear sister. Not from no dream leftovers. Real as you and real as me and real as the grass we be sitting on and real as the stream that babbles mad at our backs. Real as all that. Real as all that."

"Sweet boy," Grace smiled, shuffling to her knees and turning to face him, "you have been through much these past days and much more still before of which I have no notion." She reached over and placed the flat of the back of her left hand upon his pale forehead. "Methinks you may still be ailing, oh brother of mine."

Stafford slowly shook his head then sighed tragic. Grace somehow evaded the dull limits of her brother's despair and instead scanned the area directly before them both.

"Those men are gone," she said plain.

The stream settled into its rhythm. The tall reeds that bestrode the base of the muddy incline did consent to waft this way and that way and that way and this way. The white surface diamonds shimmered ballet and waltz in the tender arms of the yellow morning sun.

The everflow.

The everflow.

Stafford made as if to stand and staggered, tottering for a moment before he was able to steady himself upright. He licked his dry lips with his dry tongue and tried to gulp some wet into his dry mouth.

"You really don't smell nothing?" he asked sad of his sister once more as she rose from the grass to stand at his side.

Grace reached out with her slender arms and pulled her bewildered brother in close to the skin and the bones of her. She then whispered atonal through the grime of his matted locks and into the deep of his shudder.

"I tell you what I don't smell," she breathed. "I don't smell *him*, which, to my reckoning, ain't no bad thing."

Graced brushed back a clump of black strands from the sharp shadows of her brother's face. She stroked the base of his neck with the very tips of her fingers so delicate and soft for fear of breaking him completely.

They stood thus, the boy wrapped up in the cherish of the girl. And then an ache came simultaneously upon them both. Grace let fall her arms fall, and Stafford, unfurled, withdrew a pace.

The everflow will never be denied.

The everflow.

The everflow.

The everflow…

…

…

By any standard measure, Linton Gauge would be considered *odd*, but no matter.

No matter at all.

The Miller was no stranger to the everflow.

"Sorry, my friend," Linton called back to the rabbit who'd just popped his head out of the ground for a chat. "Please do not think me rude. I'll explain later if you have the time! The time has come, it seems, for old Linton to groove! I do hope you understand!"

The rabbit gazed on ahead as The Miller slipped out of sight, those long strides consuming the space to the west in huge gulps. "If I were a sparrow, had wings even," muttered the rabbit long after Linton had left the scene, "it'd be a different story, I'll warrant!" The disconsolate fellow popped himself fully out into the green of the meadow and proceeded to lurch awkward into the air in an ever-increasing circle, landing each time with an indignant thud until he was as invisible as pain.

FROM THE BRANCH of one of a copse of stubby trees, a pair of tiny chaffinches had been watching this display of floppy-eared petulance

"Rabbits," one of them sighed.

"Rabbits," intoned the other.

A third chaffinch fluttered down from the depths of the large willow at the western expanse of the huddle of trees.

"What's happening?" she chirped.

"Just rabbits is all," said the first chaffinch.

"Rabbits being rabbits," confirmed the second.

"Ah. Those rabbits," nodded solemn the new arrival, "they just can't seem to keep themselves from being rabbits."

LINTON WAS FULLY immersed in the gorgeous of his rhapsody. He was heightened in every way conceivable and in every way inconceivable. Each time his feet touched the ground, the very earth turned upon its axis, beholden entirely to that man's ravishing rhythm and faultless momentum.

That tetchy rabbit had been unfortunate indeed in his timing, for ordinarily, Linton Gauge would have happily stopped awhile for an innocent exchange of pleasantries. But when you absolutely *know* that everflow has swept in all mighty from the sumptuous startle of the outer sway, just like it did the last time and just like it did the time before that – well, you've got no choice but to let it take you where it do decide to take you – rabbits or no rabbits.

The Miller traversed the swathe of land from where he'd been to where he'd come to be in a single bound. He was still, and then he was in motion. And then he was still again. By the time the stream was in sight, he was utterly sublime. The bright and glare of the yellow sun drew no moisture to the surface of his skin, nor did it bring sweet agony to his everloving, everloving ache.

The blue and white of the stream danced sensational when it glimpsed that Small Mercy Miller.

You've got to love the everflow.

The two children were still lost in a rank reverie of their own. Linton was upon them before they even had a chance to think to blink.

Ah, that old everflow!

"Now," The Miller did chime melodic, "there ain't no way I can explain just now, even if I knew how, but you be coming home with me."

Grace and Stafford knew not of the workings of the everflow yet consented to the request of the slim, pallid fellow without complaint.

With bounding strides, Linton Gauge led Martha Chuck's young 'uns through one field and then into the meadow that adjoined the land upon which stood the Small Mercy mill.

The everflow may be miraculous and all, but the only thing that little rabbit wanted to know was just why the evenings of late had been so very, very cold.

27. That Old Universal Void

THE WIND DREW its breath from the oceans unseen. Then 'midst the slavering motion of the assembled firmament there did grow a swirling whose gasp was of sufficient and wondabulous wow to propel anticlockwise the wide wooden sails of Linton Gauge's mill. The shudder up above and on the outer brought a crack and a thunder to the inner in the form of the discs of flat rock that ground graining against one another, against one another, lamenting in torrents the glorious malice of times long gone and times to wide-eyed come.

And as a consequence of the swirl, gasp and groan, flutterings of flour drifted down all painless and snowflake upon the pale, upturned faces of Stafford and Grace Chuck.

Linton Gauge stood just behind them, a foot or so away from the arched wooden door he'd just gently pulled shut. "It is quite something, is it not?" The Miller did ask of the stupefied young 'uns.

"Yes, sir," Stafford said soft, as deep in his awe as ever he'd dared to be.

Grace could only manage a nod, such was her reluctance to disengage in any way from the momentous heave of the moment.

Linton set himself down on the floor and shuffled back until he was snug against the slow curve and shadow of the inner wall. He sighed a little to his left, a bulging hessian sack of freshly milled flour taking his weight to the extent his contorted form wholly belied the majesty of his divine slouch. He closed his eyes and succumbed holy to the fact that he truly wanted for nothing. This supplication of his had become a ritual in which he engaged sometimes as much as a dozen times a day. Never once had he ever been anything but grateful for the good fortune visited upon him that allowed his working-man's blues to croon day and night within the bounds of such spectacular parameters.

Outside in the lowlands of the skyway, the languid whapping beat of the windmill sails sliced serene through the dour of the day. That whap, whap, whap would have swiftly developed into something to be resented by those who have not the courage to dream but choose in its stead to wallow incessant in the orgasmic tragedy of their meaningless life. But not our Linton. Oh, my, not he!

It was Stafford who was the first of the two Chuck children to break from his reverie and turn to appraise The Miller in his loafing.

The slim man looked up at the boy and smiled a smile that fell just short of a grin.

"I had you for being under a spell of sorts," he said. "Not a statue as such, but as good as."

"Don't know what you be meaning, Mister," replied Stafford. The tired little boy did his best just then to wriggle out the raggles from the muscles in his neck.

"Please call me Linton. Even those birds who are prone to holding me in ill-favour are not so prissy as to address me by anything but the plain of my name."

Stafford spluttered out a crack of a cough that had clearly seen fit to give him no warning and, once recovered, turned to face his sister who, in that instant met, with no evident discomfort, the deep of his eyes with the deep of her own. Grace chewed for a moment upon the corner of her bottom lip whilst simultaneously scratching out an itch from the tippytop of her head. She too turned to face The Miller.

"Before you ask," said Linton, "I am afraid that I know as much or, which is more likely the case, as *little* as you do about why we three have come to be within these walls just now. Furthermore, I must confess to knowing even less about what is to come of it."

The children lingered before him in ghostly form, spectral emissaries sent unbidden into the dismay of his day.

"I think first it may be well if you would come over here so that we all can just sit for a while together. That at least would make some kind of sense, if only to poor me. Come. Please. Sit."

After a brief hesitation, Stafford and Grace Chuck did as they'd been so sweetly asked. They possessed not the spirit to dream themselves to a finer place and were swaddled in such a paucity of imagination and desire that in time their minds succumbed wanton to the devastating lure of the Universal Void.

There was a slurring where a purring had ever raised to floating the fantabulous funk of the whap and the thud. The whirl, sway and waltz crooned out the luscious lament of the extraordinary firmament that some say's called heaven yet is most likely no more than the lurid lusting of the filthy, wide-eyed and gorgeous.

That old Universal Void will not be forsaken.

Linton Gauge eventually conceded that it simply would not suffice for him to remain a passive participant in the hope or expectation that all would come good in the end. Whilst the serenity of the life he'd these many years negotiated had granted him a fundamental understanding of the wonder of what it is to co-exist with the incomprehensible and the marvellous, it had clearly rendered him ill-equipped to accommodate, with any degree of finesse, such circumstances as those with which he was now presented. In short, to put it plain, he was as wild adrift just then as the baleful babes on the ground either side of him, who had at least somehow summoned the good sense to submit to their everloving fate.

28. Mischief Gasps

THE WHAP WHAPPED.

Then some sort of thud or beat or whatever.

Oh, Universal Void of olden times, will you never cease in your universal and your void?

There was no rhythm, no charm to which The Miller could tether his lonesome self. He considered momentarily that he should rid himself of the dust and the groan in favour of wild outerdoors. Perhaps some flighty pal would be as astute as to recognise the disorder in his aura and furthermore see fit to advise him accordingly. He was halfway to standing when he slumped back down again. This was not like him at all.

Get thee back in the moment, you sweet, sweet man.

Get thee back to where by rights you ought to be.

Now, Linton Gauge had never uttered anything close to a profanity his entire life, had never felt the urge or the need. Even in this moment, whatever curse it was that had sparked ugly in the rage of him took full form in nothing more than a bleary blurt. But that was enough for him to divest himself of whatever glum had seen fit to embalm him. He alone was cognisant of the three one-syllable words that had for some reason been denied expulsion from the inner of him to the outer of him and that was fine enough.

Get thee back.

Get thee back.

The Miller stood without ache or elegance and in wow silence did make for the door. He pulled it open as if he'd yawned it that way and closed it behind him in the same glorious fashion, leaving the children in the full bleak of their black.

The bruise of the day greeted Linton Gauge with a rare kind of awe. The yellow sun was balled tight up to his left, the white moon translucent way up to his right. The sky was all colours and of none, the meadowlands and the hills to the north too. That man gave due deference to the arc of the light and to the harsh spray of black shadows cast crass and defiled by each small copse of trees and each wayward clump of shrub and gorse. Just as there was no sense or logic to any of it, there was nobody could rightfully deny that all was just as it was meant to be.

"Well, well," said Linton Gauge to this particular groove, "it seems to me that what has ever been can on this particular occasion not wholly be relied upon. Is there any about these parts, be you bird, beast or other, who have the sweet time to dissuade me from such an assertion?"

He stood there as solid as ever he got, his tender feet set wide and flagrant upon the solemn of the earth.

And he waited serene and beautifully bemused, as was his way.

The whap, whap ebbed away.

The thud beat too did excruciatingly recede.

And then speaketh a smalleth starlingth.

It was just like that and in that particular way.

The smalleth starlingth speaketh.

"They tell me you are The Miller."

"I am he."

"The Miller, Linton Gauge?"

"The same."

"Then I have not been deceived."

"You have not been deceived."

The sun boiled into orange.

The moon melted. Simple as that. The moon melted.

"They say you are in need of wise words just now," sayeth the starling. "And as I look upon you this day, I see that only a fool chaffinch would be oblivious to the import of your predicament. And I, dear sir, am no chaffinch."

The starling fluttered close to The Miller's left ear, causing a shiver of improbable grace across that permeated palpable, the entire expanse of his mind.

Linton lowered himself serene to the ground. He then called Stafford and Grace over to sit either side of him. He had them close their eyes and seek as restful a repose as they were able. And thus were the three of them arrayed when that lovely man did impart verbatim to those two young things just what sayeth the starling…

…blue wind blows in midst of whatever pout white feather kiss has on offer as raw tongue drips sop and soulful from out of the black and into the wow. It's all orange anyhow, these days, purple at best, but old blue wind heaves unbowed this a-way and that a-way, throwing out cruel mischief gasps of such timbre and tone as to compel the lifeless and the limp to sway, twirl and flounce with the sort of rueful acquiescence as will ever attend so devastating a capitulation.

…ah, but ain't no shame to sway, twirl and flounce…

…blue wind is childless orphan of timeless universe, itinerant vagabond, indomitable trespasser, beholden to no mistress, master, doctrine or paradigm; conduit 'tween firmament, earth and ocean, indispensable force of devious design, indiscriminate troubadour of ballads all tragic and lullabies sublime crooned crazy from black hole galaxy alleyways with no regard at all for such banalities as linear consequence and base logic.

…ah, but ain't no shame to sway, twirl and flounce…

…'tis breath is all, in some regard, that blue wind, but breath prised at inception from sumptuous breast of ancient immortal dreamer who dreams still and ever will dream, for it is upon the boards of her fantastical imaginings that all humankind do tarry inept, in effort to dissemble and codify the holy groove of the holy wonder, decaying pompous by degrees 'til disintegrated into mound of dust whose stench has no equal, save perhaps in the unapologetic farts of older folk for whom such sweet delights are at least a music of sorts.

…though blunt and raw in force of course, that old blue wind ain't no witless dolt content to thump, whomp, wriggle and cough, delighting facile in the crashing and tumbling, maybe only shrugging unimpressed at the sway, twirl and flounce, such as is surely obvious given the tantalising repertoire of any who once did one time reside fallow within sumptuous breast of ancient immortal dreamer.

…painter, sculptor, tale-teller is that blue wind, possessor of palette of all colours and none from which is daubed shade and wow in fantabulous juxtaposition, moulding, transforming by puff and mere murmur, form, structure and the undreams. Ultimate artist of universe, undefiled, impulsive, bothered not by self-doubt or posterity, unrepentant, splashing and splurging in perfect disharmony, stupendous bard belting out gargantuan poems, prose whisperings and worse comprising terror nightmares and rare serenity of gentle optimism when all is patently lost.

…blue wind sings song of universe

…blue wind pulses from white star to yellow moon to yellow sun to black of night to pale of day to splosh of sea to swish of trees to crack of spire to in of me and out of me to in of you and out of you to white star to yellow moon to yellow sun to black of night to pale of day to splosh of sea to swish of trees to crack of spire to those four wooden sails that turn the stone that grinds the grain that turns to flour and surely that is magic?

…blue wind sings song of universe

…ah, but ain't no shame to

sway
twirl
and
flounce…

THE MILLER STOOD with a jerk, strode over to his mill, pulled open the door, entered and was gone all before the two Chuck children had even opened their eyes.

"You alright?" Grace whispered to her young brother.

"Not sure. You? You alright?"

"Better than I was, I think."

"Than you was when?"

"Before."

"Before what?"

Grace was all out of words. She stood, grabbed Stafford's hand and dragged him up the hill and away from the whap of the huge wooden windmill sails. They walked awhile and came at last to rest beneath the shade of an old and ancient tree, just as evening was turning to night.

Lost time is not found again.

…

…

"What's that noise?" asked Stafford as he sat up groggy and rubbed his eyes. The white stars just then were at the very peak of their spangle.

"Just that old blue wind, far as I can tell," his sister replied.

"Thought it was," the boy nodded slow. "Just never figured it would sound so old," he added.

"Or that it be so very, very blue," said Grace.

"That too, sis. That too."

BACK IN HIS gloomy quarters, The Auditor was dragged free from his grizzle by a buzzing noise. The sound was coming from the other side of the room in the vicinity of a desk which was being hastily constructed before his eyes in order to deceive all dear readers into believing it had actually been there all along. Singe awaited the completion of the cheap flatpack literary device with uncommon patience.

That scurrilous individual pulled open the simple drawer from which the buzzing had emitted to discover a small mobile phone. His initial fear on realising he had received a text message was that it was the garage informing him that the Ford Fiesta he had pranged on his way back from the in-laws the previous weekend had been so badly damaged as to have required scrapping.

But it was not the garage.

The Auditor read the message first in silence and then out loud, perhaps to affirm its very existence.

We have something of a problem. It seems The Writer
– Miss Miriam Malone – has all but lost her mind…

Intensive Care Unit – Colchester General Hospital, Essex

Miss Miriam Malone

WHETHER OR NOT she had all but lost her mind or had merely misplaced it, there's none could deny that The Writer – Miss Miriam Malone – had led some kind of life…

3rd April 1938

Wah!
Wah!
Wah!

4th April 1938

Mummy where are you?
What is a Daddy?

6th April 1938

Nothing.

9th April 1938

Wah!
Wah!
Wah!

10th April et al.

Wah!
in excelsis…

...thereafter...

...and thereafter...

...just fragments is all...

...fragments in time...

...fragments out of time...

...just fragments of some kind of life is all...

1.   The train makes squealing noises much louder than I am making even though all these hard boxes and things don't stop from hurting me. Two big lumpy bags keep falling on me, and I am getting tireder and tireder each time I try to push them away.

It's like everything is moving except for me – the train, the boxes, the lumpy bags. My legs are so cold but get not as cold when I hold them close to me. When I do this, it makes my hands feel warm for a bit, but then they start getting cold like my legs were. When the train jumps really hard, my hair falls into my eyes, and I play at trying to blow it off without using my hands, as I feel safer when I'm all wrapped up in a ball like this.

I don't know when any of what is happening will finish. I don't know where I am being sent to and can't even remember if they told me. I do know that Liverpool – where I've been living – has got too dangerous for little girls like me because of the Germans. I do know that. Everyone knows that, so it must be true. They just put me on this train with these hard boxes that hurt me and these lumpy bags that fall on me. I have never been on a train before. I have seen them go by, I think, but maybe I haven't. Maybe it was just a picture in a book of a train that I'm remembering.

When I cough, I try and make the cough come out in time with all the different noises the train is making so it is like music. It's a good game I have made up, though I'm not very good at it yet, just like I'm not very good at the hair-in-my-eyes game. Whatever happens next, at least I can say I've been on a train now, which makes me lucky, as I'm still only five or six or seven.

2. My eyes have stopped working. They definitely have. I try really hard to see, but still everything is black. I know I am on a bed because when I sit up and swing my legs around, I can't feel the floor, and when I lie down, I can be all flat. I want it to be a bed even though it is not my bed because at least I know what a bed is. I really wish my eyes would start working. I hope I haven't been made blind by a witch or something.

My mouth is dry, and my tongue is as well. I hurt in my arms and my back, but I'm too tired to rub the hurt better. When everything is quiet, my breathing is loud, which is good because it means I'm not dead. But then there are other noises, which I don't like because I can't see what's making them. I keep telling myself it is just the silly old wind playing a game with me because he knows I'm just a little girl with eyes that don't work. I tell myself as well that it must all just be because the moon is asleep and the stars are being lazy and that when the sun wakes up my eyes will be all better and my legs won't be so cold.

I am very tired, but none of the little songs I sing in my head are making me sleep. I will just stay like this, I think, until the dark goes away. I've been in dark before lots of times. It always goes away in the end because it gets tired as well and that's why the sun is yellow and big. I know stuff like that for definite, even though I never even been to no school or anything like them others who are sometimes younger than me and who have a mummy and a daddy who haven't gone away yet.

3. There are hills and trees everywhere around here, and all the grown-ups are very big and very loud – even the ladies. They have red faces and black hair, the ones I've seen anyway.

There are lots of animals, too, that I only ever saw before in pictures. They are loud like the people but in a different way and dirty as well like the people but in a different way too.

Other children have come since I got here. Some of them scream things at night in the place where we all sleep. I am more scared of some of them, the boys especially, than I am of the biggest cow or the grumpiest goat. Mostly, they leave me alone, but sometimes they don't – the boys, I mean, not the cows and the goats.

I have some dreams where I turn into a bird.

I have other dreams where I don't.

4. I am going to stink forever. I just know it. Stink and stink and stink for ever and ever and ever, all because of this boy who hates me even though I never did anything bad to him I can remember. Each time I think I can lift my face out of the smelly cow muck, he pushes my head back in with his hand or his foot. I hear him and some others laughing and shouting as the stuff gets in my ears. When I open my eyes, it hurts because the cow muck gets in them. Even before all this, the yellow dress I am wearing was torn at the bottom. I hope it can be yellow again.

The stink of mud goes away a little bit each time they splodge my face in it. Also, the boy and his friends are laughing not as loud like when they started. Then the laughing stops, and it's like they are gone. I wait for what seems like a day, and they must be gone because boys get bored after a while even when they are hurting girls. I crawl onto my knees and pull myself up by holding on to the wooden fence. It is just when I start to rub the muck from my eyes that I get bashed in the back harder than ever and fall splat down where I just was. Then it all starts over again.

I decide to sleep where I am, out here in this field, which is somewhere near the big house where I can hear the grown-ups singing. They like to sing and they do it a lot.

I am going to stink forever. I just know it. Stink for ever and ever and ever, all because of this boy who hates me even though I never did nothing wrong to him. Nobody comes to find me or look for me. I wake up when the cockerel crows and the sun is coming over the hills. My yellow dress is not yellow anymore. My yellow dress isn't even a dress anymore. The wet cow muck has all dried onto it, but at least it falls off when I start to walk back to where the pigs live.

There are yellow flowers in the grass that are as pretty and yellow as my dress was that time when I kicked that funny-looking girl who couldn't walk properly and kept on kicking her until she gave me my yellow dress as a present. I don't know when that all happened, only that it didn't happen today or last night when I didn't have that dream where I turn into a bird.

5.   It has been raining and raining so much I don't think it will ever stop raining again. The raindrops are coming through a big scary crack in the wall between the pillow end of my bed and just under the window above it. I watch as my little pillow fills with rain, and it looks like it is bleeding or something but not with red like blood but with black, although the rain isn't black. I don't know what colour rain is even though I stare at it as hard as I can.

One time, when the rain was like it is now and my pillow even more wet than it is now, I decided to sleep with my head at the other end of the bed, but the fat lady with the spots on her face who smells worse even than all the cow muck in the whole world made me sleep out in the dirt the next night and the one after that, I think, so I didn't do it again.

The wet patch on my pillow goes from being like a little circle to a wobbly shape as if it is growing into a horrible ghost. I know it is only rain, but what the rain is doing to where I have to put my head is not a very kind thing to do. I decide to pretend to be a fish because fishes love being all wet. This works for a little bit but then stops working, so then I turn into a duck and make-believe I am asleep on a lovely pond in a lovely place where all the little girl ducks are treated like princesses and given beautiful yellow ribbons to wear whenever they want to look extra pretty. When I wake up, I can't stop coughing and I feel like I am definitely going to die.

6.   This church is so cold that I think I am not just shivering on the outside but on the inside too. There are seven others here, and some of them look like they are asleep. Nobody is talking. I try to remember what I had for my breakfast at the long table in the big house, but I can't, even though it was only a short time ago. Everything is dusty in here like it hasn't been cleaned for longer even than I have been alive. The stones in the walls have black bits everywhere in them like cracks but not cracks. It looks like somebody has tried to bash them into pieces then stopped like they got caught doing it or something.

Everything looks dead – the floor, the ceiling, the benches, the walls; all dead like the people buried in the ground where you walk in. It was the old man with the big dirty beard who told me and the other children about the dead people in the ground. I don't know if he was just trying to get us all scared. I so wish he would open the door so I can get to where the sun can maybe make me not quite as cold.

I look up and see someone standing behind the tall wooden thing at the front of where we're all sitting. I can't understand why I didn't see this man before. Maybe he's a ghost or something. He starts saying words like he's worried about talking too loud. I know most all of the words he says, but when they get said in the order he says them, it's like he's talking like a Jap or something. I know he can't be a Jap because the Japs are on the other side of the world, and most of them are dead anyway because of the war thing.

When the man stops his talking, nobody says anything for ages, and then the smelly lady from the big house pokes me hard in my shoulder and pulls me to my feet. She pushes me until I am outside like I've seen some of the men do to the cows to make them go where they want them to go. I smile when I see the sun is yellow again and the grass and the trees are shining. I want to say hello to them – to the grass, to the trees and the wildflowers too – but I don't because I know what will happen if I get caught. The older I get, the more some things just don't make sense to me – like it's fine to talk to the dead people in the ground out the front even though they're dead, but when you're telling a pretty flower how very pretty it is, you get dragged away by your hair and beaten with a stick until you stop crying even though you want to go on crying forever.

7.   There are coloured flags on long bits of string that go from one side of the road to the other, lots of rows of them, all zigzag from up here in the square to down where I can hardly see. There are sudden bangs that make me jump in fright, and everyone is shouting but not in the angry way people usually shout. I am standing in the middle of more people than I can even count and my counting is as good as my reading these days. When there is a tiny gap in the noise, I ask a man next to me what is happening. He looks down at me, and I see he has a black patch over one of his eyes and a splodge of pinky red underneath it on his cheek. I can't make out all what he says because the noise starts up again, but I think he was trying to tell me that the war thing has finished. Somebody else shouts out something about us having won. I thought you could only win games, and I know for definite that even if he was in the war, I wasn't, so I don't know why he says us and not him or them or something.

Me and the other children have been all made to look clean, and I even got to get in the bath when the rest were done. The water was cold and a bit dirty, but I really loved the way it felt on me.

The long cut on my right arm went a funny colour when I was getting dry by the fire, but it seems more normal now. I have been scratching it lots since the blood got hard but have got better at not doing that so much, I think.

The church bells start clanging, and they are really loud even though I am not inside the church but out here on the street. It doesn't sound like music to me. The boy who used to hurt me is standing next to me. I am much bigger than him now, and he hasn't done anything horrid for a long time. I think I heard he has been sick. He looks sick, though I don't tell him. I could push him over and kick and punch him if I wanted to get him back for everything he's done to me, but I decide that wouldn't be very nice. I look down at him, and he turns his head so I can't really see all of his face. He is like one of the old chickens the old farmer man kills for the fat lady to cook. I have never eaten a chicken. This boy, I am sure, would taste disgusting, and I know for definite that I wouldn't eat any part of him even if I had to or be dead if I didn't and even if everyone said he tasted better than the fat lady's chicken.

The church bells are still clanging. I hope this war-being-over thing doesn't happen all the time because it is making everybody around here be all different to how I know them. There is another very loud bang followed by laughing and shouting that is just as loud as the very loud bang. I cover my ears with my hands and close my eyes. All I can smell in my nose is the horrible stink of cow muck. That happens a lot even though it happened a long time ago when I was a little girl and I'm not really a little girl so much anymore.

8. Children come and children go. For some reason, I stay. The pigs and the cows and the other animals never seem to go anywhere either. The nights are dark, the summers warm and the days dreary. I discovered this morning that this place I've been living ever since I can remember is not in England but somewhere in Wales. It feels good to know that, at least. I have been here the longest out of all the others except the adults, but there is not a moment goes by when I don't feel like I'm a stranger. Sometimes I wake up and it takes me a while even to know who I am, which sounds silly, but at the time it's pretty scary.

9. There is some kind of singing, but I can't quite tell where it is coming from. Somebody somewhere is definitely singing, though, and I have never heard anything like it. It is a man's voice for definite. A man is singing. I think it must be a very big man, a giant or something, because his singing seems to be everywhere. I put down the brush I have been using to scrub the floor of the kitchen at the back of the big house and stand up to try and listen more closely.

My knees really hurt now I've got taller, but the hurt doesn't last as long as it once did. I begin to feel as if I am floating in the sky like a cloud or a butterfly and not standing in the puddles I have made with my bucket and my brush. That is what this man's singing is doing to me. Then I realise I am not at all cold like I always am, although I am not warm either. I am so happy. I realise I am crying. I feel extraordinary.

10. Blood is coming out of me from where only my wee should come out. I look like what they did to the pigs so the fat lady can cook them in the place I've just come from. I have only been in this new place they move me to for a short while and am terrified if anyone finds me in this field with all this blood coming out of me. They would maybe send me somewhere else not as nice or even to a hospital for mad people. That would be just awful! The blood just keeps coming and coming, and I can't stop staring at it. Then it stops, and I watch it as it goes from red to brown as it dries on my skin.

I get back too late for supper and am chided for my tardiness. I try and stay awake for as long as I can and hope the girl in the bed next to mine doesn't try to talk to me. I am so scared that the blood will come out of me again if I fall asleep. The girl in the other bed is two years older than me. She has been here since before last Christmas, or so she says. I think about waking her in case I am dying but decide not to.

The moon must be behind a big cloud or a hill, as the night is very dark. I can see a few stars and think for a while what it must be like to be up there shining with them. When I wake the next morning, the stars are gone and there are dark spots of blood on my bedsheet. I see that I am alone, and so I spit and spit and spit on the dry blood then rub and rub at it with a sock I have scrunched up until the blood is all but gone. I try to make myself believe it was never there at all, but I'm nowhere near as good at make-believe as I used to be.

11.   A boy from the village is holding my hand. He is one of them ones whose dad is the blacksmith. The boy tells me that I am pretty and that me being tall is a good thing, but I think he is only saying that because he is bigger than me and also to make me feel better as he knows some of the girls in the village tease me about my height saying that I am cursed or something. Then he holds my hand a bit tighter and leads me to one of the narrow alleys that go between the ruined houses where nobody lives anymore. He stops us about in the middle and turns me so my back is against the wall. He starts to stroke my face with both his hands. His fingers are rough on my skin, but I don't tell him that. My hand hurts where he was holding it so hard.

The boy starts making grunting noises like he's a pig or a dog or something. My eyes go wide. He pushes my shoulders back against the wall so hard and leans in to me so much it's like I am chained to the filthy black bricks. His face goes all cruel as it gets nearer to mine. He tries to kiss me, and I can't get out of the way of it. His mouth feels disgusting. My lips sting like they've been stabbed.

The boy takes one of his hands off my shoulder, and before he can put it somewhere else on me, I bash him with my knee where it hurts boys most. He falls to the floor and screams like he's been shot or something.

When I get back to my room, I wait until I can breathe again and pick up my little mirror. There's blood on my chin. I hope it is mine and not his. It might be his. I scrub at it so hard that my skin is as red as his cheeks were when he was trying to do that stuff to me.

The night comes.

I pack up my things and leave this place that's been my new home since the last new home I left.

The stars look like they are made out of silver or something. The sky seems purple in places, but mostly it's just really black. With almost every step I take, I can't stop myself from turning around to see if that awful blacksmith boy is coming after me. I think about going back and killing him, but I don't because I know killing is wrong except when it's done by our soldiers to Japs and Germans so we can win wars.

12. The older I become, the less I seem to dream. I fall asleep tired and I wake up tired. Even since I've had a room all of my own way out here where I am now, and even though the men who took me in couldn't be kinder, I hardly ever dream at all. The three men are brothers, and they're all a lot older than me, though one not so much as the other two. There is the one who laughs, the one who sings and then there is the youngest one who doesn't say much at all except, from what I can tell, to the little birds that follow him about like he's their leader or something.

I haven't locked my bedroom door for ages even though I could lock it if I wanted to.

13.   I am in love with books. When I am not working, I am in my room reading. The three men who are so kind to me are always saying this place is as much mine as it is theirs, and that goes also for the things in it, which is how I started on the books that live on the two shelves in the main room. Each time I finish one, I go straight to the next one. I think they are for me like I have seen beer be for some people, although of course, my books don't make me all angry and sick like I've seen beer do to people.

I have no idea how I ever coped at all before I started all this reading. I know that I will never be lonely again as long as there are still books in this world to read. I am changed by each line and page. It is like I am growing in my heart and my mind in some sort of magic way, almost as if all the words I've been speaking all my life have been no better than the moos of cows and the oinks of pigs. Or it's like I was once some sad little tree, but now I've got leaves and fruit all over me. That's it! What I'm trying to say is that I used to be dead, and now, thanks to these stories and the people in them, I am as far away from being dead as I ever thought possible.

14.   My husband is over there on the other side of the hall holding court with some more people I don't know. Though I can't hear what he's saying with the music being so loud, I can tell he has something of his old self about him. He has them under that spell of his, and I bet not one of them even knows it, just like I didn't know it those three or so years ago when he caught me good with his charms.

I'm standing on my own in this far corner. The air is full of cigarette smoke and the floor is sticky with spilled drink and the spit and urine of drunk men. I am sure I am standing quite still, yet through the smoke, everything I look at seems as if it is on a slope or something. I hear my husband roar out the finale of his tale and then watch as he grabs the shoulders of one of the women in front of him. He lifts her up so her face and his face look like they're touching. The smoke grows thick, and when it clears, I can't see either of them despite how hard I silently try to seek them out amongst the bawdy gaggle of strangers that comprise what remains of our wedding guests.

A terror so plain and irrefutable sinks its mirthless thorns into the flesh of me. The smoke returns billowing and black, and I hear my husband's voice call out a name that is not even a little bit like mine.

15.   My precious darling is crying again. This time, she is crying so loudly I just know that whoever hears her will think even worse of me than they likely already do. The more tightly I hold her tiny body to my chest, the less real she seems. I feel her stiffen in my arms, and I have to touch her red cheek with my finger to check she is still warm and hasn't shouted herself to death. There is music in her shrieking, nothing you'd recognise as coming from a child but more like an animal that's been hurt bad and knows only worse is to come. The screaming of this girl I'm holding is brewing in me a swelling that must be the work of the devil himself. I will my pale and colourless arms to cleave not to the will of that which is all but devouring the rest of me and fashion a sudden notion to bash the back of my head against the wall behind me in the hope I will knock myself clean out. Then, at the very instant I am about to give myself over to fate, my little girl ceases her noise. It is I, now, who is shaking and red of face. I gaze down at the slump of skin and bones that seven or so months ago was dragged bloody from out of me by the doctor who has since passed away. I feel only sorrow for my little girl and for me, her weary and hopeless mother.

16. There is flour everywhere in our kitchen! It's like it's been snowing on the three of us. I am beginning to think it is not bread we'll be making this day but a fabulous snowman! Becky is on the tips of her toes, swishing her hands across the wooden top of the counter, giggling like a riot of birds as the flour dust takes off in all directions. Not yet able do anything more than crawl at best, my barrel of a baby boy is all wide-eyed and gawping as the black curls of his hair turn first grey and then white.

Becky is unstoppable in her moment of joy. I take a step back so I can better see her. She is wild and she is unruly but also dainty as a ballerina. She swirls around and around as the flour renders our simple house just a little less wretched than it ordinarily is.

Ned tries to pull himself up but flops back down, and still the torrents of white dance gorgeous and haphazard at my daughter's ravishing behest. I stoically decide that not only will there be no bread this day but no clearing up either. Nor will there be any admonishing of these angels of mine, even though I know what will happen as a consequence if that husband of mine bothers to come home tonight.

17. I don't think I will ever get used to the stench of stale beer even though I've had this cleaning job at The Working Man's Club since not long after Ned was born. That I do not throw up my innards with each sweep of my broom is in itself a miracle. My mind empties as I mop and clean and dust and wipe. I cherish that emptiness. I am as lifeless as the stains on the tables when about my work. I adore the bliss of base function.

The door opens. A slash of white light strikes out across the stone floor, and the first clomping boots of the early shift thunder into this grim sanctuary of theirs within which I am no more than a phantom.

And then I become horribly aware that something is wrong. I stop what I am doing, though nobody notices, of course. The usual cacophony of grunts and shouts has been reduced to a morose simmer. It is as if they have had their souls ripped from them in the same way they rip the slate from mine. They take their seats, but there are no crude calls commanding I fetch them bread and beer. Not a single glance even flashes leering in my direction. An unholy pall descends upon the scene.

There comes a loud boom as the door is kicked open. The head foreman fills the gap in the doorway and then, without hesitation, strides over to where I'm standing in these far corner shadows. He tells me low and stern to follow him through into the back room. I glide shabby in his wake, and with appalling tenderness, he guides me to a chair.

"Sit you down, Miss."

I sit me down.

"There ain't no way to say what I got to say, so I'll just get on and say it. Your husband done and got himself hurt bad, real bad. He ain't dead, and that's a blessing. All the boys said so right off, seeing as how dead and gone he looked. Think of it as a blessing is my advice, Miss, the fact he ain't dead."

"A blessing," says I, staring, just staring.

"Fact is, and like I said, only way is to tell it straight up. Well, fact is while he ain't dead, he won't be...well, he won't be in some ways like he was before. Busted both his legs, one so bad I ain't in all my years seen nothing so smashed. Can't move one of his arms right now, but Doc reckons too early to say, far as what the future be in that regard. Good news is his noggin didn't hardly get a scratch, far as anyone can tell. If him being not dead is a blessing then that handsome face of his still being handsome and all is a fucking miracle if you pardon my French, Miss."

"A miracle," says I, staring, just staring.

"You be in shock, I can tell. Seen it before in wives and the like. Just why it is I got you to be sitting down like you be. Some of the lasses have been told of what's gone on, and they'll be here to sort the men out with their drinks and all, so don't you go fretting far as all that goes. I'll leave you be now, Miss. Just you keep telling yourself about what I said about the old blessing and miracle. Won't do you no good doing otherwise."

He leaves me be.

Alone in this back room, I notice the air has a sweetness to it that I can almost taste. I breathe for maybe the first time today, and my lungs fill up sudden with this strange fragrance that emanates from no source I can discern.

A tremendous surge begins in the doom of my stomach and rises through my chest. And then, as the surge subsides, I realise that a smile has broken out wide across the filth and the raw of my face.

18. One of my teeth is sloshing around in the blood that's pooling in my mouth. The blood tastes like metal. I try and get the tooth on my tongue so I can spit it out and not swallow it, but it keeps slipping away. I cough and blood spatters out down my chin and onto my nightgown. I cough again, and I feel an awful pain in my ribs. I make it worse by trying to stop the next cough, so eventually, I just let it go. More blood comes out of my mouth. As my breath returns, I see that my tooth is on the floor next to the broken chair. I pick up the tooth and examine it briefly as if I've never seen anything of the like before in my life. And then I gently set it back down.

The noise in my head is like the sound of a train that's going through a tunnel. Not a single part of me feels like it is mine. I resolve to remain here where I am until my arms are my arms again and my legs are my legs again. He'll be snoring in his bed by now and will likely stay that way a long old time, given all the drink he's got in him.

Ned and Becky are at their auntie's and will be back the day after tomorrow, whatever day the day after tomorrow might be.

19. I don't often come down to the club these days, but here I am, eyes closed, sitting alone at this faraway corner table, gazing across the smoke and the sweat at my fiend of a husband. For all else he is and in spite of all he has become, when he sings I cannot help but hate him just a little bit less than he deserves.

I give myself up to breathing in each note that floats from the deep of his throat just so I can have within me for a rare moment the taste of that which once led me to fall in love with him. His horribly misshapen legs and the stoop of his back imbue each song he sings with a poignancy that is excruciatingly excessive. It's like he is some kind of singing defective.

As he comes to the end of his final song, there is a smattering of applause that reeks of pity.

Now he has stopped singing, I find I can't bear to look at him. I hear him bellow out for another drink. I can smell him even from way over here on the side of the room. I watch as he takes a huge gulp from his glass and then spits loudly onto the floor near the feet of a young woman. Nobody says anything. He finishes his drink in the next gulp and demands another. An odd feeling suddenly comes upon me. It is as if the drink he is throwing down him is working its devilry not just on him but also on me. Though I've not eaten since yesterday, I can sense a gloop of vomit forming in my stomach. I don't have to touch my face to know I'm sweating as if I'm in a furnace. And just as quickly as it came upon me, this awful uneasiness leaves me. I am left with the stink of vomit on my tongue but all else is as it should be. My husband suddenly decides to lurch into yet another old lament from his baleful repertoire. I am not the only one who, at that point, takes the opportunity to leave.

20.   I'm on my knees at the edge of the stream that comes down between the northern hills and through the meadow of heather. The awful smells of the factory where I've been working are so strong in my nose, it's like I'm still pumping the pedals and threading the thread. I cough to try and rid myself of the smell because it feels like I'm somehow infecting this place, but when I do, I am forced to spit out an awful splat of stuff into the grass like I'm a foul creature or something and not human at all. The heat of the evening sun is prickly on my neck. I ache but not in a hurting way. My clothes are stuck to my body with the soak of my sweat.

I look into the stream, and it definitely seems the stream looks back at me. The incline of the hill makes the water move constantly this way and that, and in doing so my reflection can never totally take shape. Now I see nothing, not strands of me in the ripples nor even the water or the plants or the rocks. Everything has vanished. I stand at first unsteady and then steady. I am hot and I am cold. Without conscious thought, I see that my filthy garments lie in a tumble to the side of me and I have no recollection how they got from me being in them to where they are now.

I am naked in the waters now. The stream and I are as one. I ripple and I float. I am the bubbles. I am the swash. I am the plosh. I gaze up from my cherish and sip soft the yellow edges of the round moon. I lick the silver from the stars until it is not them that sparkle and shimmer but me.

21.   "It's great!" Ned yells over at me. "Are we really going to live in it? Can we? Can we?"

"You be careful, now. Not too close to the water."

"It's a boat, Mummy," Becky says to me softly. "Without the water around it, it would just be a funny-shaped house. How can we not be close to the water if this is to be our home?"

I rub the top of my daughter's head, and she smiles up at me. She is beautiful in so many ways. I can scarcely believe she is even related to me at all.

My indomitable little boy has now decided to try and pull open the door at the side of the hull so he can get inside the houseboat and explore. Although it is far too heavy for him, he does not relent until we are at his side. He takes to pointing up at the words that are painted in italic script further along the boat towards the bow end.

"*Y Meirw Bach*," I say slow as if they are not letters I'm reading but some constellation of stars.

"What does that mean?" Ned frowns.

"It's Welsh," says Becky. "That's all I know."

"Will Daddy be coming?" Ned asks of me, his frown untouched by his sister's reply.

"Later today, maybe," I tell him. "He has to do some things first."

"What things?"

"Oh, just boring things, I should imagine. Just daddy stuff."

"What sort of boring things?"

"Things to do with your Aunt Bessie. This was her boat, and she wanted us to have it. Your daddy is just making sure nobody else can take it from us."

Before any further questions come my way, I pull open the door and secure it in place so it doesn't fall shut on us once we're inside.

Having negotiated the few steps down, Ned runs around like a trapped fly. Becky sits on a long bench along the left-hand side, in front of a long, narrow table. She has that look upon her face that is so identical to the one I have borne for as long as I can remember. I am never less than startled when it manifests itself in one of such tender years.

"Does Daddy have to come?" Becky says soft to me.

I slide in and sit beside her. I pull her close to me. I kiss her twice on her forehead. Such is the intensity of the fearless love I hold for her in this moment, I forget even to answer her question.

Becky shuffles away from me. I suddenly feel terribly weary.

I watch my daughter as she walks through the door at the far end to my right, only just avoiding Ned as he races past her. I tell myself as I sit here in this boat that things have been better of late. A fresh start away from that awful village, the sea air, well, I can but hope. Ned is five, Becky nine – both young enough to create childhood memories of sufficient splendour and scope to, in time, render obsolete those they have accumulated thus far in the sorry little story of their sorry little lives.

22.   He is slumped shabby in his armchair like a colourless wad of rags. The light from the log burner by his side flicks yellow and orange splashes upon him. "What you doing, woman?" he snarls at me surly.

"Writing is all," I reply, having developed the ability of late to give him response without breaking the flow of my scribblings.

"All you do these days, it seems."

I pause a moment before putting down my pencil and turn to look at him. "This boat takes not too much to clean and keep in order," I say plain. I have no idea even if he has heard me. He lights another cigarette then sits back even deeper into the sagging upholstery. He closes his eyes, and I watch him descend further still into lonesome decay.

I look down at my notebook and read back to myself the paragraph I've just written. I am pleased. Whether it is good or not I neither know nor care. Up until a few weeks ago, the idea of writing anything at all, let alone a story, was as unlikely as waking up one morning to find I've turned into a bird.

I cannot honestly say what it was that first led to this pencil being in my hand. It just happened as if it was always meant to happen. I am starting only to feel complete when I am getting on with this thing, this writing. As each day passes and each blank page is filled, I am increasingly aware that the mere act of writing is as essential to my continued functioning as the beating of my heart. Perhaps this is how alcohol was for him over there when he still drank. He hasn't touched a drop since the doctors told him if he continued the way he was going, the drink would kill him for sure. His idea to move into this boat, I think, was as much to get away from temptation as it was anything else. He looks shrivelled from where I'm sitting, older, dying by degrees. I wouldn't begrudge him one last drink, if truth be told. Doctors aren't always wrong.

23.   The air is heavy with the lingering aroma of last night's rain. As I stand here, on the bank where our boat is anchored, and look across the bay, I feel I could reach out and grab myself a handful, put it to my mouth and taste it. The mountains on the far side of the water seem to me to be breathing. The myriad paths, trails and fissures that bleed out in trickles across the surface are mesmerising.

Like me, the waters across the expanse of the bay are waiting patient and enchanted for the moon to ease into the black blue grey of the firmament. The final drops of sunlight some minutes ago dripped their final drop, and all within and about me is serene.

The curved ripples that spread out in row after row from where the grassy bank juts out crude make their way from here at my feet to the Irish Sea and beyond. They aren't waves as such. There is no haste to them, no bluster, more a steady and majestic outpouring of melancholy. For the briefest moment, I understand just how it comes to pass that from time to time some person or other chooses to fill no longer their lungs with oxygen but instead gorge upon the salty waters of the sea in the hope that an existence far finer in nature may by some miracle or alchemy result.

24.   The moment I get out of the car, I know something is terribly wrong. I am breathing fast and hard by the time I pull open the door to the boat. He is asleep in his chair. The log burner is on. I am momentarily soothed. But then it comes back, this terror. Ned hasn't come running over to see if I have a comic book for him. Becky, well, she could be anywhere in one of those little places around here she likes to spend time in, reading or just watching the birds. It's cold outside, though, and I know she doesn't like this type of weather at all. Despite that, I feel certain that neither of my children on the boat. I'm sure of it. He has not stirred at all. The thought he may at last be dead barely registers in the frantic of my mind.

I clamber out onto the mud and the grass of the bank. Over and over again, I call for my Ned and for my Becky. I call out for them until the sun is gone and the moon is on the rise. When, finally, I go back into the boat, I am thoroughly spent. That husband of mine rumbles into waking.

"What time is it, woman?"

I am all menace.

I drip with rancour and with rage.

The voice that leaves my mouth is not my own.

"What have you done with my children?"

It is the voice of menace.

It is the voice of rancour.

It is the voice of rage.

"What have you done with my children?"

25.   "To Miriam Malone!" the elderly woman cries as she raises a glass of white wine in my general direction. The elderly woman is my publisher.

I lower my head a little in an attempt to hide the red flush splodges that have come to my cheeks. I have never really been one for this sort of thing.

"To Miriam!" declares the bald man seated to the left of the desk that is a few feet in front of me and behind which is a large floor-to-ceiling window that looks out on to the street. The bald man is my agent.

"This is the start of great things!" my publisher tells me as she sits back down in front of the large window and rests her elbows on the desk. Her untouched wine slops slowly from side to side in the bowl of the glass.

"Great things indeed!" echoes my agent.

I am not so sure but, of course, say nothing. From the very start, they seemed to like this book of mine far more than I ever did when first I wrote it or even do now. They keep calling it my 'debut novel' whereas in truth it was no more than something which, a few years back, I turned my mind to lest I lose it.

"You know what they say?" my publisher asks me shrill.

"No. No, I don't."

My agent is grinning with such glee I fear he may explode.

"My dear Miriam, it is a well-known industry aphorism that an author is only as good as their next book. Now, you get along and leave all the boring stuff to us, for that is what we do best. You provide the magic, and we two old hands will ensure your spells are cast far and wide so all may be enchanted! Get along now, my dear, and deliver us up another winner! Off you go now! Off you go!"

So off I go, wondering just what it is that I have gotten myself into.

26.   A change has come upon him. It is as if the weight of his contempt for me along with the dread consequences of his ghastly disdain for all but himself has wrought some devastation overnight in every hollow and blister of him. I stand as close as I dare, for though he be deep in sleep, the depth of the terror that has for so long been the spike upon which he has ever sought to impale me has become as much a part of me as the wet of my eyes and the rough skin of my heels. Truth be told, he has worn me down almost to boredom with his blows and his swipes. As I look close at him now, I am startled by the complete absence of malice his wretched form exudes. When he breathes out, he exhales merely air, and when he inhales, he takes in only air too. No putrid doom oozes unseen from his innards nor is there anything about him that is at all extraordinary or malign. He whose presence in my life has cut such a vicious swathe is quite clearly now, as I gaze full and wide upon him, nothing more than a pathetic jumble of blood and bones.

I step back a pace then forward two. I reach down and forward and crudely jab him awake with one of my fingers. He sniffles and coughs then sloppily rouses himself all slovenly and bleak. He opens first one eye then the other and blinks discordant until he sees my face but a yawn away from his own. I remain rigid, the loveless dull of my pity too much for anything he has to offer. He moves his grey lips as if to speak but manages only to dribble spittle down his unshaven lump of a chin. I can see he is appalled by the extent of his ruin. He tries again to speak but instead slithers silently from his chair and onto our newly carpeted living room floor. Having plenty of time to react, I take now to looming over his curled and broken body as it shudders and shakes at my feet. Without a moment of thought, I turn away and go upstairs to my bedroom that is further down the corridor from his. My study is opposite the bathroom that separates our two rooms.

I spend the day writing and reading and putting some of my files in order. I take a long bath and eschew supper for an early night.

When I come back downstairs the following morning, he is still on the carpet where I left him. He has stopped his shaking and is snoring like a beast. I make myself a cup of tea, listen awhile to the morning birdsong that jangles merrily through the kitchen window and then go up to the study to finish the second draft of my seventh or eighth novel.

27.   The Clinic smells of dead flowers and bleach.

"Miss Malone?"

It is The Consultant.

I bend down to take hold of my husband's left arm. At first, he jerks it away and grumbles, but then he relents and I'm able to help him to his feet. He slopes visibly from one shoulder to the other. There is no symmetry to him, no order. He is a shambles of a man. I long ago ceased to be by any definition a wife just as he, from the moment of our betrothal, took it upon himself to be unrecognisable as a husband.

The first time we came here, The Receptionist referred to me as his 'carer'.

"Thank you for coming," says The Consultant as we follow him into his office.

I nod and try to look sad.

"Well, let's get straight to it," he says. "The results of the tests have come back, and I have had time to examine them fully alongside the scans we took the last time you were here."

"I see."

"Before we go into things, have there been any, well…I mean how has it all been?"

"Much the same."

"That is not unusual in these cases. Sudden deterioration will at times be followed by a period of relative inertia in terms of the illness."

"So I understand."

There is no tone to my voice, no timbre.

"Your husband's brain shows evidence of significant atrophy. It surprises me somewhat that he is able to function in some areas as well as you describe."

"He has always been a stubborn man."

"Well, good for him."

"Yes. Good for him."

"Going forward, the dementia nurse specialist will arrange a package of care, with your full involvement, of course. There is no cure for dementia, but there has been much progress in the ways in which we are able to enhance the well-being of the sufferer."

I tug at my husband's coat. He stands almost by instinct. I turn him around and lead him out of the office, down in the lift and back into the car. I drive him in silence to our home. When we're there, I turn off the engine, get out, pull open his door and guide him into the lounge where he then stumbles into his chair.

Satisfied that he will soon slip into a heavy sleep, I fill up a bucket from the kitchen with hot water and detergent, arm myself with a sponge and a towel and return to the car to see to the dark patch of urine my husband has left for me. There is no doubt in my mind that this rancid expulsion of his was entirely intentional.

28. "On the sofa now, we have a successful novelist who, I'm sure wouldn't mind me saying, is also a woman about whom much remains a mystery, which is absolutely the definition of irony given the genre she has dominated for so many years. I am super excited that she has agreed to join us for one of her very rare public appearances. Ladies and gentlemen – Miss Miriam Malone!"

"Thank you, dear."

"The pleasure is all mine, Miss Malone, and from that reaction, your fans in the audience are clearly as thrilled to have you on the show as I am."

"That is nice."

"So then. Your latest book is due for release on Thursday, I believe?"

"Yes."

"The fifteenth in the Penelope Welch series?"

"So I've been told."

"Some people have, rather unfairly in my opinion, accused you of no longer *writing* books these days but of *churning* them out. I wonder, have you over the years grown used to such unpleasantness?"

"Yes. I have heard that. I have never considered myself to be an author as such, just a plain and simple writer. That is all."

"Well, I must say I'm intrigued. What then would you say is the difference between a *writer* and an *author?*"

"I think that is a question best asked of an author, my dear."

"Hah! Very good! Very good! Now, I would not be doing my job if I didn't press you just a little on your famed private life. Famed, of course, not for what is known but for the remarkable extent to which it remains a mystery. So then, care to offer any titbits to your legions of devoted fans?"

"I'm afraid I have led a particularly uninteresting life. Why else would I have persisted for so many years in *churning* out fiction?"

29.   I look up at the sky, and the sun is so bright I find I must close my eyes to its glare and wonder even if it is possible that I may never again have the need to open them at all. The lullaby birdsong swirls about me like a magical spell. A tender breeze soothes the back of my bare neck as I sit enchanted here in my own private corner of this earth.

I fancy I hear the trickling of water but know it must be that old mind of mine making mischief with me. These days, I am far from mountains and streams and pebbles and rocks and the commotion of their melding.

I feel myself drifting out of base consciousness into a state of serenity that is as beguiling as it is transient. There is so much talk these days of meditation and the like, about what is referred to as *being in the moment.* I begrudge no-one their chance to experience such things but confess that so often such talk irritates me more than it stimulates. I find that I am just too weary to engage in anything that has the potential to transform me. I may not as yet be ready to concede that I have for almost twenty years been *churning* out books for a living, but I can no longer avoid the fact that the events that have comprised my life to now have consigned me to a fate far worse than that which has all but finished off my husband.

As the heat of the sun begins to burn into my saggy cheeks, I desire only to be set fully aflame like the witches and hags of olden times. With something like relief, I condemn myself to the pits of hell for having been a rank traitor to the young woman I once was and all she endured. I abandoned her with callous disregard, deciding instead to pen insipid tales whose inspiration and genesis was from some awful soulless wretch who has ever dwelt within my carcass.

Beneath this sun, I am suddenly overcome with the knowledge that I am just an old charlatan who somehow got lucky. And then, with equal rapidity, another feeling simmers to the surface, a feeling far finer – so fine, in fact, that a scintillating tingle gets to ravishing the whole of me. I open my eyes to the full glare of the sun and find I am at last its equal.

Well, well, Miriam, my dear.

Well, well.

30.   I wash his bent back with soap then rinse it with warm water. I lift up the folds of skin that flop across his stomach and clean them after the same fashion. His hair I washed but a few days ago so am satisfied just to offer it the briefest of splashes. Through all this, the hollow object of my ministrations barely moves at all. He is knees bent and chin on chest, sitting thus on the tiled floor of the walk-in bathroom that was finished more than two years ago now. I turn off the shower, and then I leave him awhile to let the steam shudder off its wetness.

Eventually, I hear him shout out something loud and incoherent, which is my cue to attend to the rest of my task. I get him into his dressing gown, haul him onto his wheelchair and then wheel him to his room.

I look at the clock in the kitchen. It's just gone seven. The night has come despite there barely having been an evening to speak of. Nothing much has happened today. I am just existing in the same way as he is just existing. There is an arc of inevitability to the path he is on which at my most maudlin I truly envy.

But just like as steam will shudder off its wetness, I divest myself of my maudlin and chide myself into something of a fervour, the result of which is a steady determination that, unlike this day, this old woman is not done quite yet.

31.   I am to bury my husband this afternoon. As of now, I am in my garden and he is at the undertaker's in his coffin. I ache with no sense of tender devotion. The skies are dull, the air chill. The absence of birdsong pleases me more than I can say.

****

"Miriam. I will get straight to the point. The many years of being your agent have led me to believe straight talk to be your preference in difficult matters, though please forgive me if I appear on this occasion to be excessively terse. In short, we have a problem. Late last night, I received word from Mr A – The Author. He informed me in that rather unseemly way he has when deep in his drink or whatever else he has a mind to indulge, that he has become weary of inventing any further scenes in the story of your life. He suggests, therefore, that you return to your unfinished manuscript – your *Small Mercy* – while there is still time."

Langham Ward – Colchester General Hospital, Essex

Small Mercy (2)

29. Oooom ara ooo

THE YAWN OF the morn was of peach and of pink as it lolloped languid into the gargantuan gasp of the day. And that yawn of the morn took its own sweet time to shudder off its shackles. The yellow sun blinked white just above the bleak of the northern hills. The long-gone moon was up there somewhere too, sighing no doubt, capricious at best. The million pinprick stars ever frozen for our facile delight are shrouded for now, though some do fervently attest that their motionless presence in our bewilderment is nothing more than the ultimate lie of the ultimate universe and that each one doth in fact hurtle and spark incessant across the extraordinary expanse of our inelegant lives. Peach and pink and lollop and gasp, hurtle and spark and wow; such are the composite charlatans of this particular post-coital dawning, way on over here in the Small Mercy outerwilds.

Dewdrop tears glistened fraught atop the unshaven acre of land upon which The Crop Farmer, Tobias Defoe, had for so many years tarried marvellous. In time, black specks of birds bespattered the scene, bringing with them belching blurt arias of notes high and low, little larynx exercises in preparation perhaps for some momentous serenade with which to astonish, somewhere further down the line, the ever so, ever so lost.

Never did the first boot clumps of Tobias Defoe's day reveal him to be anything less than amazed by whatever his eyes beheld. On this day also was this held to be true as he watched the pitiful figures of Grace and Stafford Chuck draw closer to where he stood in the black shade of doorway. He heard the squelch of their steps long before he was acquainted himself with the sag of their bones and the grime of their countenance. He interspersed the faint thud of their hearts with the squidge and the thwop that accompanied each of their little steps. By the time two children were but a few paces away, he had hit upon a rhythm and a beat that jived jaunty through the whole of him. Those big hips of his rolled and swayed as he thudded into the earth first one big boot and then the other. His face grew raw with red as he breathed to the booming, the stomp and the holler. And so that was the sight that greeted that boy and that girl as they came to a halt just where the black of his shade met the lush green of the meadow.

"I recall you, sir," said Grace, looking up at Tobias, "but I fear my recallings be more like from a dream though I am lost when it comes to knowing if it be the good kind or the other."

"Well, you are very formal in your speakings, young lady, I do declare!" grinned The Crop Farmer. "And you, young man," he said looking down now at Stafford. "How are you set on this matter?"

Stafford lowered his head. "Don't rightly know, Mister," he mumbled. "My sis here does the dreaming and like for the both of us, is the plain truth, I reckon."

Grace put her arm out and across the young lad's bowed and puny shoulders.

"Well," boomed Tobias, "you will be pleased to know that I never been one for details and such, 'specially when it comes to the when and the how of things. I tells the time of day from the sun and the old of me age from the moon. Ain't ever had call to do different. I have my dreamings when full awake, but still I be blowed if I could remember a single one of 'em! Now how about that?"

Without waiting for a reply, Tobias, with a single, marvellous stride, launched himself past those two fraught young things and deeper into the fields then, without turning, called out for the children to come over and stand either side of his heft. Grace and Stafford complied with neither consultation nor delay. The man dropped swift to the floor, and as if chained, the boy and the girl followed him down. No sooner had he flopped forward onto his belly and stretched out his legs, his companions found themselves doing the same until all three were thus arrayed upon the earthy bosom of the land.

As Defoe turned to his left, he cherished to the point of ecstasy the scratch and the scrape of sharp stones and sod upon the filthy blast of his forehead. By pure consequence of motion, his right eye was now ostensibly near the top of his face. It was only saved from slipping into the hairy well of his ear by the crude slash of his eyebrow and the wedge of black and gold sproutings that dripped from the base of his upper curls way on down to the full flop of his jowl. By some power or other, Stafford Chuck felt compelled to move his head around to where he was looking directly into that single wild eye.

"Now, though I be addressing you, boy, what I say goes as well to you, my pretty Miss. For a starter, I be taking you in, so to speak, same as I do when I harvest my crops. That being clear, best you be knowing I won't be taking no blade to your bones or heaving you into no sack. This be a different kind of harvest and no mistake."

Stafford mumbled something through the scrunch of his mouth, but it went unheard by all but the worms in their holes and the ants in their scurry.

Tobias inhaled hugely, closed tight his eyes and slipped all humble into the peculiar state of startle and bliss necessary for what he had a mind to do. He did not need to tell the girl on the ground to his right or the boy on the ground to his left to close their eyes nor even to slow to almost imperceptible the come and go of their breath. It just seemed to happen and they gave themselves up to it entirely. Each had an ear flat upon the warm soil, as perfect a conduit as could be between the virgin wow of their melancholy and the sumptuous soul of the universe.

All was silent.

But all was not silent for long.

In such a circumstance as is above described, as the world doth turn relentless and the rancid rags of those defiled by unimaginative despots do unfurl, only music will do. Tobias Defoe knew that well, knew it better than anybody.

So let us all get down on our bellies, stretch out our legs, close our eyes, open up our gorgeous and slip into the same scintillating swathe of pure rhapsody inhabited just then by the ever so, ever so lost.

And so beginneth The Song of the Earth...

...ah yeah
that soft drop doomph is there and gone then back again,
all lilt and sway and
swagger and swoon
ah
soft drop doomph de doomph, doomph, doomph,
lilt and sway and swagger and swooooon
ah yeah, ah yeah, ah yeah;
now deep down tuts and tedium too dumb
to drop or doomph
ah
then come bursting cherub orbs ablaze
squealing wild around and round and
up and down,
untime skipping,
cracked with grin of taunt and dares,
disintegrating raucous diamond blizzards
'til all is naked and translucent;
ah
then getting back some circuitous how to
lilt and sway and swagger and swoon
though with less conceit this

second time around;
ah
glee shorn horn
dribbles and pouts dismay of decay
as stumble staggers into
the holy swirl,
but not so fast ye rank of heart for
with cool defiant tooting toots
and boogie-woogie startle bops
there comes a final bugle bounce;
ah
then irreverent
groove serene
doth whisper of such mysteries that even this
old earth divine must cease
awhile the rolling of
its hoary bones.

...oooom ara ooo
ma
...oooom ara ooo
ma
...oooom ara ooo
ma
...oooom ara ooo
ma
...ooom ooooh
araaa wah
...araaa wah
...whaaa
wah...
wa..
w.

. . .

.

. .

and step it
up

. . .

…flung flaming outta foetal furnace
stonefree pumped and bursting
into the day
frantic crazy cackles
rip jagged doom of black
then drip crimson globs and canker gulps of
ravenous heft that
spark horrific into hurtle frenzy;
shameless
whammed-up spiral spurts rise to
avalanche heights then
quaking
stutter 'til upstanding;
ah
licentious hipsway orgies
do rain down their mighty jangle
crescendo crashing admonitions of
such demonic drench that
sinew vines do bend and snap
like serpent fiends sprung free and
drooling;
ah
higher than hell 'n'
way on down to wretched heaven's
glum and sulky bluster and
then and then and then and then
stupendous wail of all our sighs
flutterfloats into foetal furnace embers with

some kinda cripple and crack
then none,
some kinda fizzle and blurt
then none,
only to bubble rancid
in the orgasmic ecstasy of
the imbecile's own interlude.

…oooom ara ooo
ma
…oooom ara ooo
ma
…oooom ara ooo
ma
…oooom ara ooo
ma
…ooom ooooh
araaa wah
…araaa wah
…whaaa
wah…
wa..
w.

…
.
..

…but rest ye now
my monotone relics
and settle to slumber your
peerless parps and whimsies that
having gained fair standing in the piece must gallantly give way
to
gentle cymbal shivers that

in turn propel to the fore
plinks and plonks and tings and toots
that would if of feudal glib be most wretched
but ensconced within the gorgeous of
some delicate denouement are
momentous hero fruits whose core and pip reek not
of the baleful blight
so redolent of those from whose sap and gawp they
one foul night
were formed;
ah
Slow and slow comes this tighter fold,
yet hewn not of
lilt and sway and swagger and swoon which
be but shadowy echoes now;
a linger sigh in major key doth
sweep good souls all clear this morn of
accumulated bewilder webs
and in their stead are sown
a seed or two that will
when in lusty bloom
implore the raw of humankind
to simply *be*.

ah
oooom ara ooo
ma

And so endeth The Song of the Earth.

30. When Writing Ain't

As The Song of the Earth leapt sublime to a key more divine that only lonesome angels could discern, Tobias Defoe hauled himself up from the ground. He rubbed his eyes with his grimy fists and then shook slow his head in wonder at the true majesty of nature's offerings.

The half-melon sun glowed green within the purple swell of the skyway. The Crop Farmer looked up at it and chuckled like a babe, almost to the point where he thought he'd be unable to stop. If any sweet soul in this universe was capable of chuckling himself into the grave then it was this fellow, this Tobias Defoe.

By the time he had returned his attention to the ground, Tobias's two young charges had managed to wrest themselves from the reverie within which they'd been so charmingly embroiled. Grace sat for a while before standing whilst her brother tarried not at all and was up in an instant.

The whole-melon moon was blue in the golden swoon of the heavens. The two children looked up at it and then at one another. The Song of the Earth still bubbled glorious through their veins, and thus were they left in no doubt of the veracity of the vision above them.

"Now, my young things," said Tobias, "I ask that you not speak of what you just heard down there from that there soil, nor go wasting your brains by ways of bringing sense to it. All you need be knowing is there is some things that we dolts have no words for because we ain't spirits or angels and the like. Such as you just bore witness has rightfully to make its home in your dreams, not your bony old heads. Music comes about when writing ain't got the worthy to tell the plain of it all."

The Crop Farmer closed his eyes for a brief moment. Then he opened them. On doing so, it was as if he had been consumed by an astonishing force for, without warning, he let out a wild and splendid howl, spun full circle – not once but twice – and then dropped with sudden halt to a low squat, whereupon he became absolutely still. Given such a display of feral lunacy, it has to be said that Grace and Stafford could in no way be scolded for the shock and dismay expressed upon their pale little faces.

Red-cheeked and eyes a-burning, Tobias addressed his guests once more. "What all *that* was meant to be a-saying is that when that old Song of the Earth gets to singing like it do, there be times when you just can't do nothing but jig a little like I just done, though that be a right basic jig where jigging be concerned."

Stafford nodded. He understood. He really did. And Grace, she really understood too. They both absolutely got it. That's children for you. That's the Song of the Earth for you, and that's the likes of Tobias Defoe for you.

"Ain't no tune, none mind, you can't get to hearing if you let yourself go a little. Now you got this start I give you, you'll be seeing that the music don't ever stop. That which be called music for simplicity's sake is nothing more than nature herself being all mischievous like she do get at times when she has a fancy for a big old dollop of joy."

Stafford smiled.

Grace smiled too.

Stafford sighed sweet in the sumptuous sway of his melody.

Grace sighed sweet too in the sumptuous sway of hers.

And then, with blistering alacrity, did Tobias leap to his feet and tremble in a moment of ecstatic frenzy before, to put it plain, he just

let

himself

go…

31. Automaton Heights

E NOUGH, FOR NOW, of this hedonistic unravelling.
Feral lunacy it seems may be, for good or for ill, somewhat infectious.

That is to say that it is the apposite juncture in our tale to accord solemn reverence to those early pioneers whose enduring legacy was the Small Mercy Constitution.

In less than one year, four individuals somehow managed to conceive of a cohesive societal construct whose foundation was based on one hundred and thirteen plainly written tenets that were to be adhered to without deviation, the consequences of recalcitrance being of an altogether different strain of genius. That framework would sustain undefiled for almost two centuries, during which time that village between the northern hills and the southern woodlands grew from barely a spark into a ferocious furnace of relentless burn. But then, breaking from the black of the night into the pink of the dawn, came a certain John Dawlish. Almost two centuries is a long time indeed, but that fiend Dawlish had never been a devotee of anything as unremarkable as a tick-type thing that is followed so slavishly by a tock-type thing.

There are some achievements that, regardless of ethical or philosophical considerations, warrant admiration. The Constitution of Small Mercy was an undeniable example of such a feat. This can be evidenced by the way in which it endured unchallenged from one generation to the next and the next, the genius of its success being that as each year passed, the compliance to those one hundred and thirteen commandments intensified to an almost rabid degree with barely a handful of recidivists.

It all began when four men of rare talent and intellect came upon the holy truth that humans are by nature feckless creatures who, if free to indulge in base instinct, will be as useful to the functioning of a productive community as would a fish be to a flower. Success depended not upon nurturing those of sound mind and unblemished character but in harnessing the brash allegiance of the lumbering masses. The black of the black and the white of the white should not be subjected to those prone to meandering curiosity. It was the dolts in their number whose lust for simple cause and effect was satiated by the stunning simplicity of the rules that were laid out before them who would drive the village of Small Mercy to automaton heights.

No commandment stretched across more than the length of a single line. When the message is so gorgeously concise, interpretation is negated, and without the need for interpretation, no requirement ever was there for scholarly critique. There was no small print other than that which would at times appear unbidden in the black of night deep in the minds of those who were prone to bouts of solemn three-in-the-morning introspection, during which times they would consider aghast the rank inevitability of their existence in their pilgrimage from the sweet sway of the crib to the dull crass of the cross.

To hold sway over a populace by such means is dependent not upon that which abounds but by that which is lacking – a lack of trust, a lack of love, a lack of conscience and so on. The demonisation of that which flows immaculate from the comingling of joy and raw wonder such as the wild imaginings of music, art and the pursuit of wonder will make a heretic of the dreamer whilst elevating the glib savage to a status of licentious invulnerability, as essential as the hammer, the wheel and the pail.

Four men.

One hundred and thirteen commandments.

Almost two centuries.

The painter, the pianist, the scribe and the craftsman must some fine day hold everloving sway.

Until then?

Well

Until then.

Dawlish snored deep in the cold grass of the northern hills. He heard not The Song of the Earth, nor was he present when that old dollop of joy was as dollop as it gets. He was as of rock as he lay there rasping his way through the black night. He was at rest, in repose, for he alone knew just how things were to play out. Though he was many things, his essence was of a relentless and awful design. His flaws were as bold in their depravity as was his blood red and his snot gooey. It was for others to acquaint the young and the wretched with what it truly was to be alive on this earth. The stink of him whilst he snored and rasped just then was putrid, yet the green of the fields kept him close not even the air so defiled felt it necessary to accord him anything but affection.

By any reckoning, it had been a strange few days for Grace and Stafford Chuck. It was clear to the both of them when they awoke from their post-Tobias-Defoe-feral-lunacy-jig and found themselves to be in some other field entirely that those days of theirs were about to get a whole lot stranger.

32. Slaughterman

Now what is it you young whelps be doing in trying to pull your funny little noses off your funny little faces? Can't say I ever did see the like of it!"

Nathaniel Wild plunged his left hand almost up to the wrist into the ragged red deep of his sensational beard. What his fingers took to doing, only they could tell. With that hand thus occupied, he used the palm of the other to rub rough his bulbous right ear. His eyes flickered all colours as if the pupils were made not of some fleshy composite but a combination of gemstone and lightning. He was sturdy in the way of The Crop Farmer yet had about him the sweet tenderness of The Miller.

It was only when Stafford and Grace were surely about to collapse from lack of air that they dared cease in their efforts to stem the awful smell that seemed to come from absolutely everywhere about them. No place was less malodorous than the other. It was as if this whole swathe of land upon which they stood was rotten beyond compare.

"That's the spirit," Nathaniel said to the pair, his hands now clasped behind his back, in repose for now. "So what do I be calling you then? Not had folk in these parts since time when that old tree up there weren't no more than a twig, so this be some mighty day indeed. So, young lad, what's you called?"

Stafford scrunched up his face in an effort to prevent as little air as possible from entering his mouth and managed a grunt of sorts through the tiniest of gaps.

"Sturf? Sturf. Fine name. Pleased to be acquainted with you, Sturf. And you, my dear?"

Grace squeezed out a tuneless squeak, having followed her young brother's lead in trying to protect her innards from the foul smell of the morn.

"At your service, Kree! Sturf and Kree it is then. Nathaniel be my name. Nathaniel Wild being the full of it. Kree the girl, and you, boy, Sturf."

Whether they had begun to grow accustomed to the rank air or there was some kind of unseen cleansing going on, the children slowly started to feel less of a need to interfere with the natural flow of their breath.

"Not Sturf. I'm not called Sturf or whatever you said, Mister. Stafford is who I am. And my sister here. She is Grace."

"I be humbled at being corrected, young Stafford. I still be Nathaniel Wild just so's you know. Always have been. Most likely always will be."

"I'm sure my brother meant no offence, sir," Grace said.

"Ah, ain't nothing can offend old Nate," Wild chuckled. "All these years I been out this way, I never been nothing but all levels of cheery!"

Nathaniel took a thunderous step forward and reached out to take the hands of the two children. He didn't care that slops of snot spurted through Stafford's thin fingers and into his hard hefty palm, nor did he pay Grace any mind when she at first tried to resist his grip. Thus attached, he dragged the two children off out into the expanse of muck that seemed to have no end.

There was nothing they saw that wasn't filthy about the place at which they finally came to stop. The weary young things discerned not even the smallest of green shoots, the tiniest yellow stalk or any sign of life at all. They yearned for the snowstorm of flour in Linton Gauge's mill, for the notes high and low of The Song of the Earth.

The indomitable Wild thudded off in the direction of a small, wooden structure some hundred or so yards away. When at last he returned, he did so with a curious retinue at his rear the like of which the two Chucks found wholly astonishing.

As he stood there defiant before the silent children, there fanned out in a row to Nathaniel's right first a huge black-and-white sow. A hairy, tan-coloured cow took up her post on the other side. Stafford stared through the cow's heavy legs and watched as a goat came up around the cow and stood still beside it. Grace had eyes only for the lamb that was doing its best to avoid being splattered by the slops of mud that dripped from the impressive pig that held its position beside Nathaniel like some faithful old hound, though that little lamb did eventually get to where it was beside the sow, albeit a polite distance away.

"So what do you make of these beauties?" Nathaniel laughed all cherish and boom.

"I ain't seen nothing of the like, Mister," replied Stafford. "Don't mean I don't like them. I got to say, I reckon I could get to liking them as much as I ever had a liking for anything before."

"And you, young Grace?"

"I don't rightly have the words, sir. I ain't feeling scared of them but don't know if I should have sort of fear in me if you take my meaning, sir?"

The lamb, the sow, the cow and the goat remained impassive as the little girl silently chided herself for fear she'd be taken for foolish.

"You been scared before, I can see that too well, but you don't go fretting yourself none. Old Nathaniel don't have no time for fear and such. There's a deal of what you might call *magic*, I won't deny, but you two is as safe out here as my old bones be in this skin of mine."

Stafford was already well on the way to being utterly enchanted. "What be they all, Mister and what do they do?"

"This big old lump next me here is a cow and other side of her with his crooked horns and bony legs is a goat. This one snuffling away just here is a pig, and that fluffy little lady is what be called a lamb. Goat, cow, pig, lamb. That's what they be called. As for what they *do*, well, boy, they can do or not do just so whatever they please far as I be concerned. Only one real beast round here, and that ain't none other than him you see before you, beard, bollocks, bunions and all!"

Grace frowned as she considered carefully her words before eventually letting them go.

"I know of *lamb*, sir, but reckon myself wrong, as I always took lamb to be grey and horrid looking and something the old men in the village eat with their hands from the big iron pot when it is their day for meat and not for flowers or bread."

"Young lady," said Nathaniel Wild sincere, "you ain't mistaken in what you be saying. That being so, I'll wager you least heard tell of such as beef and pork and such, perhaps even seen like you did lamb but in its stead goat?"

Grace Chuck nodded. "Yes sir. All of 'em after a fashion, though none in their particulars."

"Boy? Young Stafford?"

"No, Mister. My sis has in smarts what I has in mischief is what I always been told. Besides, she got more years in her than I have."

"So then, it seems that what we got here right now is the need for some learnings and I don't see no honest reason for stopping 'til it be done? What say you, imps?"

Nathaniel need only to look at the haze in those little eyes to see fit to continue.

"Sit you down then. Don't mind that soggy mudwhomp monster whose back we be standing on. He don't mind it none, so we shouldn't be minding it none neither. That's it. Sit you down comfy like, and I'll fill in some of them big holes you got in them kidaroo brains of yours, though it ain't be no fault of your doing that them holes be so big and all.

"Well, it ain't from the ground like potatoes and corn and all that other stuff him across the way sings about. No, my dears. I have no notion how it came to be that people got to be needing to fill their bellies with something more than what the earth gives freely, but once they did, there weren't no stopping them. I'll say it plain as plain is all I know. Dead lambs get chopped up, and that's where you get that meat you saw before. Dead pigs get chopped up and are called pork. Cows like our fine boy here get bashed to death and chopped up like the rest, and they slice up the pieces and call them beef. Dead goats get chopped up and don't get called nothing other than goat still or so I been told."

The two children stood with their mouths slack, their eyes wide and wet. Neither had the vocabulary to adequately express how they felt in that moment. They just stared intense at the animals arrayed before them – the goat, the cow, the pig and the lamb. There are certain truths that, when you learn of them, are far too big to comprehend. Such it was for those two little souls.

All was profound and solemn in the universe.

An hour and more passed before Nathaniel sought to lure Stafford and Grace from the dread silence into which each had slipped.

"Don't you get to being all of a misery," he said. "Some things just be is all."

Then, of a sudden, Stafford became engorged with a terrific fury. His face went from white to crimson, his eyes once dull, now ablaze. His voice, when it found form, simmered with rage at a volume no more than a whisper.

"I ain't fooled, Mister, by your fancy words, though I don't doubt the truth of them. Clear to me as the filth 'tween my toes that it be you and none other that do the bashing and the chopping you talked of. I might be young and all and simple, no doubt, which ain't my fault, but if you ain't him that is the slaughterman then you can do me like you do them pigs and them cows and them goats and them lambs."

Nathaniel lowered himself into a crouching stance without taking his eyes from the boy's glare. And in such a pose he did waddle slow towards him. For a moment, he said nothing. And then he said something.

"Boy," he said low. "Time is right for you and that sister of yours to come along now with me. There's something I been just *dying* to show you."

33. Sprouts Forever

T HE STRUCTURE BEFORE the two children was somewhere around sixty feet in length and had no doors or windows across its front aspect. Nathaniel led the children around the northern side, which was no more than fifteen long strides across but did contain a narrow wooden door at its centre, bolted shut across the top. A tour of the circumference revealed the rear aspect and the southern end to be identical to their opposite sides. The only difference was that the door to the south was ever so slightly open.

"This, my darlings," Nathaniel stated gravely, "is where the *magic* happens."

Stafford and Grace looked at one another and then back at that barrel of a man. Nathaniel Wild was standing just to the side of the unbolted door, thick, hairy fingers wrapped around the chunk of wood that served as a handle of sorts.

"*Magic?*" asked Stafford.

"Magic," came the reply.

"In there?" asked Grace.

"In there."

Wild paused for a moment, during which time neither child breathed a single breath. And then that strange old man did speak once more.

"Once this here door is closed on us and we be in and not out, you ain't to do nothing but watch – no talking, no moving, no nothing 'cept watching. You find your little heads starting to bubble with questions then best you get rid of them soon as they appear. In there ain't a place to be doubting and figuring. Magic don't have no truck with logic and the like. That clear for you?"

The children nodded.

Nathaniel pulled open the door and waved the children in with his outstretched arm. He then pulled the door shut, and it seemed to the boy and the girl in that instant that day had without pause become night.

Stafford saw only blackness. Grace too. Being well used to things most magical, Nathaniel saw no blackness at all. He nudged them forward and to the left until their backs touched the western wall. Then, with a rough yank on their heads, he ensured they faced forward to the middle of the barn, though of course, the black was still the black as far as they were concerned.

They stood, the three of them thus, for a time that neither Grace nor her brother could afterwards accurately specify. The one thing they could agree on was that where you may expect your eyes to become accustomed in some way to the circumstance, adjust a little so as to provide perhaps a modicum of vision, theirs did not.

From what began as barely a distant murmur, Grace discerned a rise and fall, a rise and fall of sound whose breadth was of barely more than four or five notes. It wasn't so much a beat that she heard ever more clearly, more a coming and going, a coming and going. By concentrating until almost in raptures, she felt sure that what she was listening to was a tremendous communal fluttering of wings from somewhere in the upper blackness.

In time, Stafford too became attuned to the tremendous communal fluttering somewhere above him to the point where he felt he was in the very centre of it.

Nathaniel let out a croon of a sigh and as if commanded, the southern door creaked slowly open, letting in a slender jagged shard of yellow light that spread out across the centre of the floor almost from one end to the other. The black was still the black but that yellow would not be denied and grew into a perfect rectangle when the door got to being fully open although the one at the opposite end remained bolted in place.

Still gawping at the wow of the yellow, the two children were to be astounded still further as first the pig, then the cow, then the goat, then the lamb, stepped from the outerworld to take their place upon the swathe of pure light.

The fluttering in the rafters intensified to an extraordinary degree. When it seemed the whole roof would blast off into the firmament, a blazing glow of all shades of red and all shades of yellow broke across its entirety. The wild sonic pulsing indulged itself wanton in the flashes of crimson and gold. Thus comingled, it became clear to the two children whose pupils were by now almost bursting through the tops of their heads, that what they took at first sight to be a morass of indiscriminate throbbing was, in fact, a gargantuan gathering of beautiful butterflies in the midst of a most staggering state of arousal.

The contrast between the blistering frenzy above and the stoic dignity of the four animals lined up one behind the other on that yellow rectangle was holy indeed.

As if directed by a conductor unseen, the cacophony of butterfly wings eased into a sublime synchronicity, the result being a low droning of devastating might. And then that shimmering butterfly blanket of hum and wow did slowly descend from the upper rafters until there was barely a slither between the lower hovering and the tips of the cow's ears.

None of the animals made the slightest move – not the pig, the cow, the goat or the lamb.

Suddenly, the humming stopped and no sound at all was there to be heard. The butterfly blanket shimmered no more in red and in gold but became as of hessian before dropping down hard and in silence upon the pig, the cow, the goat and the lamb.

For a breathless moment, all life was gone from that place. Grace dead. Stafford dead. Nathanial dead. Animals as good as dead, the butterflies too.

Magic is what magic is.

And ever will be.

The bolted door at the far end crashed open, and all was alive again, *more* than alive even. Red and gold flames flickered across the dread shroud in a crescendo wave, and the billions of butterflies splashed rampant into the air, swarming out into the tumultuous night, the very last of them leaving behind a single salacious trail of orange which was there and then gone.

Grace eyes wide.

Stafford eyes wide.

Nathaniel – though he'd seen all this so many times before – eyes wide.

Silence throbbed in the silvery light within that outbuilding. The animals had not moved since the moment they had come to a halt. Yet now, in perfect unison, they stepped slowly out through the open door through which the butterflies had exited.

Nathaniel led the two Chuck children to the centre of the barn where the yellow rectangle of light was beginning to fade. He ushered them to their knees and he did join them. Arrayed on the floor before them were small piles of meat – beef where the cow had stood, pork from the pig, lamb from the lamb and goat from the goat. The various meats were perfectly chopped, and rivulets of blood oozed from them just where they ought.

It was a while before either Stafford or Grace could bring any words at all to their sweet mouths. It was the boy who broke first.

"How can that even be, Mister?" he murmured.

Nathaniel Wild put a large hand first on Grace's head and then Stafford's.

"Just ain't no explaining some things," he said soft. "Can't no more explain what you just saw than I can why it be that folks all over see fit to eat animal innards when there be potatoes and carrots and beans aplenty. Beasts eating angels far as I be concerned. Nothing less than that."

Grace seemed as if she was about to say something but then held back. Moments later, she held back no more.

"Sir. If you don't mind me asking – that what them animals left behind after they walked out all alive and all – them piles of meat – if that be how it be done then what for did you go scaring us with all that talk of bashing in heads and chopping and stuff?"

"Young lady," Nathaniel replied, a tender smile just about visible through the coarse hair of his beard. "I telled you more than once that this here be *magic* – meaning there ain't nothing ordinary about it. I takes these piles in sacks and leaves them at the edge of your village, and that's what them folks down there chew up and shit out. Ain't nothing like this anywhere in the world. Nothing but slaughtermen all other places with their axes, their blades and their buckets of blood."

"Don't make no sense, Mister," Stafford sighed weary.

"No, it don't, boy," said Nathaniel, leaning forward to ruffle the boy's already tangled hair. "And you know what is the saddest thing of all?"

Grace and Stafford looked up at that man and shook sweet their little heads.

"Saddest thing is that if them folk down there in that village knew that what they chomp down is made like you just seen, they'd be accusing old Nathaniel here of being a demon and worse, doer of devilish deeds and consorting with warlocks and wizards. But – and here's the thing – when it comes to that slaughterman bashing and killing and chopping up the likes of pigs and cows and goats and lambs into pieces, in their minds, there ain't nothing more natural or appealing."

"I'm going to eat potatoes and carrots and nothing else the rest of my days," Stafford said with as stern and determined a voice any eleven-year-old lad could surely summon.

"Peas and beans and sprouts for me," Grace affirmed, her eyes sharp beneath the faintest of frowns.

"You ain't ever liked sprouts," said Stafford plain.

"Well, I do now, little brother. Peas and beans and sprouts for ever and ever and ever."

Nathaniel Wild looked on as Martha Chuck's two young things got to be hand in hand. He noticed how the sky seemed less black and the moon more glowing and golden. He felt also the raw chill of some errant breeze that had seemed to come from over yonder where the northern hills lay sullen.

A change was a-coming along.

That which is will ever be that which once was.

Raw chill.

Errant breeze.

John Dawlish was on the move.

34. A Magnitude Inconceivable

IT HAD NEVER been a trait of any Small Mercy Auditor to accord merit to the fantastical. Franklin Singe did not stray from this particular edict. No dream had there ever been that had lingered sufficiently long in his dread night for him to have the slightest recollection of it. Where imagination was the waif, cunning was the lord and the king. The very concept of *magic* he considered nothing more than the nonsensical whimsy of the intractably foolish. The Constitution of Small Mercy was clear in that respect as it was in all its other tenets. That which could not be explained by simple logic, so said the founding fathers, had no place in the functioning of a productive society. There was, though, a single unwritten, little-understood but powerful exception – namely *intuition*. And as far as *that* was concerned – *intuition* – Franklin Singe had no equal.

On the morning in question, Singe awoke in his low chair as if sparked into action by the hottest embers hell itself had to offer. There was no aching in his wretched bones as first he flung himself forward then launched himself upright. His sallow skin tingled all over as if a million tiny insects roamed ravenous beneath its surface. The groan of a grin broke across the lower half of his cruel face, the force of which pushed him back down into his chair.

The Auditor was aroused.

The Auditor was very, very aroused.

John Dawlish may have just heaved himself upright so as to get to being on the move way up there twixt the northern hills, but in the shadows of his cabin on the desolate eastern fringe of Small Mercy, Franklin Singe was appallingly ready to set in motion some moves of his own.

Opposite the Chuck household that once comprised a husband, a wife and two young children yet was home now only to a hollow and lonesome widow, there lived two brothers, twins in fact. Barnaby and Eustace Tretton, they were called, and they were identical in almost every facet – each horrifically obese and stunningly incapable of engaging in any behaviours that were not senseless and crass. The dull of their eyes did not lie, nor the gawp of their slavering mouths deceive. The two misshapen black holes in the rough centre of each saggy wet face was recognisable as a nose by dint only of where they were set. Filthy squirms of hair bled out in greasy clumps on either side of the head, beneath which were inexplicably small ears of wretched design.

The Tretton twins were ghastly within and ghastly without. Were you to merely appraise their physical form, you'd be forgiven for considering the one in all form and function to be the equal of the other. Ah, but in so doing, you'd be more fool than fine. Barnaby, you see, was born deaf, whilst Eustace had ever lacked the ability to speak. Bizarre as it may seem, there was no disputing the fact. One twin able to talk but not hear, the other to hear but not talk. And, as you can imagine, given the character of these men and the particular afflictions under which, night and day, each laboured, the Tretton household had never been anything other than fraught.

Barnaby and Eustace would fight with one another on almost every day until each was at the point of exhaustion and could continue the fight no longer. Many a time was it that they would awake to the day, supine on the grime of their living room floor, battered and bruised and bleeding. The memory of what grim altercation had ignited their fury would be erased from their memory by putrid blasts of morning flatulence. And then, as the hours passed, for some reason or other, they would go at it all over again. They were humourless hulks, the Tretton twins. That did not mean, though, that they did not have their uses if engaged with sufficient cunning and malice.

Sullivan the baker was no Tretton, but there was no denying he was in many ways of their ilk. He had not the crass paucity of charm redolent of the twins, neither did he reek of the sly dank waters in which The Auditor had ever bobbed supreme. But he was of they and they were of him. Though each may have been appalled at being presented with such a construct, there was no doubting the cruel threads that bound them together nor the bleak pall each cast without care upon the weary earth.

Just as there is no explaining *magic,* so perhaps the fact that Eustace, Barnaby and Sullivan happened to approach at the very same moment the very same tree whose shadows had spawned John Dawlish at the outset of this tale, should be free of scrutiny. Some things just happen. That is all. They just happen. For good or for ill, or even, from time to time, if truth be told, to salvage most holy the most tenuous of plot lines.

There is no fine time for a gathering of creatures so reeking of havoc as those just latterly described.

'twas not day.

'twas not night.

'twas mainly just dark is all.

…dark and red and raw in places.

Such is the way when such creatures do unbidden collide.

The shiver and tremble in the air was born not of any kind of cruel chill but of a trepidation of sorts. To remain inert is to succumb. At least a shiver, a tremble or both speaks of a sorrowful headshake even though it be token resistance at best. Though nature in her humble beauty be indomitable when gazed upon deep, humans of a certain disposition will, if drawn sullen together in mutual malice, sully even the most tantalising of sumptuous cherishings.

This was such a moment.

This was such a fracture.

And then Franklin Singe did enter the travesty. There was a booming of the blank between heart-thuds. What a mighty sound that was, that booming of the blank between the heart-thuds. Singe let go a gargantuan groan of a magnitude inconceivable.

None shook but them who had no choice but to shake – the sort of dreadful and tantalising shaking that only the truly dissolute and ragged will ever wholly comprehend.

Sullivan the baker shivered of a sudden as if run through with electric that left him completely drenched in some kind of gruesome glee, simmering with the knowledge that his Mary was back down at the southern end of the village, spent to dry off her tear torrents and her once full tongue now but *half* a tongue whose bloody remnants had turned from raw red to a brownish black.

Barnaby Tretton dribbled out from his mouth a stream of saliva that at one point appeared to have no end.

Eustace Tretton belched hearty, then heartier still, then belched no more.

Franklin Singe waited until Sullivan was free of his ecstasy, Barnaby's dribble dried up and the stench of Eustace's foul innards dissipated into nothing more than a sulky gasp.

The Auditor was one who was ever apt to have his way.

"Look at you," he rumbled harsh and without love. "Just look at you."

Eustace Tretton sat fat cross-legged whilst his brother was flopped flappy belly side down on the wet gloom overgrowth. Sullivan the baker was hinged tight and right angle to the trunk of the sopsap tree trunk.

The universe was lost.

Dreamland was dry.

The twinkle stars oozed into blob bruises.

Decay held its hover.

There was no boom bend, just crack and consequence.

The Auditor did then address his stricken flock 'neath the firmament tears. It was more an incantation than a discourse, his words at times more comprehensible by the manner in which he spat them into the night than had they been scrawled upon a page. He said much. The sway was his. His final dronings lingered so long that they almost bled into the pursuant dawn.

"Hunt them down hard, bring them back careful and no more than that. I am done with nails and with doors. We are in dread times now."

Sullivan nodded, though understood only the basics of the task assigned him and his charges.

Eustace Tretton vomited up the full gloop of his innards.

Barnaby kicked those innards right thwap into Eustace's face.

It all made sense to them there present.

Even that last bit concerning the full gloop and the thwap.

Dread times.

Dread times indeed.

35. Alchemic

MARY AWOKE TO the day to find Sullivan gone, She blinked twice then blinked twice more. The only evidence that her tongue had been removed was that it was no longer in situ. There was no blood around her face, or down her neck or upon her sheets – wet, congealed, dried up or otherwise. Her mouth no longer housed a tongue. That was all. She experienced no pain as a consequence nor horror at what had passed. A curious feeling of peace eased through her as she sat there on the edge of her bed. Mary looked down at her bare feet and continued staring at them for quite some time. And then, well, she just got up and left.

There was birdsong in the air. Mary listened to it as she padded away from her home as if she had never before in her life heard birdsong at all. The swish of her thin dress against her thighs enthralled her with equal wonder. She saw colours she swore were beyond classification.

No pain, no horror, no tongue; but such birdsong, such swish and such colour.

The southern reaches of Small Mercy had seen Mary grow from a bright and quizzical girl into little more than a spectre of a woman. Only when occasion or happenstance demanded had she ever tarried further north than the centre of the village; rarely had she ventured sufficiently far east or west without being accompanied by even the faintest scent of baked bread. Where others within her community oft were brought to raptures by even the hint of fresh loaves, for Mary, it only served to remind her of what she'd become.

But now, right now…

Mary's lungs were drenched with untainted air. There was no burn or flame to its edges, no rasp, no crass and simmering indifference. Instead, a sumptuous sigh it was that so, so soft, kiss, kissed her lips, slid down the red of her throat, then, as a whisper, slipped through the gape of her mouth and out into the midst of the morn.

"Woman! Where are you? This bread is for baking!"
No more, sir
no more
"Don't dawdle, woman. Put these others in to bake. Can't have the fire burning low before the bread is baked. Now quick about it."
No more, sir
no more
"There is nothing as inefficient as sleep, particularly when you are akin to a stinking corpse beneath your sheets at four chimes and your working day commences at five!"
No more, sir
no more
"Woman! What are you doing woman? Is that fire out? Where are you, you bloody woman?"
I am
no more, sir
no more,
sir
no more.

Martha Chuck was face down and motionless in the fetid filth of a loveless field when the baker's woman happened upon her. As if all was as it should be, Mary lowered herself down elegant to where she was stretched out beside that stricken widow for whom life had been so cruel. She turned her face not to the dirt, however, but lay instead upon her back, her gaze set full and ravishing into the deep of the upper skies.

Each could have been taken for a corpse such arrayed. Given the travails to which they had been subjected, death for the pair of them just then could perhaps have been perceived as a blessing. To suffer in torrid isolation is to be tortured in a most unspeakable way. But what if in the midst of such agony, there came about a comingling of alchemic majesty? What if by such means, a single entity of indomitable power was spawned? What then?

Martha Chuck rolled over slow from her front to her back as if manoeuvred by pulleys and wires. She turned her head to the left just as the woman on the ground beside her turned her own head to the right. Red-veined eyes fell into red-veined eyes until the red was gone and a gleam did shimmer resplendent. Soul became entangled in soul. The lingering was long and the lingering was fine.

Martha had been a wife since birth, a mother since she was a child and a widow from the moment her husband chose to die. All colours she'd seen had been shades of black. The only sounds she'd been besieged with had either been screams of varying duration and pitch or, when momentarily freed of such spite, the hollow thudding taunts spewed out by her heart as a reminder that she was to sustain for a while longer yet. She'd ever been smeared in a thin layer of grime that had become a second skin of its own. She'd existed all her life streaked in her own sweat, coughing never laughing, her back ever so slightly bent, her hands and feet dry and cracked. She had been recognisable as a woman in large part due to her having been wed, widowed and spawned. With him whom she'd wed and fed long in the ground and those she'd spawned departed, there were those in the village who would have deemed her, given such circumstances, indistinguishable from a plank of wood.

But now, right now…

It was Mary who was the first to stand. When both were upright and adjacent to one another, the utter holiness of the scene was palpable. Martha embraced Mary, and Mary embraced Martha, then each sweetly let go, save for the right hand of the one that grasped still the left hand of the other.

How free must be their dreams?

How free must be their dreams having no further place to fall?

How free must be their dreams?

How free must be their dreams having thus transcended the malice of man?

Broken slivers of purple cloud drifted from west to east upon some tender breeze that served not just as courier but cleanser also. In time, the sky became free of its succession of bruises and pouts. It grew stark and immense, unadorned by dots of birds or the latent glow of sun and moon. Were it not for the grim efforts of the horizon line that stretched out in a clumsy black smudge, the earth itself would surely have been summarily jettisoned to some space in the galaxy from which it could maybe start all over again.

Martha withdrew her hand gently from Mary's grip. There was barely a discernible gap between them as they faced one another. They were of equal height, both slight of build and pale of skin. With the Small Mercy Constitution given more to function than fraternity, it will come as no surprise that Martha knew Mary only as that young girl who helped out the baker and Mary didn't know Martha even by sight – but no matter. Far greater even than the bond between blood relatives is the ancient bond between those for whom life has seen inordinate suffering. Then, as they stood there so close and so still, something remarkable did occur.

A churning succession of smoky green rings took shape in the slender, ragged space that separated them. It began where their chests almost met then extended in both directions until it stretched from the ground upon which they stood and up to the level of their foreheads. It began to rotate with ever-increasing speed, whirling around and around like a raging emerald tornado. When it seemed the force of that vision could be contained within the bounds of the universe no longer, it descended of a sudden into a colourless blur, then a steady vertical stream of mist and finally into nothing at all.

No more were they strangers. Though the wild frenzy of vapour had gone, it had somehow left each of the women with full knowledge of the life the other had led in such intricate detail it was almost as if they had lived it as their own. Martha let go a soft breath and smiled. Mary felt that soft breath of Martha's upon her lips and returned one of her own that was so gorgeous it could in other circumstances have been mistaken for a lover's kiss.

So it was that even though one had been parted from her children and the other from her tongue, they, in that moment, experienced a most sweet and astonishing serenity.

Ah, and what a day it was just then as those two women moved at their own pace, in their own way, free from the treachery of men and the merciless constraints of linear time and its heathen hordes.

Trees bent near to breaking so as to be nearer the beat of the feet that passed them by. Trunks of ancient birth sought to shed the coarse streaks of their outer layers in the hope of beckoning back into being the supple sinews of their younger days. No talons up above now, but yearning fingers seeking only a tender touch of the enchantment that from out of nowhere had of a sudden revealed itself.

BE EVER CURIOUS
BE EVER TENDER
ah
take me
to the river…

36. 'Twixt

*A*LL THIS THAT *by my doing has been set in motion will be brought to an end not because I will it to be so but because the earth must ever turn relentless.*

Dawlish chuntered these words to himself – or some similar – as he thudded awkward his huge heft into the weeping of the day. Mud pools sploshed their brown filth into spatters that landed invisible here and there, this way and that, yielding to the immaculate inevitability of it all.

There was nothing Dawlish had ever done during his entire existence that did not have a purpose, even if that purpose be known only to him. Although it is true that he did indeed, by his doing, set this here tale in motion, and it is also true that the particulars of its ending were not his to know, he was in no doubt that he was pivotal in all aspects.

NATHANIEL WILD HAD become aware that Dawlish was headed in his direction long before that craggy form appeared from out of the outer bleak, He was alerted by a squeal from one of the long lengths of timber that stretched from one corner of the barn behind him to the very end of the other. Most all the wood that comprised that structure within which such magic was done would sing its song in snippets or full verse at any time it chose, but the pitch and the tone of this particular note had a hint of disquiet discord about it.

The smell in the air was comprised of the lingering rancour of the night's tumultuous downpour, but there was a simmering sweetness at the edges, some fragrance redolent not of maudlin disdain but mischievous somehow, an impishness tinged with a certain kind of cunning. Nathaniel took down a big old gulp of it, for he was that kind of fellow.

When he was but ten feet away from Nathaniel, Dawlish came to a halt. He spat on the ground and nodded his gruesome head by way of a greeting.

Nathaniel paused a moment before making reply.

The air was still.

The time of days was of no consequence.

With some reluctance, the earth did sullenly turn.

Wild's blistered lips widened into a smile, which fell just short of a grin. The myriad of crimson veins that had, it seemed, since his birth sought sanctuary in his cheeks blossomed into two wavering pink orbs that glowed like some far distant moons.

"So there you be," he said. "And here I be too," he added. "Here we *both* be. Me and you. You and me. Both here and the two of us all a-being and the like. By my rememberings, it be what, three days, maybe more, maybe less, when last you be round these parts?"

Dawlish dripped with a stunning absence of emotion.

"I been gone. Now I be back," he stated plain. Every syllable that left the black of his mouth pulled at the air, dragged it close to the hairs and the welts and the bones of him, until a crude silence fell upon the scene. It lasted many moments, did that crude and that silence, until at last, that fiend did go on. "We needs sit awhile, me and thee. 'Neath that twisted oak yonder be as fine a place as any."

Having finished his piece, Dawlish turned like a steamer of old, and though it would go against how things should rightly be, Nathaniel figured the man increased in mass with each stomp that took him closer to the oak. He attributed this anomaly to the work of an angel up in the firmament who had, in that moment, perhaps a little too much time on their hands. None knew more than he that even angels are wont to indulge in a little innocent mischief from time to time.

It was some such day or other.
It didn't matter which.
Just some such day.

The sprawling roots of the tree beneath whose shade Dawlish and Wild sat were set in the ground like serpents that had been frozen in perpetuity to roam no more earth's green and muddy lands. A breeze blew through the ragged spaces between the branches that struck out from the deep of the riven trunk. It was as if the crooked talons in which each branch culminated were imploring all unbelievers to show themselves in order that they may be stripped clean of all gleaming acolyte garb and by so doing regain the sweet wonder they'd somehow lost along the way. There was no malice to that tumbling oak, no malice at all; more a sorrowful dismay at the insipid manner of humanity's importunate decline.

No living soul – that old oak excepted – bore witness to what passed between Dawlish and Nathaniel just then. Having instigated the meeting, it would not be remiss to presume that it was the former that did the bulk of the talking whilst the other listened only.

Done at last, Dawlish coughed putrid. With a startling degree of supple and lithe, he rose to his full height even before his rotund companion had made it to his knees. Having lurched to a point where he felt solid again upon the earth, Nathaniel Wild noticed then just how enormous the stranger appeared when apprised from certain angles. It was as if the awful rags that passed as clothes and the amalgam of sinew, muscle and bone beneath them were in constant flux, forming and reforming at the behest of whatever it was in that wretched skull that drove that man on.

When both were back outside the barn, Dawlish took to walking slowly around the circumference of it, his stride stealthy, wary almost. On returning to where Nathaniel Wild stood, he addressed him thus.

"This be the place then?"

"It be."

"Then it is settled?"

"It is settled."

"At the river's bend when the whole of the moon be 'twixt the northern hills?"

"At the river's bend when the whole of the moon be 'twixt the northern hills."

Nathaniel stepped back into the shadow of the barn and leaned his back against its boards. He watched as the stranger made his way back up towards the old oak tree. And he watched still as Dawlish threw himself to the ground some thirty yards or so from where the two of them had been sitting.

"Hmmm," Wild muttered, baffled yet somewhat amused at what he'd just seen.

But it didn't end there.

Dawlish spread out his misshapen limbs and proceeded to thrash them into the ground as if he were gripped by a momentous seizure. His body remained inert throughout, although in time his head joined the fray, his forehead banging off the dirt like a piston. No matter how hard Nathaniel concentrated, he could discern absolutely no pattern or scheme to the flailing. All initial brevity left his soul and was replaced instead by an overwhelming sense of awe. The mystery of why men eat dead creatures was one thing – what this fellow was doing, quite another. At no point, though, was he tempted to intervene. He had learned well enough over the years that some things – particularly those inexplicable in nature – are best left to do as they will.

Just as suddenly as the frenzy had begun, it was over. Dawlish got to his feet as if propelled from the earth – one moment flat on the ground, the next erect as can be.

But still it didn't end.

Nathaniel looked on as a small swift flew out from behind him and over to where Dawlish stood all statue and scarecrow up ahead, his avalanche of a profile in the mid-distance, the old oak tree beyond. The swift glided with barely a flutter of his wings as if drawn in by that fiend on a length of string. When the little bird came to a halt, hovering in the sky two feet or so above Dawlish's head, Wild (yes even he) was astonished to see that ghoul of a man leap fully into the air and grab hold of the swift with both of his filthy hands until the sky was once more just the sky.

His feet set steady once more, Dawlish inclined his head to one side and raised his cupped hands to his ear, that poor creature trapped within the rancid walls of that loveless cage. Nathaniel Wild stared at the scene, still with no inclination to intervene. Had he been able to peer close into the eyes of that man just then, he would have found them to be of all colours yet of an ember quality rather than ablaze. At last, Dawlish straightened, lifted his arms and let go the small swift into the expanse of the day. His curious endeavours thus concluded, he strode with unaccountable ease to some other place far from Nathaniel's vision.

"Well, well!" said Tobias Defoe to himself with more than his usual glee. He had, you see, just raised himself up from the ground, having listened intrigued not to the Song of the Earth but to a music of far more prosaic design. Had he been pressed at all to give a name to the composition that had so enthralled him, there is little doubt he would have entitled it *At the River's Bend When the Whole of the Moon be'Twixt the Northern Hills*.

Now, swifts are not starlings just as starlings are not chaffinches. Linton Gauge had learned throughout his life, sometimes by chance and invariably through his innocent bewilderment at just how astonishing the living world truly is. Though he'd at times partaken in conversation with many of his wilderness companions, swifts themselves were rarely seen in the vicinity of his windmill and the surrounding meadows. Thus it was that his heart became even more emboldened than ordinarily it was when such a bird emerged from the deep of the sky and settled down soft upon his bony left shoulder. What he heard, however, drained what colour he had from every inch of his skin. It wasn't just what the swift imparted but the manner of its voice. There was no singsong to it, no merry lilt. It spoke instead in a rough and low atonal drawl that was horrific to poor Linton's ears.

The swift tore two tiny rips in The Miller's shirt as it took once more to the air and let that tender man be.

"At the river's bend when the whole of the moon be 'twixt the northern hills," he whispered to himself as if terrified of being overheard. "The river's bend, the whole of the moon, the northern hills."

Linton Gauge sank to the ground and covered his gaunt face with his thin hands. Of all things he did not understand with regard to his fellow man, murder was uppermost. The very concept of it appalled him, sickened him to his innards. If the little swift had spoken true – and he had no reason to doubt it be so – then he who had spent his quiet life grinding grain into flour would in short order commit as foul an act as any could conceive.

37. Malevolent Joy

WHILE SINGE WAS some paces off lost in his nefarious thoughts, Sullivan set about casting as surly an eye as he could upon those he considered his charges – those calamitous Tretton twins. Lacking The Auditor's gruesome ability to perceive ruinous traits as absolutely fundamental in the pursuit of devilish deeds, Sullivan at first struggled to quell his contempt for the slavering duo that even then were squabbling like flies over a dead pheasant. At first, he saw only oafish ineptitude, but in time he began to realise that it was he who had been, for a moment at least, the biggest fool of all. He had considered Barnaby and Eustace to be base men when in all aspects they were nothing more than beasts. They were of a rare species indeed, perhaps even unrivalled in the extent and quality of their comingled imperfections. The matter resolved in his mind, Sullivan intended to wield the Trettons with a most malevolent joy.

Having disentangled himself from his brother, Barnaby wailed a cacophonous wail as he lumbered to his feet. Eustace heard the malice in his twin's blurt but, being mute, was incapable of mounting a verbal response – not that Barnaby, being deaf, would have heard it anyway. A lifetime of such bloody scuffles had, however, equipped Eustace with an armoury of effective retorts, the most foul of which he employed once he'd managed to stand. He turned, bent low, bared the rotten sagging flesh of his arse and blasted out the loudest, most decadent fart that even his now-vanquished foe had to accept was an admirable way with which to end this latest spat of theirs.

The soiled and sweating brothers shook hands then in unison set their small, dull eyes to Sullivan and Singe, who stood now before them. Despite his newly acquired sense of superiority, Sullivan was sufficiently astute to know now was not a time to indulge it. The air was heavy with menace, though he believed it was only he who felt it to be so – the Trettons being too ignorant and The Auditor no doubt having inhaled no other such scent for many a year purely because what was menace to others was purity itself to him.

Barnaby it was who first sought to prove his worth as far as indelicate sensibilities were concerned.

"He done gets me with that every time!" he bawled, unable to moderate with any consistency the tone and volume of his expulsions. "Every bleeding time! I ain't be lying to you none neither. He'd tell you himself if he could, but he ain't able."

Sullivan felt the hot heat of The Auditor's frozen breath on his left cheek. It was awful. Worse even than the countless years of kisses he'd been deprived by that harlot, Mary, if that can be believed. A furtive glance, in which he realised Singe faced not him but the brothers, did nothing to ease the baker's discomfort. And then, just as suddenly as it had assailed him, the hot heat of that frozen breath was gone. He was mid low sigh when The Auditor chose that moment to make clear what was to be done in the name of consequence.

"We have two days for that Chuck woman's children to be rendered whole before Judgement. None here present will be held to account for the manner in which the deed is done, such is the import of this endeavour. You will do my bidding in all respects. I, Franklin Singe, The Auditor of Small Mercy, hast spoken."

Eustace Tretton nodded his accord.

Whether it was the subtle changes in composition of Singe's cruel features as he spoke or the way in which the scent of that magnificent fart had been displaced with an odour more indescribably malign, Barnaby was left in doubt as to what was expected of him.

Sullivan was momentarily aggrieved that he had not been singled out by The Auditor as deserving of any more details than were the indolent lumps before him, but of course, he made no mention of his surly chagrin.

Way up in the heights of the universe, the sky raged with itself. It was a frenzied assault of epic dimensions that was all the more devastating for the complete silence with which it was accompanied. Huge, jagged shards of blue and orange crashed reckless into rampaging hordes of yellow and crimson and green. There was a bursting and a startle from the charcoal horizon line that went all the way on up to the hint of the glint below, which had ever dangled the silvery thread of the galaxies from which all moons and planets and stars had been from the very beginning of time suspended.

On and on, raged the upper skies.

On and on, they raged, those upper skies.

No place was this for the glib pouting of clouds or for yellow sun flirtations or for the wistful digressions of half-moons or full.

For when the sky sets about raging with itself, then and only then is it apparent that all else is meek and superfluous when thus side by side compared. The upper skies and beyond hath it in their power to compel all that turns to cease in their turning, to command all that breathes to breathe no more and to render all that ever was to never again be. Just like that, with a mere finger snap, should it so feel the need.

The silvery thread twists this way and that.

That way and this, the silvery thread twists.

The silvery thread from which all else is suspended possesses a boundless compassion that is unquantifiable by even the most ingenious of measures. It is the source from which the stars themselves startle the heavens, evertwirling, ever seeking a place to settle and to shine.

It is from the silvery thread that the sun draws its everblaze.

It is from the silvery thread that the moon owes its everglow.

The puffclouds even, with their vapour and their hush, are summoned magical from the copulation of the evertwirl, the everblaze and the everglow.

Then the seas.

Then the mountains.

Then life itself.

The silvery thread twists that way and this.

This way and that, the silvery thread twists.

The skies relent at last in their solemn dismay.

There are no victors.

There never are.

It is just the way the universe sometimes expresses its sadness is all.

Franklin Singe and his crass cohort remained unmoved by the visceral outpourings of the upper skies. Not a flicker of a notion did they have that it had even come and gone. Those of their kind are blind to such wonders, a deficit which is not always to their detriment. It has, and will ever be true, that those who aspire to be angels must by necessity imbibe the rancid juices of the devil himself.

THE AUDITOR STEPPED lightly to his left and on past the Tretton twins. Uninstructed, Sullivan stumbled forward in his wake until he was no more than a pace behind his leader. With no thought as to why they were doing it, Eustace and Barnaby heaved themselves around, remaining adjacent to one another, and took up their place behind the now-stationary baker, in front of whom Singe waited. Thus arrayed, these loathsome fellows formed a crossbar of sorts – Barnaby and Eustace being the handle, Sullivan the shaft and Franklin Singe the sharp and unforgiving point.

None among them other than The Auditor had ventured any further from the village than where they all now stood. All other than he were automatons now, his to command in any way he saw fit. And with that next unholy step of his did the march of the loathsome commence.

38. Undulations

THE VILLAGE OF Small Mercy was as precisely circumscribed as that which lay beyond it was not. It stretched six hundred and twenty-two yards from its northern point down to its southern. When measured from its centre, it was two hundred and eleven yards across – one hundred and fifteen to the west, ninety-six to the east. There was nothing within its perimeter that could be considered remarkable other than the fact no physical structure had ever been required to delineate where the village ended and its surrounding environs began. A yard was a yard, a half a half. The passage of time from minute to minute, hour to hour, veered not from its eternal brief, and ever had it been the case.

None of those four whose intention was anything but malignant could by any measure be considered to possess the necessary physical attributes for the task upon which they'd embarked. Each wheezed and panted after his own fashion. There was much coughing and spluttering, all of which was unmusical indeed. With every crude expulsion, heads bent down ever further. Galvanised only by a cumulative desire to do ill, they fell into a kind of trance whereby only they existed in that particular time and space. So it was, as they crossed over from the realm of base logic and into the lands where no man held sway, it all started to get just a little bit strange for them.

Being of less natural cunning than The Auditor and lacking the gargantuan ignorance of the Trettons, and in part due to his being in the central position as the group moved on, it was perhaps unsurprising that Sullivan was the first to become aware that not all was as it should be. For some reason or other, he glanced back over his shoulder. Where he had expected to see the diminished images of the homes that lined the eastern track, he instead saw nothing but an expanse of purple heather. There were two things that perturbed him about this – the first being that he had been certain that given the time elapsed since they set off, it was impossible for them to have covered sufficient distance to have left even the faintest speck of the village behind. Second – and perhaps more concerning – was that he had no recollection at all of having trod through anything but dried mud and dead grass. He looked ahead and saw just that – dried mud and dead grass. Not for the first time, he chose not to address The Auditor with his disquiet lest he be judged a fool at best, a Tretton at worst.

"I done be needing to get me some food or get me some sleep 'fore I ain't nothing but dead as dead can be!" blurted Barnaby, each word punctuated with a dribble, a wretch and a croak.

Eustace nodded his accord and in so doing almost fell over, such was the impact of even this small action upon his fragile equilibrium. His stumble went unnoticed by Sullivan and Singe but brought a modicum of mirth from his brother, which, for a moment at least, satiated the latter, though not in the way that nourishment or rest would have done. The brothers were lagging ever further behind the baker, who, in turn, was doing his absolute best to keep pace with The Auditor. What had begun as a relatively tight formation resembled now a slack and fraying length of cord that, if fashioned into a noose, wouldn't hang even the tiniest mouse.

Sullivan looked once more behind him. Still just purple heather. Rather than fall deeper into his unease, he set his focus on gaining on The Auditor, which had the additional pleasing consequence of extending the distance between him and those two slovenly lumps at his rear.

The stick that Singe gripped in his left hand was as gnarled and unbeautiful as the man himself. It had been passed down from generation to generation of his kin, fashioned long ago from the fallen branch of some surly tree. It was almost four feet in length and of a pale grey hue which lent it an appearance more of bone than of wood. A bulbous knuckle of twisted sinews served at one end as a handle whilst the other had from years of use been worn down into a callous as impermeable as any stone. Thus did The Auditor leave in his wake for the baker to follow, not so much the boot prints of an elderly man but a triumvirate of indentations – the two at the base being rather indistinct, whereas the one at the apex was deep and unholy like the single, misshapen eye of the devil's own design.

As the group moved on after their own fashion, the sky shed itself of its birds and its butterflies. The grass and the leaves sucked in their juices, appeared brittle in aspect, the former aching to be crushed, the latter desperate to fall. Where but hours previous, the land revelled in its subtle undulations, splashing about the full range of its palette with a joyous disregard for all things symmetrical, a baleful watercolour wash drowned out even its most fantastical tints. There was no breeze to speak of. The ambient temperature was identical to those who disturbed the air with their passing and therefore was not discernible at all.

Soon, even the chuntering of the awful Tretton twins dripped itself dry. The only sound at all, as they left the village farther and farther behind, was the rhythmic thud of The Auditor's loveless staff as it impaled the earth with each step he took. Of course, it was inevitable that the heart within each of those who trailed behind him, as if by some spell or other, began to beat in sublime synchronicity with that primitive entreaty.

Be that as it may, these were humans, after all, and not automatons comprised of wires and thingamajigs. The fact that they could not go on indefinitely was less surprising than the identity of he who saw fit, without equivocation, to address the matter at hand.

Sullivan had to repeat himself twice before The Auditor, with audible rancour, came to a halt. Barnaby and Eustace were by this point perhaps twenty yards or more behind the baker though, on being aware that the opportunity for rest may be nigh, found sufficient energy to close the gap with a comedic absence of poise.

"My apologies, sir," Sullivan said to the pale and simmering Singe. "It's just my old body has these many years been accustomed more to kneading dough to bread and not much else, and even in that endeavour I been known to sweat and puff."

Franklin Singe may have been a statue just then, so devastating was his inertia.

"What I mean to say," the baker continued with laudable pluck, "is that if you could see your way to permitting all us here the opportunity to sit awhile, there might be some merit to it when it comes to when we get to doing what we all set out to do."

It may have been the fact that neither of the Tretton twins took it upon themselves to express, in their own peculiar fashion, their support for Sullivan's case that The Auditor assented.

"Very well," Singe sneered. "Very well."

"Thank you, sir," sighed an immeasurably relieved Sullivan.

Singe turned away and remained standing the entire duration of his wretched crew's repose, examining his stick throughout as if engorging ravenous upon its remarkable propensity for unspeakable harm.

As if summoned by a power unseen, Barnaby, Eustace and Sullivan rose in unison, unaware they'd even done so until it was too late to do anything other than resume their shambolic trudge.

39. Forlorn and Sorry Bombast

A ND THE RAINS came down.

The rains came down, and all men, women and young 'uns back in the village of Small Mercy did with mutual wonder leave their grim hovel homes in the chill bleak of their eternal lament to behold the immensity of the ancient universe. Each of that staggering array of human tatters creaked skywards, first neck, then brow, though the droplet torrents did slash them harsh and the rampaging wet did all but drown them where they stood. No notion was there, once all were assembled in the comingling of their drudge, that did not have at its source nature's forlorn and sorry bombast.

And the rains came down.

Them old rains came down like you wouldn't dare believe.

The burgeoning upper skies roared purple and crimson, then of a sudden did crash white emblazoned as they partook of a tender breath before resuming redoubled the indignant manifestation of dismay upon which they had so stunningly embarked.

The rage raged on without relent.

Without relent, the rage raged on.

A tremendous blast cracked immutable from the eastern extents to the western hollows then turned full northwards, where it rang out flagrant from the shudderhill peaks down to the very deep dense of the southern woodlands. That blistering sound resounded, pumping its pain to an unbearable pitch as it howled wanton in torrents of end-of-days wowness.

Still, no notion was there, once all were assembled in the comingling of their drudge, that did not have at its source nature's forlorn and sorry bombast.

The soil gulped gluttonous from the pools that spread sloppy between the lumpy clumps that had for so long been emblematic only of dire impotence.

The sumptuous precision employed in the intertwining of the hallowed disparate elements that comprised that momentous tirade was of profound majesty to the few among them in possession of the courage to submit humble and dreamy to the repugnant swooning consequence of glorious moments forsaken. For all others, it reeked simply of retribution.

Yet it was no biblical flood in progress. This was a drenching whose portent, whilst ominous indeed, had been sent wild into the scene not to massacre but to cleanse. The northern hills knew it to be so and took to shuddering cool as evidence of their respect and accord with the necessity of the act. Some who bore witness to that cool shudder of the northern hills became more terrified still in their sodden static state yet had not the capacity to bemoan the wretchedness of their souls. Others, though eyes wide open, remained stupefied by the roar and the purple and the wet and the harsh. There was not one there present who did not conclude swift that a force unstoppable had been mercilessly unleashed.

Then at last the rains did cease and the purple and the crimson did fade into pale and blue and the booming did subside 'til it was barely a gasp.

Even as they ever so slowly regained the ability to shake off their rigid and their static, the men, women and young 'uns looked not at each other as they shuffled back into their grim hovel homes. Nor did any of them ever discuss for the remainder of their days just how it could have been that not a single stitch of their clothing, swathe of their skin or clump of their hair was even remotely wet. All else, however – the land, the leaves, the flowers and more of that ilk whose very essence was the product of the outpourings that issued gargantuan from the fabulous fornication referred to these days as *the Big Bang* – was saturated to a most astonishing degree.

The white stars blinked back into the sullen of the sky. They had many times seen a similar kind of tumult as that which had latterly befallen the small village of Small Mercy and its environs to the east, the west, the north and the south. Hardly a smattering of them were of a mind to summon up even a sizzle of curiosity with regard to what, if anything, might next unfurl in this tale of which they had, at times, been only peripheral participants.

The night that followed the tempest oozed on until the pink talons of a scintillating dawn poked every baleful star into the recesses of the firmament until they were visible no more. A yellow whisper sauntered all shimmer first shapeless then bulbous across the black horizon line until the intensity of the glow to which the residents of Small Mercy awoke led most all of them to believe that the very universe was on fire. On realising their error, each indulged in a sigh of such tragic harmony that never again would the prospect of death be anything other than sweet relief. The consequence of such a shift in the minds of the populous, regardless of the genius of The Constitution to which they had so long been acolytes, was inevitable. What once was, never quite again would be.

Small Mercy, as a concept, as an entity, as a novel (you may be relieved to know) tumbles now to its denouement.

40. Prettiest There Is

STAFFORD AND GRACE were on the grass side by side near the bend in the river that swept down from 'twixt the northern hills. Stafford's weary head was nestled into the grubby droop of cloth that flopped from his sister's left shoulder. Neither was quite awake, nor quite were they asleep. They were in that in-between stage where reality itself is a mischievous sham, the two of them oblivious to the forces that were then arrayed across the Small Mercy landscape. As had ever been the case, their ultimate fate was not theirs to determine.

Those poor things.

Those poor, poor things.

"Little brother?" Grace whispered soft.

Stafford rubbed his eyes hard with his balled bony fists.

"Huh?"

"It's just I was wondering if I could ask of you something."

"'Course," coughed the frail boy.

"Well, please don't make me for being foolish and the like, but would you consider me pretty at all?"

"Prettiest there is that I ever did see or ever knowed of," came the instant reply.

"Really?"

"Yep."

"You're not just saying that to be kind due to me being so very, very weary?"

"Nope. Like I said. Prettiest ever."

"Thank you. Thank you."

Grace closed her eyes and smiled so beautifully and only opened them when wrenched from her reverie by what her brother said next.

"I think I just pushed one of my eyes into the middle of my head."

"Really?"

"Yep. Right into the middle of my noggin."

"Does it hurt?"

"Not like before."

"Well, that's good then."

"Do I look right to you?" Stafford asked, looking direct and plain at his sister.

"Handsome as the moon itself and the sun and stars too."

"Thought as much." He nodded. "You being pretty like you be and me being like you said even when we be dirty like we are and tired like we are and you being scared sometimes and me being brave all the time – well, ain't we really something?"

"Indeed we are," smiled Grace. "And I don't think I be wrong," she continued, pulling him real, real close, "to declare that it be better to be *something* in this life than to be *nothing*."

And then they both fell instantly into a most gorgeous and ravishing slumber.

41. Some Aplomb

T HE MOON NOW be 'twixt them old northern hills.
          At last.

The river that pours down from up there to down here must pay full homage to the curvaceous bulge of its bend. It was a whore of a bend, a mysterious raggedy of a bend, whose presence had ever been destined to one fine day play host to events at once tragic and momentous.

That one fine day?

Well, it had arrived.

At last.

The moon now be 'twixt them old northern hills.

Though the river splurged fulsome seemingly from where the tapered base of the central two northern hills met, its source was way on over and beyond where any Small Mercy inhabitant could ever have conceived. For them, as cunningly intended by the four founders who'd written The Constitution, the northern hills were where their world ended. They were as impenetrable as the night sky itself. The notion that anything lay beyond them was considered by not even the most erudite amongst them. It's a powerful thing, is the written word, when wielded with dread intent. If any dared dream at all, their dreams focused on what was above, not what stretched north, east, south or west. That river was bound by no inky shackle. It had in centuries past sprung in the form of a single tear from the highest mountain in the furthest land and cried itself senseless night and day until it became what it had become. Small Mercy bore witness to but a thimble of those tears in terms of the entirety of that everflow.

Those northern hills knew all that, of course. All that and more besides.

The moon now be 'twixt them old northern hills.

The river water flickered green and blue and purple and white as the moon splashed down its fair light. There was no order to the flowing. Nothing but chaos and collision attended the downward spurts, whose fury burst full to overflowing until a levelling out brought some sense of demure to the wild. Over rocks and detritus the river poured, all motion and fervour though the day be done for most mortal men. The muddy banks that did their best to contain that relentless outpouring succumbed more than once, offering up its clumps and its chunks as some sort of tawdry sacrifice to that mighty, mighty flow.

That bend in the river grooved to a groove all its own. Whatever the force, however rampant the surge, there was a bowing down took place when the tumultuous waters reached the first sway of the bend. It was as if some dam unseen arrested the dash and the roar, transforming all that once was furious into a sedate and sorrowful weeping. The bend itself was maybe ten feet across at its widest point, its central swathe pitted with a copse of grey and blue boulders of various dimensions. At its southern tip, it fell away sharply and thus it was at that point where the dash and the roar did resume untethered.

Stafford and Grace Chuck were huddled together asleep on the grass barely a step away from the apex of the bend in the river when Dawlish came upon them. He had them in the raw of his grasp before either had even the slightest notion of his presence – his right arm wrapped around the boy, his left the girl. There was no forgiveness in the way in which he held them, no semblance of angst, nor pity nor sorrow. The children knew instantly the identity of their captor by the putrid wail of his stench, which was as incomparable as it was unforgettable.

As Dawlish reared up silent to his full height, Stafford and Grace dangled witless from his huge fists like small sheaths of riverbank reeds. Neither spoke. Neither moved. They just let the dangling do its thing.

And then came in balletic majesty all those others who had been either directed or destined to gather at that spot at that time of night when the moon be 'twixt them old northern hills.

From the east, Linton Gauge appeared as if out of a whisper.

On the western side of the river came into view first Tobias Defoe then moments later Nathaniel Wild. The two indefatigable men stood beside one another, heavy arms twitching, hearts all hurricane poised.

Up from the south came Martha Chuck and the tongueless Mary, who at first glance seemed bound so tightly together it was as if they were a single, billowing entity.

With far less swoon than those two women for whom life had been such a terrible strain, Franklin Singe and his barbarous battalion stumbled to a halt. Ahead of them some fifty yards or so were Defoe and Wild, whilst Martha and Mary were a similar distance to their left. By some odd quirk of design, The Miller, though on the other side of the river, was almost exactly diagonal to Sullivan, who by now was flanked by Eustace on one side, Barnaby on the other. The Auditor, murderous staff in hand, had somehow managed to take up a position behind his wretched charges.

All the pieces were in place, all actors on their mark, as was always the intention from the outset. Some things just take a little time is all.

But there was nothing the slightest bit slovenly about what then came to pass.

John Dawlish lurched mighty into the river, splashdrops leaping startled into the night as he landed hard and with some aplomb steadied himself brazen. The water came up almost to the filth of his crotch. Grace's feet just touched the cold wet surface of the river whereas her brother's hovered tantalisingly above it.

The splashdrops had barely begun their woeful descent when Martha and Mary charged banshee and heroic towards the stricken children – Martha to the left, Mary to the right. They clambered sopping but undaunted onto the treacherous midstream boulders and wailed all banshee and howl as the white moon looked on aghast.

The speed with which Tobias Defoe and Nathaniel Wild reached Singe, Sullivan and the Tretton twins was by any measure unholy – as was the manner in which they laid that awful quartet to waste, rendering each unconscious by some means or other in less time than it took Linton Gauge to cover his timid eyes with his dovelike hands.

The Miller let drop his veil just in time to witness Dawlish let go his hold on Stafford and Grace, who as a consequence fell like corpses into the water. Dawlish for his part seemed to have lost all capacity for motion. It was as if he'd been turned to stone there and then. Martha lunged forward and dragged her son from the depths. Mary hauled Grace out of the wet and into the dry, and both women somehow managed to get to the eastern bank whereupon they flopped to the grass no more than a breath away from where The Miller stood stupefied.

The white moon dipped beneath the black of the northern hills, and for a while, all was in darkness.

Nobody moved – even those who still had capacity for motion.

The only noise was that of the river careening down past the bend to vent once more its indolent fury.

The whole wide universe sighed, for there are some things that can't be undone, that will brook no bulge or bend of any description.

You're a fool, Miriam Malone.

A fool.

Didn't he always tell you that?

42. This Very Human Travesty

Tobias Defoe dragged The Auditor from where he'd lain unconscious by the river up towards a patch of land that was overrun with ivy for fifteen feet or more in every direction. The long, thick roots snaked out of the ground, criss-crossing all over the place, no discernible rhythm to their rampage. Their foliage gleamed not at all, even in the brightest of beams, ever sullen and hard of edge.

Singe regained his senses only when dumped full force into the very centre of the ivy swarm. Defoe stood astride him, the ivy roots barely cognisant of the albeit negligible weight and heft of the man who had without warning invaded their territory. Defoe bent over and with no more than a flick turned The Auditor onto his side. He then searched about for any roots that looked like they could be fashioned into some design of loop and, having found sufficient for his task, used these to tether Singe to the ground. The ivy talons crawled across Singe's ankles, his wrists, his waist, his shoulders and his neck. It was as if he were being consumed alive. The final thing Defoe did before leaving Singe was to ensure that the awful fellow's right ear was in contact with the soil, for The Song of the Earth will ever be there to be called upon to belt out its righteous boom.

As the seasons rolled into one another, as year begat year, the thick ivy roots grew with astonishing vigour. Barely had another winter set in when not the slightest essence of The Small Mercy Auditor could be seen. Defoe could not be sure when Singe actually took his final, rancid breath. For all he knew, the despicable rogue lived on beneath his rank ivy blanket. Not that

Tobias really cared. For he'd already decided with unwholesome glee that henceforth would that very spot atop where Singe lay in crude decay serve as his favoured place of defecation.

And with The Auditor gone, Judgement in an instant was no more. For the incoherent tyrant will ever be nothing when not enabled by those of an envious and malevolent disposition.

WHEN SULLIVAN THE baker eventually came to, he thought at first that he'd been paralysed. It wasn't long before he wished he had been. To add to his dismay, it seemed to him that although he was clearly inside some sort of building, it was snowing. Yet he was not cold in the accepted sense of the word. And what was that unbearable thrumming noise that appeared to emanate from somewhere high above him that had no source he could immediately discern?

Linton Gauge was outside the walls of the Small Mercy mill, staring through a small hole in the arched door. His back was slightly bent, and there was an aching in his knees due to the hunch of him. He was alone just then. Not a single one of his animal or avian brethren were of a mind to be anywhere close given the grim nature of this very human travesty.

The two huge circular stones high up in the upper reaches of the windmill rumbled against one another. The crushed white remnants of the grains fluttered down in white swirls through the gape of the floor. They fluttered down in white swirls, landing where they may, joining those that came before them in an ever-increasing mound of flour whose mass increased with startling menace. Atop the mound, visible (though clearly for not much longer) from the base of his chin upwards was Sullivan's head. The chair to which The Miller had bound him had long since disappeared in the relentless flurry.

The Small Mercy windmill sails turned at the behest of the unseasonal gale.

The huge circular stones ground on.

The flour fluttered on down.

And ever so gradually, Sullivan the baker breathed his final breath, buried deep within that astonishing mound that should have been used to make bread but, on this occasion, was not.

His woeful deed concluded, Linton Gauge sought solace away from the worst of humankind. He slumped to the ground, his back against the wooden fence he had built many, many years ago.

A squirrel he had never met before approached him uninvited. Without hesitation and lacking due regard for bland niceties, it popped onto his lap and then scurried bawdy to rest upon the slump of his right shoulder. The curious little creature proceeded to lean forward and begin a discourse of sorts.

"You didn't have to do it," whispered the squirrel. "You really didn't have to do it."

His message thus imparted, the squirrel leapt down and raced off to wherever it was he had a fancy to go.

Many hours passed between the squirrel's departure and the arrival of a young starling. The young starling was of the excitable type, but Linton welcomed his company all the same. He told the young starling about what he had done and what the squirrel had made of it all.

"Was it a red squirrel or a grey squirrel?" asked the young starling with laudable earnest.

"Red."

"Are you sure?"

"Yes. Red. It was a red squirrel."

"Then I have good news for you! Red squirrels tell nothing but lies! Whatever a red squirrel says must be reversed in order to find its true meaning! So in fact, you did have to do what you did, and you should have done what you did!"

The young starling almost fell from the sky, so joyous was he at having rescued his human friend from the deep of his maudlin.

Linton waited the whole of the rest of that day for the young starling's testimony to be corroborated, for everyone knows that where starlings are concerned – particularly those in the eager flourish of their youth – such corroboration is essential.

He waited and he waited in vain, in fact, for the entire remainder of his sweet, bewildered life.

NATHANIEL WILD IT was whom Dawlish had tasked with dealing with Barnaby and Eustace Tretton.

Nathaniel tied their hands before they regained consciousness and with inhuman strength hauled them to their feet. He poked and prodded them across the fields and up the northern slope until they arrived panting and sweating at the door to his wooden barn. Wild pulled open the door, pushed the twins inside and bolted the door shut behind them. He then walked slowly around the front and up to the far end, whereupon he unlatched the other door. And then he waited. He waited some more. There was not a single sound that came from within the barn, but that was ever the case. Whichever of his animals he led through it, none would so much as fart.

After what must have been almost an hour or more, Nathaniel sensed in his soul that the time had come to reveal what magic had been wrought. He flung open the door and at first saw nothing but the empty insides of the barn. It was only when he looked down that he fair chuckled with joy. For there at his feet were two of the ugliest chickens he had ever seen in his life. The moment they were free of the darkness, they began pecking fiercely at one another. Their fury was awful. Wild watched as feathers were ripped off and red streaks of blood splashed onto the ground. Wounded as they were, those ugly chickens did not relent in their murderous pursuit until each was more dead than alive. It was the slightly smaller one who was the first to thwap down and perish. After a brief stagger, the victor keeled over to rest at the side of his vanquished foe and died barely a breath later.

Nathaniel shook his big fat head and laughed so loud and for so long it was a wonder his beard did not fall from his face.

So it seems that it's not just the vile and depraved but the mighty also who have it within them to be foul.

43. Unsheathed

I T WAS SOME sight to which the villagers of Small Mercy awoke. The news spread like a virus from which none was immune. It began with the children, who were immediately scolded for their indulgence in churlish fancy. Only when the first of the adults creaked open their door and yawned gormless into the day was any veracity accorded the scurrilous youthful bleatings.

To give some credit to the multitude of Small Mercy villagers gathered at the top end of the dirty main track, the awe with which they clothed themselves was admirably appropriate. A solemnity hung in a haze above their heads. Mouths were either wide open or on the way to being so. All eyes spoke of ecstasy and wonder. All hearts thudded in perfect unison. Each and every shack and hovel had been emptied of its residents. Not a single soul that morning was there alive within the slender parameters of those environs who was not present amidst that holy throng.

It was the figure and frame of John Dawlish that so enthralled the heaving mass of heathen folk. He stood at the very end of the track, as motionless as he'd been after he'd let drop the Chuck children in the cold river water.

In a place for whom the presence of any stranger was rarer than, say, a starling that could talk, the mere presence of Dawlish in their village would ordinarily have alone been sufficient to induce such a response from the populace. But there was nothing ordinary about any of this at all.

The point need not by now be laboured that as a specimen of his species, Dawlish was unique in the ramshackle nature of his constituent parts and the slipshod manner in which they intersected. On any normal day (which, of course, this was not) the spittle hanging from his cracked bottom lip or the horrific lifelessness of his gaze would have driven most all the crowd to their knees in terror. Yet in time, having become accustomed to the sight of the static stranger, the expression upon his ghoulish face inspired in the onlookers a feeling more akin to pity than of terror. It even reached a stage where one or two began to mutter amongst themselves, having gained enough control of their sagging mouths to have been able to do so.

It was what happened next that was truly memorable to all who were there to bear witness on that spectacular Small Mercy morn.

From out of the shadows behind the static hulk of the inert stranger stepped first Martha Chuck and then Mary. They were followed swift by Grace and Stafford, each holding the hand of the other whilst Grace's free hand carried a wooden pail of water, Stafford's a bundle comprising three rags.

There was complete silence from the crowd. Not even a gasp kissed the air.

Martha and Mary took up a position in front of Dawlish. Stafford came to Mary's side and handed her one of his rags. Of the two remaining, he gave one to his sister and kept the other for himself. Grace moved around to where her mother stood and without a word handed her the wooden pail of water.

Still all so quiet.

Still all so humble.

Mary and Martha turned inwards to face one another. Mary put down her rag, Martha her wooden pail of water. The two women leaned in and shared a devastating kiss. They then turned once more, this time to face the rigid stranger, their backs now to their Small Mercy brethren, who as a single entity stared stunned as the two women began slowly to relieve Dawlish of his fetid garments.

Dawlish did not resist. He did not move at all. Were it not for the fact he was upright, none would have mistaken him for anything but a statue. And there he was at last displayed. Naked. All his rottenness unsheathed. He was, if it were possible, even more wretched unclothed than clothed. It was as if he were decaying from his head to his toes.

No muttering now. Nothing but hearts thudding. Nothing but black-hole mouths in bone-white faces.

Martha picked up her wooden pail of water, Mary her rag. Then, one by one, beginning with Grace then Stafford and lastly the baker woman, each dipped their rag into the water and proceeded to cleanse John Dawlish of his lifetime of detritus.

Now not so quiet.

Now not so quiet at all.

For as each crust of filth was washed away, a sound began to emanate from deep within the hollow of the naked stranger's chest. By the time his left leg had been all but shed of its grime, that noise lingered for a moment in the deep of his throat and then burst out magnificent into the day. It was the voice of the valleys, the boom of the mountains, the sweet crashing of the waves upon the shore. Though his mouth barely moved and the rest of him remained absolutely still, he sang with a pure and astonishing beauty. As the women and the children continued undaunted in their washing of him, tears came to the eyes of the crowd. Where they had at first been in awe, they now were utterly overwhelmed. As the song went on, a torrent of love fell down upon every man, woman and child there present, shaking them to their bones, ridding them fully of the callous chains with which that Small Mercy Constitution had enslaved them and their forebears.

When fully free of the dirt of his days and the rank of his nights, John Dawlish brought his song to an end.

Martha Chuck took the hand of her son and her daughter and drifted off through the small copse of trees just beyond the northern end of the village. Mary the baker woman set down gently her rag and sauntered with some style past the stricken masses and on down south. She didn't stop at her home, where for so many years she'd baked her bread and suffered so much misfortune, but continued instead into the deeps of whatever lay beyond.

Not one of them – Martha, Mary, young Grace or little Stafford, were from that moment ever to be seen or heard from again.

Peldon Ward – Colchester General Hospital, Essex

I

"MY DEAR MIRIAM, we have known each other for many years, have we not?"

"Indeed we have. And I could never have wished for a better literary agent, of that you can be assured."

"You are very kind. That being so, I must ask of you a question which is derived purely out of necessity to perform my professional duties to the standards I hold sacrosanct."

"Go ahead, you dear man. Ask your impertinent question. I will even put my telephone as close to my ear as this blessed arthritis will permit in order that I do not miss a single breath or syllable."

"Then I shall get straight to it."

"Please do."

"Well, that *Small Mercy* novel of yours that you kindly sent to me – is that the *first* draft, a *rough* draft – my apologies if this phrase sounds crass – for which you await my comments?"

"Ah, what you feared may be impertinence, I fear *ridiculous* would be an adjective more apt for your query. You alone must know that Miss Miriam Malone is famed, amongst other things, for never having written more than a single draft of any of her novels. It has been remarked upon with malice by those who would denounce me for slovenly practice, lauded by those who would have me as possessing some demonic talent or other. Of course, neither is the case. It is just the way I have come to do things. Furthermore, at my advanced age, do you really think I am capable of changing my literary modus operandi when it is oftentimes such a chore even to change my clothes?"

"I was afraid that would be your answer."

"Afraid but not surprised?"

"A little of both, Miriam."

"I confess this *Small Mercy* is not in my usual style."

"It will be the ruin of you, Miriam. I beg of you to dispense with it. You know as well as I do that The Publisher will release it regardless. The furore it will cause will lead to untold publicity. It is an undeniable truth in our profession that a bad book will sell just as well as a work of art. People will go out and buy it in their droves, motivated by the same fascination that causes them to stare at a car crash. The Publisher will make his millions, but your career, my dear, will be over."

"Sweet man. I am eighty-five years old."

"And what, may I ask, has that to do with the price of beans?"

"The price of beans? My dear, you are incorrigible."

II

The Daily Record

UTTER RUBBISH!

I WILL CONFESS at the outset of this brief review (I see no merit in using any more words than are necessary) that I have never seen in Miss Malone's 'work' quite what it is that has elevated her to the pinnacle of her profession.

Even more remarkable is that she has remained there for so many decades. I may have read one of her early novels out of curiosity, back when I was eager to discover the secrets of being a bestselling author, though I remember nothing at all of the experience. That being said, one must admire, albeit grudgingly, anyone who is able by their own wit and guile to inspire such universal adoration as Miss Malone has achieved.

Caveat complete, I have little more to say other than this latest offering of hers is a supremely unedifying example of that old boxing cliché about the champion of the world being allowed to participate in one fight too many. I can say without equivocation that Miss Malone should never have written this book and that it should never have been published. It is at best an embarrassment, at worst a crude jumble of nonsense. Were it not for her advanced age and elevated status in our nation, I would even go as far as to speculate on the soundness of her mind, but I will leave such conjecture to those more qualified than I to explore.

MORNINGTON TIMES

Oh, Miss Malone!

OH, MISS MALONE! Miss Malone! What have you done?

By page five, I was horrified, by page ten, in tears, and by page thirteen, furious. Your loyal band of readers, I fear, will react in much the same way. If this Small Mercy of yours is some kind of private joke then it has fallen flat with me. Even as I type these lines, I am aghast. All that makes sense to me is that you have been kidnapped and some illiterate philistine has coerced you into putting your name to his drivel. If that is the case then I hope you are safe. If not, then please forgive me if I scream!

Oh, Miss Malone! Miss Malone! What have you done?

THE STANDARD

An Opportunity Missed

MIRIAM MALONE is famed as much for her strict adherence to her private life as she is for her extensive output. For one so ostensibly in the public arena, it is nothing short of a miracle that so little is known of her life. Now very much an octogenarian, she could be forgiven for deciding the moment was at hand to tell all. In fact, last summer, I was party to a very forceful rumour from a very reliable source that indicated an autobiography was imminent. But instead, we have _this_.

Unlike many other reviewers, I will not dismiss Small Mercy as being entirely devoid of merit. Some of the descriptive passages are wonderfully conceived, and many of the characters are imbued with qualities that mark them as memorable. But that, I'm afraid is where my praise – such as it is – must end. On the brief occasions when the plot attempts to make itself known, it is drowned out by a deluge of stream-of-consciousness ramblings that would make the local dope fiend blush. This is a mishmash of a disaster, bland social commentary rolling around in the mud with shallow spiritual epistles, intertwined with the sort of juvenile humour that appals more than it cheers.

They say that to read an author's work is to learn something of their experience of life. If that be the case with this awful Small Mercy of Miss Miriam Malone then I am afraid I must decline the invitation whilst awaiting the as-yet-unwritten biography of this National Treasure. I can only hope, for her sake, it is not of the posthumous kind.

III

Miss Malone: Good afternoon. Please sit down. Would you like me to sign your copy of my new book?

Fan: Oh, it is so great to finally meet you, Miss Malone! I just can't believe it's you!

Miss Malone: Well, I can confirm it most certainly is.

Fan: You are a national treasure!

Miss Malone: So I've been told. Now, what would you have me write by way of inscription?

Fan: Oh, erm. Just 'To my friend, Tracey. Best wishes Miriam.' Could you do that? Oh, if you would, I would love you forever!

Miss Malone: Of course, dear. Now, whilst I'm doing that, do you have anything you would like to ask? By the look of things, you are the last of the day. The bookshop will be closing in ten minutes, according to the note I was given before you came in.

Fan: A question? Oh, I wish I'd known I'd get this chance. Let me think. Come on! Think! OK. Here's one. What is the secret of how you do what you do? I know you've probably been asked it a thousand times, but I'd just love for you to tell me.

Miss Malone: The secret? Now, I must disappoint you, I'm afraid. I personally have absolutely no idea.

Fan: You don't?

Miss Malone: You see that gentleman over there in the far corner?

Fan: Him? The homeless man?

Miss Malone: Well, I cannot attest to his choice of abode, but I can guarantee that he will enlighten you as to your query. He is *The Author*, you see. I am but *The Writer*.

Fan: I didn't know there was a difference.

Miss Malone: Apparently, there is. Now, go and see him while there is still time.

****

Miss Malone: That was quick, my dear. What did he have to say? I would be very much interested to know just what it is that has been the secret of my success.

Fan: He was very odd.

Miss Malone: I don't doubt it. You seem somewhat downcast if I might say so. Did he give you an answer?

Fan: Yes.

Miss Malone: And?

Fan: He wrote it down on this scrap of paper.

Miss Malone: May I?

Fan: Here.

Miss Malone: *1. Be kind to midgets. Especially the disproportionate ones. They have a hard time. 2. Never let a day go by.*

Fan: Thank you for everything, Miss Malone.

Miss Malone: Fare thee well, my dear.

****

Mr A: I reckon that time has come, Miriam.

Miriam: It does appear to be so.

Mr A: Just wanted to apologise for that *Small Mercy* fiasco. Not an ideal end to your career. From what I have heard, everybody hates it.

Miriam: Young man, of all people you have no need to offer me your apologies.

Mr A: Yeah? How come? It was a disaster.

Miriam: That may be the case. What you seem to be forgetting, however, is that were it not for you, it is all but certain that I would never have existed at all.

Mr A: I suppose there is that.

IV

I THINK IT'S A Monday, but it could be a Friday. Doesn't feel like a weekend, that's for sure – not that it really matters round here. Whatever day of the week it is, you can't get a drink in. Staff won't even take my money. Last ward was better. They're like the Gestapo in this place. It's definitely March though. Yeah, pretty certain it's March.

At least they took me off that breathing thing this morning. Been on it so long, I began to think it'd become a part of me. One of the doctors told me yesterday I really should have died. I still don't really know exactly what he meant by that.

They say they want some mental health lot to see me before I'm discharged home. Don't really see the point but guess I don't really have any cards to play just now.

Miriam: Afternoon, Mr A.

Mr A: Miriam? I thought you'd gone?

Miriam: You and me both, dear.

Mr A: Well, it's nice to see you. How you doing?

Miriam: Better than you, I fear. You don't look very well at all, if I might say.

Mr A: Ever the charmer…

Miriam: I'm a national treasure, don't you know?

Mr A: They're sending me home in the morning if they think I haven't totally lost my mind since I've been in here.

Miriam: Sounds sensible. You are prone to your cerebral meanderings, are you not?

Mr A: You think I'm mad?

Miriam: It really isn't for me to say, but the fact we are engaged in this discourse at all…

Mr A: You might have a point.

Miriam: I think I do.

Mr A: Could you do me a favour while you're about?

Miriam: If it is within my power.

Mr A: They say they won't give me any Tramadol when I'm out of here. Apparently, I'm the sort that could get addicted to it. You couldn't have a word, could you?

Miriam: They know you too well, it seems.

Mr A: I take it that's a 'no' then?

Miriam: There is one thing I can do, though.

Mr A: Yeah?

Miriam: I could sing for you?

Mr A: That would be wonderful. Let me first close my eyes, though. I get so very tired these days.

…and then did sweet Miriam Malone go ahead and sing to me soulful the most beautiful song that I ever did Tramadol hear…

The End

About Stuart Ayris

Stuart was born in the summer of 1969. He wrote his first novel, *A Cleansing Of Souls*, when he was twenty-two years old and then wrote nothing, until he began the FRUGALITY trilogy, the first part of which was published in 2012.

Over the years, Stuart has set up stalls in Romford market, spent two years working as a road sweeper and some time as a council gardener. He has been a psychiatric nurse since October 1997 and currently lives in Tollesbury, Essex, England.

He is married to Rebecca and has three children, Matthew, Daniel and James.

By Stuart Ayris

A Cleansing of Souls
Bighugs, Love and Beer

Frugality (Trilogy)
Tollesbury Time Forever
The Bird That Nobody Sees
I Woke Up This Morning

The Buddhas of Borneo

The Magical Tragical Life of Edward Jarvis Huggins

Elysian Wonderland

Merzougaville, Baby

Albion Calling

Bolivian Rhapsody

This Awful Small Mercy of Miss Miriam Malone

www.stuartayris.com
www.beatentrackpublishing.com/stuartayris

Beaten Track Publishing

For more titles from Beaten Track Publishing,
please visit our website:

https://www.beatentrackpublishing.com

Thanks for reading!